BECKONED
PART 3

From
LOS ANGELES
with Love

by Aviva Vaughn

Table of Contents

Praise for "BECKONED, Part 3: From Los Angeles with Love"

It has been so long since I have read a series that has kept my interest like this one! I literally couldn't wait to jump into part 3 of this series and again as with the first two books I wasn't disappointed! I just can't help but be swept up in the relationship between Angela and Soren! I really am drawn to them. Again the author did a fabulous job with the writing in this book and I really do love her writing style – I honestly feel like I am on the journey with these characters through the author's fabulous descriptive writing! There were some good twists in the story and just when you think Soren is finally making his move along comes someone new to throw things up the air again! It's getting harder to review these books without giving away too much of the storyline but without doubt if you have read any of this series then you will not be disappointed with this one! It's about to get pretty sexy!!!! I am so excited to read part 4! -Katie from the United Kingdom, 5-star review

Aviva Vaughn just keeps bringing it. Another book in the Beckoned series that I could not put down. The way Ms. Vaughn writes, always is so descriptive and makes you feel like you are right there with the characters. She keeps you on your toes with all the twists and turns. You keep reading because you want to see what is going to happen next. I cannot wait to read Part 4 in the series. -Dori from Florida, 5-star review

Something I've always admired about books is that when you find a well written series each book may even be better than the last, unlike motion pictures where the second rarely adds up. This is just one of the many reasons I've always favored a good book over a movie. My point is that I feel this way about Aviva Vaughn's Beckoned series. I was completely drawn into Angela and Soren's story in book one, book two blew my mind and yet somehow even after following their story a third time, I NEED to know more. Unfortunately I can't divulge too much information without giving the storyline away but once again I enjoy the storytelling, the wording is somehow deep while having a storyline that is true to life and very relatable. The characters are once again relatable and enjoyable and there were times I felt conflicted for Angela. I'm really looking forward to continuing the Beckoned series and following Aviva Vaughn's writing. -Felicia from U.S.A., 5-star review

This lady has completely captured me with this series, at first I was intrigued to see how a American author would write about the UK and she definitely did it justice. I really feel that Aviva characters really pull you into the story and plays wonders with your imagination not many authors can really do that for me I've only got a hand full I will read hundreds of times over and over and she has definitely gone on that list for myself. -Claire from the United Kingdom, 5-star review

The more I get to read about these two, I love the person that Angela is becoming and seeing Soren coming into his own is a great experience as well. This book is more about the difficulties of a long term relationship and just how far those difficulties will push these two young lovers to the breaking point for their love. The deeper I get into this serial read, the more I grow attached to how Soren and Angela will turn out in the end. Will they finally get their happily ever after or will they allow the distance between them to end what has only just begun for them? Don't miss out on this great read, and fantastic author, jump on the Vaughn train and get to reading this amazing series! -Ashleigh from Iowa, 5-star review

The whole story/series has been fascinating and captivating- but this book takes it to a whole new level. Ms. Vaughn has upped the ante, so to speak, and produced a story that I devoured in matter of hours. I couldn't put it down and HAD to find out what was happening. The books just seem to get better and better.... And the love triangle of sorts/the 'threat,' and the emotional roller coaster that this story took me on had me sooooo conflicted. I love the characters and thought I knew how their story would play out. But Ms. Vaughn brought in a bit of a twist, a surprising element, that really drew me in and held me captive the entire way! I read this book about a week ago and have been mulling over how to do it the justice that it deserves. The whole series has been a surprising find, I never expected to love it as much as I have/do. Ms. Vaughn had my emotions and allegiances all tied up in knots, And I loved every minute. This book gives a new meaning to the word sizzling! There are some no-holds-barred romps that singed my eyebrows and melted the screen on my kindle! This is definitely the best of the books, so far. It had everything you could want in a great read- it was captivating, sentimental, emotional, romantic, seductive, sexy, realistic and entirely believable. I am now really anxious about the next book, and to find out how the story will end. Thank you, Ms. Vaughn! -Angela from Australia, 5-star review

Woah part three! This series just keeps getting better! I read this one in just a few hours because I could not stop reading it! After finding out this is the author's favorite book of the series, I was so excited to read this and Aviva Vaughn did NOT disappoint! This book gave me a new appreciation for California and seeing it through the eyes of someone who truly loves it is wonderful. Every time Aviva Vaughn describes a new location, I can picture it in such vivid detail. She really has a way with words! Bring on Part 4!! -Emily from Ohio, 5-star review

I enjoyed how much this was written with vibrance, much like the first two, but even better! Just when you didn't think that it could be any better! You really feel as if you are taking in the City of Angels in for yourself. Aviva's ability to bring to life food and locations completely transform you to each and every place that the characters visit. It is of course written in a fan-fiction of sorts to Jane Austen's works. You can't deny the connections of writing styles between Aviva Vaughn and Jane Austen. Throw in some awesome lustiness and you have one heck of a nice afternoon all in the pages of this wonderful book. -Liz from Nebraska, 5-star review

I loved that we yet again get to delve back into these two's lives. Their journey has been so tumultuous and has had me on the edge of my seat that I couldn't wait to jump right back into their story. If you expect they might catch a break in this book then think again. The writer takes you on just as many twist and turns as the first two books. I always find myself hoping that they will make it work, that everything be will ok in the end. The fact that I have been this invested in the characters for all three books is testament to just how well they have been written. I cannot wait to jump into book 4!! -Kerry from the United Kingdom, 5-star review

I'm not even sure I'm even capable to begin to describe how much i enjoy this book (and series). Wow, it's such a roller ride! So much attention to details, scenic scenes and characters ! I can picture it all in my head and hear their voices. Phenomenal story plot, with drama, suspense, intrigue ... oh and sooo much love!! We can't all forgot that! The characters are relatable and entertaining! Such an amazing story, once you read one, you'll want to read the others ASAP!! -Nicole from Missouri, 4-star review

This series just gets better and better with each book. The chemistry between Angela and Soren is stronger in this book and we get to see a bit of a stronger side of Soren. Aviva Vaughn continues to guide her readers through a descriptive journey of all the cities she has the readers travel to with her characters. This book really takes you into an emotional roller coaster and Angela batters with inner turmoil regarding her relationship with Soren and the new temptation. I can't wait to read book 4 to see what finally happens between Angela and Soren. -Lisette from Florida, 5-star review

Beckoned Part 3: From Los Angeles with Love by Aviva Vaughn is absolutely my favorite book by this author! Angela and Soren's story is so sweet, charming, steamy and full of discoveries both individually and as a couple. I feel so emotionally invested in their story, being able to read their story from the beginning and seeing how it developed over time as they overcame many obstacles made them seem so real. I absolutely loved how this story had some added drama as new characters were introduced, it had me reading this book in one sitting as I just had to know how it was all going to play out! This book had some twists and turns I didn't expect, but really enjoyed them. I feel like I have gotten to know these characters very well and consider them my friends. Aviva writes with such color and I am transported into her book experiencing the sights and sounds of her locations. I couldn't wait to read this book and am diving right into the final book. -Kristi from Oklahoma, 5-star review

Legal Stuff

AvivaVaughn.com

This is a work of fiction. Names, characters, businesses, places, events and incidents are either the products of the author's imagination or used in a fictitious manner. Any resemblance to actual persons, living or dead, or actual events is purely coincidental.

Cover Art: Les Solot
Cover Location: Newport Beach, California

ISBN: 1-947420-06-2
ISBN13: 978-1-947420-06-9

About the Author

Aviva Vaughn (ah-VEE-vah) loves reading, traveling, and eating…preferably all at once. She isn't afraid to try new things, which has made for an interesting—although not always straight forward—life.

She is an avid reader and especially likes books with multifaceted characters who reveal something about that most compelling of all subjects: human nature; no matter what species they are or what planet they are from.

For a list of her favorite books visit her website at
AvivaVaughn.com/about

Other Titles From Aviva Vaughn

Novels

BECKONED join the conversation at
Facebook.com/groups/AvivaVaughnBookClub
-Part 1: From London with Love AVAILABLE NOW
-Part 2: From Bath with Love AVAILABLE NOW
-Part 3: From Los Angeles with Love AVAILABLE NOW
-Part 4: From Barcelona with Love AVAILABLE NOW
-Part 5: Adrift in Costa Rica AVAILABLE NOW
-Part 6: Adrift In New Zealand AVAILABLE NOW

Short Stories

-PRESSURE (available now and included in Beckoned, Part 4)
-Knotty Naughty Bits Volume 1: a collection of tangled romantic shorts PREORDER NOW **SmartURL.it/KNB1**

Subscribe to Aviva's list to be notified of new releases and special offers—and get her favorite **FOOD | BOOK | TRAVEL tips** by clicking SmartURL.it/BECKONEDfan

Dedication

September 2016

To my parents who gave me the blessing/curse of figuring it out on my own. Thank you for an interesting life. I love you.

And to my own little who—unfortunately(?)—will not have the same luxury. Thank you for choosing me to be your mommy. I love you.

With thanks to Edith Wharton and Margaret Mitchell who taught me that sometimes the best romances are also tragedies.

Wishing you love and romance,

City of Angels

If you feel like
you don't belong anywhere.
Try L.A.
~Aviva Vaughn

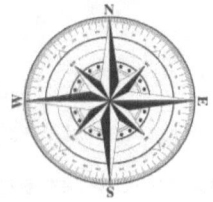

Chapter 1: Uncertain

July 12, 2001 somewhere over the Atlantic Ocean

Angela turned back from the jet way, brushing past the flight attendant who had just taken her ticket, and ran toward Soren, his dark, Savile Row suit moving farther and farther away from her.

"Soren, wait…" she called out, extending her arm, reaching out for him.

She grabbed his shoulder, but the fabric felt wrong. Instead of worsted wool it felt like cotton knit.

"Don't go…" she tugged on his shoulder, waiting for him to turn around, tears streaming down her face.

She awoke with a start.

"Would you like a tissue my dear?" The kind elderly woman sitting next to Angela held out the white paper like a surrender flag and smiled through her thick glasses.

Angela looked at her right hand, wrapped around the peach-colored, cotton knit sweater of the sweet-looking woman. She released the woman's arm.

"Sorry," she said quietly, reaching for the tissue, which felt like a security blanket to her swollen, tear-stained face.

She pulled her light, cashmere wrap tighter around her to stave off the chilly plane cabin air. Now that they were above the clouds, the bright light through the window burned her eyes. She pulled the shade shut and leaned her head against the wall.

She had been crying off and on, ever since the plane had taken off from London on her return trip bound for her native city of Los Angeles and far away from Soren.

Soren Lund, the man of her dreams who had suddenly become a surprising reality during her just completed trip to London. She couldn't think of the brooding Dane without thinking about his stormy, blue eyes that seemed to look right into her soul.

Her elderly neighbor stole a concerned look at Angela.

Angela turned to the woman. "Thank you," she said, wiping her nose. "Please excuse me, I'm just sad to be leaving."

The woman patted Angela's arm comfortingly. "No need to explain darling, you go ahead and cry. It's good to get it out."

At the word "darling," Angela began crying harder. "Darling" was the word that Soren always called her, and hearing it again—even from another person—was like tearing the bandage off a wound.

She didn't know why she was crying so much. It wasn't like she and Soren had been dating long. They had met almost a year ago as MBA students at the *Barcelona Instituto de Negocios*—or BIN—but it wasn't until they reconnected in London last week that their long-burning desire was ignited. She closed her eyes and remembered the feeling of his lips on her neck and it sent shivers down her spine.

At least that was better than crying.

Inhaling slowly she took stock of her situation: her eyelids were almost swollen shut, her cheeks hurt, and she was starting to have difficulty breathing out of her nose.

She needed to calm down.

Pulling out her black sketchbook/journal, she turned the pages past the sketches and journaling she did in London and Bath, found a blank page and started writing.

7/12/01, on the plane home

Has it really been only ten days since I left Los Angeles? I feel like I stepped through the looking glass when I got off the plane in London. So much has happened.

The most important thing is that I've fallen in love with Soren Lund. Oh God, how ridiculous does that sound? I guess the many months in Barcelona made it easy to fall fast here in London…and I thought he was falling in love with me too, but the words were never said.

I'm such a blind idiot. How could I mess up so badly in only ten days? How could I have hurt him unintentionally so many times without an alarm bell ever going off in my head? Am I that naive? Am I that selfish? I'm sure Marco would answer "yes" to both of those for me.

She paused, shaking her head as she thought of her dear friend Marco Lucian. Marco was one of Soren's fellow MBA classmates at BIN. With a wicked sense of humor and vivid, green eyes, he was a firecracker of an Italian: a Roman candle. Marco was instrumental in helping Angela and Soren overcome some of the misunderstandings they had experienced during their nascent relationship.

The bottom line is, whatever mistakes I made...they were mistakes. They were innocent. I never meant to hurt Soren by having lunch with Marco, dancing with Rolfe or having my Peter issues resurface. And then, when it was time to say goodbye, it was as if he didn't even know how he felt about me. He gave me lots of gifts and gestures, but he never said the words I needed to hear.

And what the hell was that at the airport? Was that a "goodbye forever" or what? I don't even know? I poured my heart out to him about Peter and was left hanging. I literally have no idea where we stand at this point. But what I do know is that I am completely in love with Soren. My heart is literally aching right now as I write this.

I know that long-distance relationships are hard, but I also know that I want to at least try to make it work. The last thing he said to me was "there's so much we need to figure out and discuss." What the hell does that mean? Is he my boyfriend or my stockbroker? His words were like a knife through my heart.

I would give myself to him completely if he would ask. I get that there are no guarantees, and that it might not work, but what I don't get is that he doesn't even seem to be willing to try.

All those kisses and gestures, and yet he didn't ask the simple question, "When can I see you again?" Does that mean he doesn't want to?

Oh God, here come the tears again, this isn't helping at all. I just wish I knew how he felt...

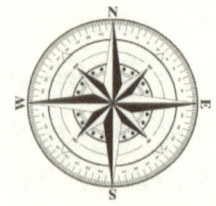

Chapter 2: Welcome Home

"Welcome to Los Angeles." The flight attendant's voice over the loudspeaker woke Angela up suddenly.

She had been dreaming vividly. In her dreams, she was walking away from Soren, toward the airport gate. She wanted to turn around and run into his arms but some invisible force made it impossible. She felt as though she had been physically fighting the invisible force the whole flight. Her limbs were heavy with fatigue.

Facing her parents at arrivals was going to be a trial.

After two hours of baggage and customs, Angela burst through into the bright, sunny international arrivals area of LAX and immediately saw her mom waving her arms over her head like she was signaling Angela in for a landing.

It was only a little after 1pm, but it felt like bedtime to Angela. She took off her cashmere wrap and threw it in in the new carry on Soren gave her. The thought made her want to cry again.

"Honey, pumpkin, baby, it's so good to see you. I missed you so much," her mother, Lillian, gushed as she enveloped her only child in a big hug, heavily scented with her favorite gardenia perfume. The powerful, synthetic fragrance made Angela feel queasy.

Angela smiled weakly. "Hi mommy, it's good to see you too." She hugged and kissed her mother and then her father, trying to be happy to see them, but she felt like a soulless shell.

"What's wrong sweetie pie, you look so glum. Are you hungry?" Her mom asked as she grabbed one of Angela's new roller bags and started weaving through the crowds, directing Angela to where the car was.

Angela's dad had her other roller bag and shouted, "Lillian, it's over that way," as he gestured in the opposite direction, clearly exasperated.

Lillian rolled her eyes and turned around, bumping into three other people as she navigated her turn on the crowded sidewalk.

"Thanks mom, but I'm not hungry. I'm just tired is all. Jet lagged. I know you want to take me out for lunch, but can we get together tomorrow? I really just want to get home and sleep."

Angela didn't have to fake anything, she really felt bone tired.

Her parents exchanged concerned glances before her mom said, "Not hungry? That's not like you, but we'll get you home right away, and then tomorrow you can tell us all about your exciting trip to England."

Angela smiled gratefully at her sweet mother. Being an only child had its perks, but sometimes she wished that her every move wasn't so very important to her parents. When she had returned from her semester in Spain, her mother had pestered her for weeks to make up for the lost time. Fortunately, she had only been gone ten days this time, so her mother wouldn't be quite so clingy.

Or unfortunately, I should say.

She wished that she had been with Soren longer; remembering his lips on hers, their bodies pressed together and the beautiful memories they had created during their short—but intense—time together.

"Here we are," her dad said as he popped the trunk on the white, 1990's-era Jaguar sedan that he had bought used. He loaded in the luggage while Angela got into the backseat.

"So did you have a good time?" Lillian asked pleasantly as her husband started up the car.

"Yes," Angela replied flatly.

"Did you see Marco?" her dad asked, looking backwards as he pulled out of the parking space.

"Uh huh," Angela murmured.

Lillian turned around, trying to make eye contact with Angela. "Was the weather nice?"

Avoiding her mother's gaze Angela answered, "Very nice."

Angela pretended not to notice when her mother narrowed her eyes at her, continuing to stare out the window, watching the landscape pass without really seeing; mentally immersed in replaying the scene at Heathrow airport over and over again in her mind.

"This is a boarding message for KLM flight #1002 to Amsterdam with service to Los Angeles. We will begin boarding first class and business class passengers."

"That's you," Soren said coldly.

Angela could feel the distance he was putting between them and it sparked a bit of anger inside of her that felt somehow comforting.

"That's my flight, but I'm not boarding yet, they just called first and business."

Soren repeated more quietly this time, "That's you."

She looked down at her boarding pass and saw for the first time the bold letters spelling "FIRST CLASS." The words seemed to yell at her from the page, and a dull roar built-up in her ears.

His final thoughtfulness made her feel off balance and confused.

She wiped at her eyes with the heel of her hand, willing herself not to cry until she got home. She looked out the window at the Santa Monica Mountains, cloaked in their characteristic pecan-brown of dry earth, chaparral, and oak tree trunks with just a sprinkling of deep, pine-green from the glossy leaves of the trees.

Her parents didn't ask her another question, and Angela fell silent for the rest of the 30-minute drive north from LAX airport to her 1-bedroom apartment in Encino.

Encino is a small, suburban neighborhood located in the San Fernando Valley area of Los Angeles abutting the Santa Monica Mountains. The word Encino is Spanish for "oak tree" and the area lives up to its name with thousands of huge, broad oaks—some hundreds of years old—peppering its streets, parks, and homes.

One famous oak tree, of the *Quercus agrifolia* variety—known as the Lang Oak—sadly perished a few years earlier in the El Niño storms of 1998 at a verified age of over 1,000 years, living much longer than most of its species, which are considered old at three-hundred.

A sleepy community, Encino's claims to fame are that it was the childhood hometown of Michael Jackson and the site of the Sepulveda Basin Recreation Area, one of Los Angeles' largest city parks covering an area of over 2,000 acres or almost two-and-a-half-times larger than New York's Central Park.

The temperature in the Los Angeles Basin was about 85 degrees, the same as it had been in London, but the air in L.A. was always bone dry, which made the heat more bearable. As the car climbed through the Sepulveda Pass toward Encino, the thermometer rose with it about ten degrees. The Valley, as locals called it, was usually warmer than the Basin.

As the Holguín car descended into the Valley, Angela saw the bone-white curve of the Sepulveda Dam come into view. An engineering marvel completed in 1941, the majestic dam was a frequent star in music videos, commercials, film and television. Angela smiled as she recalled the time she recognized it in the movie *Gattaca*. She double-exhaled at the site of the dam's beautiful, Streamline Moderne lines which always felt like a "welcome home" sign from the city she loved so much.

"Here we are sweetheart," her father said, shooting Angela a concerned look as they pulled up to her mid-century apartment building with its strong, linear angles and glass and stucco façade. "Are you sure you're okay? I've never heard you so quiet."

"Just tired dad." Angela inhaled a stuttered breath trying to align her mental reality with her physical one. It was hard to believe that she had been in Soren's arms earlier this morning, although technically it was already a new day in England; flying backwards across time zones was always such a mind game.

"Can we help you with your luggage?" Her mom asked gently.

"No mom. I got it." Angela felt relieved as she looked toward the bright white building that had been her home for the last few years. Her bed beckoned.

Her parents exchanged looks again.

"Are you sure you're okay honey?" her mom asked.

The worried tone in her mother's voice was enough to get her going. Angela started moving quickly. She wanted to get into the safety of her apartment before her parents started to overreact. "Yes mom, I'm fine." Her dad opened his car door, "Dad, don't get out. I'll get my bags. You guys get going…really, I'm just exhausted," she said as she made a big show of yawning, hoping they would back down.

"Okay sweetheart. Just let us know if you need anything," her mom said through the window.

Angela pulled her roller bags out of the trunk, working hard to make it look easy so her father would stay in the car. She waved at his reflection in the side-view mirror. She rolled the bags to the glass and aluminum security door and gave her parents a final wave. When they finally pulled away, she sighed heavily, grateful to let her guard down.

She fished her keys out of her carry on and pushed through the security doors, grabbed her mail, and walked through the lush, palm-tree courtyard of the small, two-story building. An elderly woman dressed in black—who spoke nothing but Russian—nodded her head at Angela as she swayed in a metal rocking chair pushing against the ground with her black, orthopedic shoes. Angela nodded back and carried one roller bag up the stairs to her apartment landing.

One of Angela's favorite things about her building was how private and quiet it was. Her staircase served only her apartment and the one across from her, and with only twenty-five units, the building felt more like a huge duplex than an impersonal apartment building.

After two trips up the stairs, Angela finally opened the door to her small but beautifully-furnished apartment that she had cobbled together with street finds, good deals at vintage shops, and fortunate hand-me-downs from her parents.

The air in the apartment was warm and stale. Angela put her keys on the hardwood table adjacent to the front door, feeling none of the joy that she usually felt upon coming home.

She looked around languidly, taking in the décor that she had so artfully picked out and arranged.

Her favorite tableau included a gilded, Peruvian sunburst mirror—a gift from her parents—that hung over two very masculine, black 1960's leather and wood lounge chairs—that she had scored for a song at a vintage shop—that were placed on either side of a small, elaborately-carved wood Chinese side table upon which two dainty, scrolled English pewter lamps topped with colorful silk shades sat. The arrangement just didn't beckon to her to sit and linger the way it usually did.

Instead, she flipped on the AC, shrugged out of her travel clothes, and fell into her bed.

When she woke up fourteen hours later, she felt groggy and disoriented. She looked around, but couldn't see anything; it was pitch-black outside. She turned on the light by her bed and saw her cell phone sitting on her nightstand, uncharged.

What time is it?

She plugged the dead phone into the wall socket to charge. Fumbling through her carry on, she looked for her watch, which she had stowed away when she went through airport security yesterday. Her watch read "4:24am."

Damn!

Her parents were probably worried about her.

And Soren!, she thought, realizing that he had no way to get ahold of her as her European phone didn't work in the U.S. and her American phone was dead. Then again, what if he wasn't trying to get in touch with her at all?

She sighed thinking how much she wished she could change their last two days together. Her heart ached at the memory of their final words to each other. She'd been so rude and cold. She needed to apologize to him.

Now wide-awake, she threw on a robe and hurried out to her living room to turn on her laptop. She paused momentarily before hitting the power key. Who knew what an email from Soren might say? Maybe he wrote saying they were over.

A chill went up her spine.

She took a deep breath and started up her computer.

When her email program began to boot up she saw her inbox populating with the many messages that had built-up over the last two weeks. The most recent ones all had the same email address "soren.lund@hotmail.dk." The timestamps read 2:36pm, 9:15pm, 11:23pm, 2:58am and 4:12am.

She smiled, happy to see that he had written. She clicked on the one from 2:36pm.

From: Soren Lund
To: Angela Holguin
July 12, 2001 at 2:36pm
Subject: Let me know when you arrive

Darling,

I'm going to bed soon, and you'll be arriving home safely in Los Angeles while I'm asleep, so I just wanted to write you a little note saying that I miss you already and to please email me when I can call you and get ahold of you (by phone I mean, I wish I could actually get a "hold" of you right this moment. I miss the feeling of you in my arms...)

Sorry, my email was hijacked by a non-Danish person who knows how to express affection. I'm back now. Please let me know you've arrived safely.

Yours,
Soren

Angela broke out into a big smile reading his sweet email. It felt like her heart had melted into pure liquid.

He misses me! Relief flooded over her. They could figure this out.

She reread the email, smiling as she did. Soren was far more playful in writing than she had ever seen him in person. What an interesting revelation that was. Maybe their long-distance relationship would reveal other aspects of Soren that she wasn't familiar with yet. She read his next email.

From: Soren Lund
To: Angela Holguín
July 12, 2001 at 9:15pm
Subject: Don't forget to let me know you arrived safely

Darling,

You should have arrived by now, but maybe you were tired or are catching up with your parents. Please just send me a quick email so I know that you are okay. I'll look for your email when I get to work. Don't forget.

Yours,
Soren

Her heart swelled—momentarily—at his thoughtfulness, but then her eye caught the subject line of the next three emails and her heart started to beat faster. Furrowing her brow, she opened his third email.

From: Soren Lund
To: Angela Holguín
July 12, 2001 at 11:23pm
Subject: Are you mad at me?

Angela,

I know that things didn't end ideally when you left, but that's no reason not to send me an email so that I know you are safe. I tried calling your American phone number, but it went straight to voicemail. I'm starting to get worried.

Still yours,

Soren

Oh poor baby. She had worried him and then she read the next one.

From: Soren Lund

To: Angela Holguín

July 13, 2001 at 2:58am

Subject: What's going on here?

Angela, you should have landed over 12 hours ago. This is getting ridiculous. Soren

Angela couldn't believe what she was reading. Was Soren actually getting mad at her? The realization both concerned her and amused her. Considering the way things had been left, she was happily surprised to see this outpouring of emotion from him. Maybe falling asleep for so long had been a good idea after all. However, she also found his tone more than a little condescending.

She narrowed her eyes as she clicked on the most recent email, which was timestamped only thirty minutes ago.

From: Soren Lund
To: Angela Holguín
July 13, 2001 at 4:12am
Subject: Is there a problem

Am I missing something here? Why haven't you emailed and why aren't you answering your phone? Ignoring me is very childish.

Her eyebrow arched swiftly as she digested the last email.
Oh no he didn't.

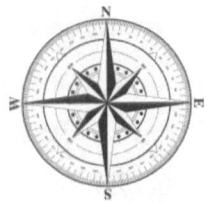

Chapter 3: Understanding

Angela stood up and paced around her living room, doing laps around her large, koa coffee table. Her mind raced as she considered Soren's five emails in their totality. The first couple had been so endearing, but the last two reminded her of their final interaction in Heathrow: cold and condescending.

She had opened herself up to him about Peter, exposed a pain that she would have rather ignored, and instead of that bringing them closer together, it had driven them apart. After dozens of laps around her living room, she walked back over to her laptop and reread his emails. Sighing, she put her fingers to the keyboard and hit "reply" to his very first email.

Dear Soren,

She scowled. Deleting the "Dear" she continued.

Soren,

I'm responding to this email because it seemed that you were not exactly in your right mind when you wrote the last two. I'm sorry I didn't write sooner but after getting home, I fell asleep immediately and just woke up thirty minutes ago. I didn't mean to make you worry.

My American cell phone was dead, but it is charging right now, I forgot to plug it in before I fell asleep. Just so you know I can only receive international calls on it, it isn't set up to make them.

Angela

She reread the email. Part of her wanted to confess to him how much she missed him, but she was still hurting from the tone of his missives. Her reply might be bland, but it was factual, and factual felt safe. She hit send and then headed to the kitchen for a glass of water.

The combination of air travel and many hours of sleep had left her parched. She drained the glass, refilled it and was just about to put the glass up to her lips again when she heard her cell phone ringing from her bedroom. She ran to the phone and saw a Spanish phone number on the display. Her heart leapt into her throat.

"Hello," she said out of breath, her lips dry with nervousness even though she had just hydrated herself.

"Oh my God, are you trying to give me a heart attack? I've been completely out of my mind the last few hours," Soren said breathlessly, the sound of cars honking audible in the background.

Her heart melted at the sincere concern in his voice, helping to repair some of the damage done by their less-than-ideal goodbye at the airport. From the background noise, Angela knew Soren must be out on the street, outside of his work. He would never speak this openly at his cubicle.

"I'm sorry, but I was so exhausted when I got home that I went straight to bed and forgot to charge my phone. I was so tired I didn't even put on pajamas. I just threw off my travel clothes and fell into bed," Angela said in one, long breath.

"That's a nice image," he said suggestively, the tightness in his voice diminishing noticeably.

"Soren!" she said with mock anger, secretly thrilled at the direction this conversation was taking. She could feel the strain between them lifting, and it was such a relief.

"I can't help it. I'll take any excuse to imagine you with no clothes on," he said quietly.

She smiled at the lightness in his voice. It was as though the airport scene had never happened.

"Angela..." he trailed off, his voice cracking.

Her heart clenched at the sound.

"Yes..." she said gently.

"I was such an ass at the airport." His words were heavy with regret.

Angela sighed, her residual anger for Soren evaporating.

He exhaled. "I haven't been able to stop thinking about it since you left. I've just been sitting like an idiot in front of my computer, wishing I could turn back time and do it all over."

She smiled. "I've been thinking the same thing too."

"Why? You didn't do anything wrong. You were right. We have feelings for each other; that should be enough. I'm always trying to analyze everything, but I don't want to analyze you, I want to…"

Love me? Angela thought, finishing his sentence, her heart beating rapidly. "Yes?" she prodded.

He sighed. "I just want to follow my feelings."

She exhaled the breath she'd been holding. It wasn't exactly what she wanted, but it was definitely a step in the right direction.

She smiled. "I'd like that too. That's all I've ever wanted."

"I know. It just doesn't come naturally to me. But when you got on the plane and didn't turn around…well, let's just say I know now why they use the term 'heartbreak.' It literally felt like my heart was broken. And I don't want to feel that way again."

Her heart clenched. "Thank you. I really needed to hear that." She stood up and began pacing again, only this time it was a casual, meander.

"But seriously, I'm just glad you're okay. I didn't like not having a way to check on you. I don't even know your parents' first names so I couldn't do a decent search for them on the internet…"

Her eyes widened. "You were looking up my parents?"

"What else could I do? I don't know anybody in Los Angeles. My next step was to call the airlines or the police. I was really starting to panic."

Soren panic? The concept seemed so foreign to her. He was always so calm, cool, and collected. Then she remembered that it was not too many days ago when he didn't seem so calm, cool, or collected as she recalled how tongue-tied he had always been around her until that day—almost two weeks ago—when she bravely took the first step and kissed him. But now Soren seemed so unflappable that it was hard to remember what he had been like before.

His version of panic probably looked like her version of meditating.

"I'll give you my mom's email address and phone number if it makes you feel better," she said uncertainly. This was not something any man had ever asked for before.

Soren replied immediately, "Please do. That will make me feel much better."

She stifled her laughter at his serious tone. "Okay, I'm sending it right now. I'll also send you Charlene's number since she always knows how to get ahold of me."

"Good thinking," he said clearly relieved.

How sweet.

She must mean a lot to him for him to have become so worried. She hugged herself.

Everything is going to be all right.

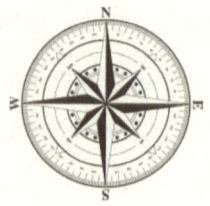

Chapter 4: The Question

"…and then Jorge straightened up, lifting his hands off the back of the person below him and looked out over the crowds around him. He felt as tall as a mountain. He did it. He climbed to the top of the *castell*." Angela smiled, pressed shift, and tapped the quotation mark key loudly, pleased with the scene she had just created. She could just imagine her young, dark-haired hero standing at the top of a human tower six-levels high, waving his right arm with infectious enthusiasm.

The last six weeks had flown by in a blur of creative inspiration. It was like her subconscious mind had been working on the story of Jorge and Estel—the heroes of her children's book set in Barcelona—and now it was flooding out of her in wild bursts of productivity. Sometimes when she started writing it was hard for her to stop, and she'd look up at her clock in shock that three hours had passed without her noticing. It was exciting.

Writing her books was so much fun that she had to be disciplined about it or it would pull her away from the work that was keeping a roof over her head: transcription.

She had been a fast typist ever since her mother enrolled her in a typing course the summer after seventh grade. By her senior year of high school, she was so fast she won a typewriter for having the fastest corrected WPM—words per minute—of any student: 69. Her typing was even faster now—112 WPM corrected—and transcribing medical and legal dictation from home was what paid the bills.

She also worked a few hours a week tutoring students for standardized tests. Her 95th-percentile scores on her SAT and GMAT tests earned her $100-$200 an hour as a private tutor via a Craigslist ad that she maintained. She figured the high price she charged would help keep the weirdos at bay and so far, it had worked.

By keeping her expenses low, including rarely eating out, she was able to save just enough for a small travel fund, her luxury of choice. Another benefit of the mindless "day jobs" was that it reserved all of her creativity and problem-solving for her writing.

In order to make sure she transcribed enough to pay the rent, she worked on her own books in the early morning and late evening, and reserved "work hours" for transcription.

One of her favorite things about working on her book was being transported back to the magical city of Barcelona. When she wrote she could feel the dark, cool, stone passages of the Old City rise up around her. The aromas of the charcuterie and cheese mongers scenting the salty sea air. The fashionable Barcelonese brushing by her on the streets.

The Festival, her book's working title, was definitely her favorite story to work on, although the one set in Bath was also fun.

She leaned back in her chair and looked out toward the large window of her dining-room-cum-office, her laptop and sketchbooks arranged on the right side of her round, 6-person dining table, leaving the left side clear for eating. The evening sky was dark, but there was a light on in the apartment across the courtyard.

She checked the time. It was almost 10:00pm. She looked at her cell phone expectantly. Ever since she had returned to Los Angeles, she and Soren had a standing, date-night call on Friday nights where they would talk until Angela drifted off to sleep. When Soren was still in London, he would call her at 6am his time, but now that he was back in Barcelona—for the beginning of his final year in school at BIN—he called her at 7am.

Soren had asked her to wear one of the nightgowns, he had bought from Selfridge's, tonight, which was the first time he had ever made such a request. She was curious to know why.

Angela jumped when her phone rang. She laughed and quickly picked up. "Hello?"

"Hullo darling Angela. How are you this evening?" His voice was low and tantalizing, like a hypnotist inducing a trance.

Angela shut down her computer, grabbed a glass of water, and padded down the short, carpeted hallway to her bedroom. She had already brushed her teeth in preparation of their phone call, and was ready to crawl into bed and talk the night away with Soren.

"I'm doing well, thanks very much. I've been making good progress on my Barcelona book. My little hero just overcame his fear of heights. It was quite exciting."

Soren chuckled quietly. "It's like he's a real person to you."

"Jorge is a real person to me...although I'm not sure about his name. I think I need something more Catalan," she said, referring to Barcelona's native language. "But anyway, Jorge was really scared about climbing up all those people, and I was scared for him," she said, pulling back her thin cotton blanket and climbing into bed.

September was always the warmest month in Los Angeles, as any school-age child could tell you. Angela could still remember how hot her trendy—but oh so thin—ninja shoes got on the black asphalt playground of her elementary school that glimmered with wavy lines of heat.

Tonight, her bedroom windows were fully open, allowing the balmy night air to fill her room; covers were almost unnecessary.

"I love how much compassion you feel for your characters. How's the book on Bath coming?"

Angela's lips twitched. "It's coming along too, but I keep getting distracted..."

"Distracted, by what?"

"By all of my delicious memories with you! I can't think about Bath without thinking about your hands on me in the bathtub or you sucking on my nipple in front of the fake castle..."

Soren sucked in his breath quickly and laughed.

"What?" she asked.

"I'm just amazed at how my body reacts to you, even over the phone."

She grasped the phone tightly to her ear. "Really? How does your body react?"

He sighed. "Your last sentence gave me a throbbing erection."

It was Angela's turn to suck in her breath. "Really?" she asked, genuinely surprised.

"Really. In fact, it seems like now might be the perfect time to segue," he said mysteriously.

"Segue?"

"Yes. Are you wearing the nightgown I asked you to wear?" His voice full of promise.

"Yes," she said quietly, almost timid. She didn't know why, but she felt suddenly shy.

"Good," he said authoritatively.

Angela felt a pleasurable ache between her legs at the sound of his voice. She was always surprised by how turned on she got when Soren took charge of a situation. She scissored her bare legs beneath her silk charmeuse nightgown, anticipating what was coming next.

"Angela," he said, his voice serious. "Have you ever had phone sex?"

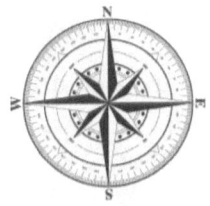

Chapter 5: An Education

Angela wanted to giggle at his tone, but knew that would be the wrong reaction.

But Soren sounded so polite, so deliberate. He could have asked her if she felt her investment portfolio was properly diversified, and the tone would have sounded completely appropriate.

She answered quietly, "Um, oh. Well…a little. I guess. But it was when I was still a virgin. It's been a long time. Why?"

"Well, that wasn't a clear answer at all, now was it?"

She giggled nervously. "Sorry, I guess I'm feeling a little shy."

"You shy?" His tone was skeptical. "I don't think I've ever seen you shy in all the time I've known you."

"Hey, I have boundaries too you know," she said defensively.

"Really? I don't think I've ever seen them before," he answered playfully. "You'll have to point them out to me."

"I'm pointing them out to you now," she said ruefully. She drew her legs up tight against her chest, and wound her free arm around them.

Soren sighed. "You seem…uncomfortable, is something wrong?"

"I don't know…I guess…well…I guess talking about sex does make me a little uncomfortable." She exhaled loudly.

"Angela, are you saying that you are more comfortable with *having* sex than *talking* about it."

She squeezed her eyes shut tightly. She had never thought about it that way, but when it was put to her plainly, she realized the truth. "Honestly, I'm surprised at the answer myself, but I have to say yes."

"Why is that?"

"I don't know. I've never thought about it," she said, biting her lip. "I guess because I didn't grow up talking about it. My parents' version of the sex talk was 'Don't get pregnant.' That was it. I've never really *talked* about sex."

Growing up with an Asian-American mother and a strict, Latino father had guaranteed that Angela's sex education had been practically nonexistent. She vividly remembered when she asked her parents where babies came from at the tender age of five. They sat her down in front of the TV and put on the *TIME LIFE* video on the miracle of birth. She was the kid on the playground who would correct her friends' use of "peanuts" and "China", explaining that the correct terms were "penis" and "vagina."

The "sex talk" finally happened sometime during her thirteenth year, and it was like the pop-up turkey timer proclaiming her season of puberty done. *PING!* The conversation came on the heels of other milestones that year including reaching her full height of 5'-4", blooming to a D-cup seemingly overnight, and starting her period.

Judy Blume would have been proud.

While she had enjoyed her early height—it gave her an edge on the soccer field—she never enjoyed being busty. It annoyed her that she always had to wear two bras while playing sports; and sometimes she fantasized about the simple pleasure of wearing a t-shirt and having it look stylish instead of dumpy.

"You're exaggerating, right?" Soren asked.

"No I'm not. Literally, the sex talk I had was a single conversation and it was with my dad. It lasted exactly as long as it took to drive from our house to my high school, which was about twenty-five minutes max. I was 13-years-old. The only message was 'don't have sex so you don't get pregnant.'"

"That's it?" Soren sounded dumbfounded.

Angela nodded. "Yup, that was it."

"Wow. I'm stunned. In Denmark we talk about sex quite a lot with our parents."

Given Soren's reserved nature, she found this surprising. "What do you mean?" Angela stretched her legs back out.

"I mean, from an early age my parents discussed sex with me and my siblings in a very straight forward and descriptive way; and I know we weren't alone in that experience."

"Really?" Angela exclaimed. "When you say 'descriptive,' what do you mean exactly?"

"My father said things like, 'when the man gets excited his penis gets stiff and he places it in the woman's vagina and if he's really excited he will ejaculate—'"

Angela cut Soren off, "What? Are you serious? Your parents said the word 'ejaculate' to you?"

"What word would you use?" he asked dryly.

Good point. "Um, well, we didn't ever need a word to describe that action because we never talked about the *act* itself. We only talked about the complications…you know, pregnancy, STDs…the fun stuff."

"That's all?"

"Yes, that's all. I told you, it was literally a single conversation." A shudder ran through her as she remembered the horror of sitting in her father's 1976 Corvette Stingray, wishing he would rev the engine just a little louder so she could tune him out completely.

Keeping his eyes on the road in front of him, he gave her his lecture. "Honey, you just can't trust boys. They'll say whatever they have to say to get what they want. You need to stay focused on your future. Getting pregnant will ruin your life. The only way to not get pregnant is to not have sex."

Angela prayed that the traffic gods would be good to her and part the cars like the Red Sea so that she didn't have to listen to any more of her father's talk. Fortunately, he didn't expect her to respond, he only expected her to listen.

She studied the back of her hands with unusual interest.

"You Americans are very interesting. You show sex everywhere, but you don't talk about it at home?" Soren's voice cut into her reverie.

She found herself nodding. She could still smell the lambskin and leather from her dad's old Stingray. "I guess so. I've never really thought about it. That's just how it is."

"My parents talked to us about it in vivid detail throughout our lives, starting with when we were children. And we didn't just talk about the *complications*, we also talked about all the pleasure that one can have from sex...orgasm and everything."

"Oh my gosh. Wow. That's...huh...interesting," she ran her hand through her hair, surprised at how flushed she was feeling...and not in a turned on way.

"Anyway, I've been missing you a lot, and I thought it would be fun to have phone sex."

Angela blushed from head to toe.

Soren filled the silence, "That's why I asked you to wear one of the nightgowns you bought while you were here. I wanted to be able to imagine exactly what you looked like while we were talking. Do you want to try?"

Angela swallowed nervously. She couldn't remember the last time she had hesitated when asked to try something new. Usually she was a "jump first, ask questions later" kind of person. She took a deep breath. "Ok. I just don't know what to do..."

"It's easy darling. Just follow my lead. Are you lying in bed?"

"Yes."

"Are you under the covers? Is the light on?" he asked.

Okay, he's setting the scene like I do in my books. I get it. "The covers are folded back and I'm propped up on my pillows sitting up. The light on my nightstand is on."

"I want you to get really comfortable, so lie down in bed and turn off the light. Just focus on the sound of my voice and the words I say, nothing else," he said slowly and deliberately.

Angela had never heard him use this tone before and it sent a warm thrill through her. "Okay," she said, snapping off the light and sliding down so that she was horizontal on the bed. "Done."

"Good. Now tell me what you are wearing. Describe it to me in as much detail as you can."

She closed her eyes tightly. "I'm wearing one of the ivory-colored, silk charmeuse gowns that I got at Selfridge's. It has four thin straps over each shoulder. Two of the straps hang straight and the other two criss-cross against my back."

Soren breathed in sharply. "Ah yes, I remember the criss-cross straps well. The ivory was so beautiful against your skin. I loved running my fingers under the straps," he paused briefly. "Continue…"

She could tell she was turning him on with her words, which helped to stoke her courage. "It's very long, it almost reaches to my ankles but it has a really high slit on either side that is open all the way to my upper thigh."

"Uh, yes…I remember," he said, his voice ragged.

Angela's nipples puckered in response. She was surprised at how open he was over the phone. Soren was still such an enigma to her.

She rubbed the silk nightgown against her body and continued, "I'm rubbing the silk against my body and it feels amazing. Especially now that I've been wearing it for a while and the fabric is the same temperature as my body. It almost feels like I have nothing on…or like I've coated my body with baby powder."

The sensation of her own fingers on her body was really starting to turn her own; a moist heat developing between her legs.

"I loved touching you through those gowns. I remember how it glided over your skin so erotically. I especially loved tugging the front down and seeing your nipple peak out over the top...uh..." he trailed off, a few guttural sounds following.

A shiver went up her neck, causing her to shimmy against her sheets. "Okay...it's your turn now. Tell me what you're wearing and where you are."

"I'm lying on my bed, but the covers are thrown off to the side. The sun has not risen yet and my blackout shades are drawn so it still feels like nighttime. It's very quiet as none of my flat mates are awake...and I'm wearing a pair of gray boxer briefs that aren't nearly as tantalizing as your ivory nightgown," he said playfully.

"That's what you think," she said as she imagined how they hung low on his body exposing the incredibly-sexy iliac crest and his sandy-colored happy trail. "The mental image they are giving me is quite provocative." After a brief pause, she whispered shyly, "This is fun."

Soren's breath caught in his throat. "God I miss you," he sighed heavily.

She replied breathily, "I miss you too. I remember how it felt when I wore this gown with you last. I remember your hands skimming over my body...over my thighs and ass and then coming to rest on my bare skin in the deep-v of the back."

"Mmmmm…I remember that deep-v very well. I loved dipping my fingers down to caress the small of your back. If I were there I would slide my hands up your legs following the slits of your gown, hike it up around your waist and then run my hands underneath and pull your ass to me so I could feel you tight against me."

Angela sucked in her breath. "Fuck Soren, this is hot."

He laughed lightly. "That's the idea. Then I'd pull down the front of your gown to expose your nipples. I'd roll and pinch one of them with my fingers while I'd swirl my tongue around the other and blow on it, alternating between swirling and blowing until you begged me to stop."

Angela moaned loudly, the intensity of her desire catching her off guard. She closed her eyes, and concentrated her entire focus on the sound of his voice.

Soren continued, "Then I'd nibble my way up to your neck and I'd clamp down hard on that spot you love right where your neck and shoulders meet. I love how you moan and writhe when I lick and bite you there. As I'm attacking your neck I'd be pulling off your panties—"

"If I were wearing any…"

She smiled as she heard Soren moan deeply.

"Oh God, Angela. I want you so much."

"I want you to," she answered immediately, her voice hungry.

"How do you want me?" he asked urgently.

"What?"

"How do you want me?" he repeated, his tone almost demanding.

Angela licked her lips, considering. She felt a hot flush creep over her face and neck.

Soren's voice oozed liquid honey. "Come on darling, talk to me…"

Angela inhaled deeply. *Fuck it. I've done worse.* "I want to ride you Soren. Once you hiked up my gown and saw that I was wearing nothing underneath, I would push you back on the bed and straddle you. I'd put your hands on my naked breasts as I look into your eyes and slide you into me…and then I'd ride you hard. Feeling you deep inside me; filling me up; making me yours as I vary my rhythm between frantic fucking and slow, sensual moments where I tease the head of your cock by bouncing on it ever so slightly and then plunging suddenly all the way down."

She could imagine Soren stroking himself on the other end of the phone, the images she was creating playing themselves on the screen of his mind.

Now for the finale.

"As I'm riding you, I can feel your pelvis grinding against my clit pushing me higher and higher with each stroke. I'll grind my hips in a circle, stroking your cock against every inch of me, teasing you mercilessly…"

"Uh…"

She ran her finger furiously over her clit, tensing and releasing her legs as she approached her own, overdue release. She'd been thinking about Soren all day long, and her lips were plump with desire. Her breath hitched. "Eventually I won't be able to hold back any longer and I'll fuck you fast and hard until I come. Grinding, sliding, fucking you hard until I...I..." words were beginning to evade her.

"Mmmm?" Soren was barely verbal as well.

She slid a finger into her vagina, her muscles convulsing around her finger. "I'd pick up speed and ride you frantically until I collapse onto your chest, spent and sweaty." She squeezed her eyes, her orgasm hovering just out of reach.

"Whu...huh?" he asked.

She sucked in two rapid breaths. Panting as she said, "Then I'd say...'finish me Soren' and you'd flip me over, taking me from behind and fucking me as hard and fast as you could until you came."

She could tell—by the monosyllabic grunts from the other side—that he was close to his release. Her own orgasm was frustratingly close.

"Oh God, yes...mmmm...uh...aaahhhhhhhhhhhh," his voice straggled out a lengthy string of groans.

Fuck that's sexy.

She slid her finger over her clit, faster and harder, flexing her legs as she quickly brought herself to her own orgasm and felt chills run up her back and torso as the waves of her climax crashed over her again and again. Suddenly, the chills began to morph into rivulets of pain, searing through her temples down to the back of her neck. It felt like someone was tightening a metal vise around her head.

"Ow, fuck, ow," Angela moaned through clenched teeth as she dropped the phone and rolled to the side, her hands clutching her temples in anguish.

"Angela? Angela? Are you okay?" Soren's voice sounded far away through the blare of pain radiating through Angela's head. "Angela! Talk to me!"

His voice grew more distant, as Angela writhed on her bed, oblivious to anything but the pain in her head.

She clenched her jaw, moaning with pain, and then, everything went black.

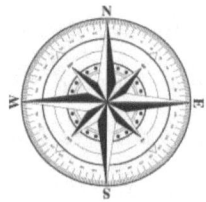

Chapter 6: What's Wrong?

"Angela! Angela!" A frantic voice was yelling.

Angela awoke to the sound of banging on her apartment door.

"Mom?" She sat up, confused as to why her mother was pounding on her door, and immediately raised her hand to her head, which still throbbed painfully. "Ow."

"Angela! Are you okay? Can you hear me?" Her mother continued to assault the door.

Angela attempted to stand up, but quickly sat back down on her bed, her head spinning.

"Yeah, mom. Hold on a sec," she said in the loudest voice she could muster. She snapped on her bedside light, shielding her eyes from the sudden brightness, which seared her cornea and intensified the pain in her head. She took a deep breath and stood up slowly, taking two steps quickly to the wall, and placing one hand on the wall for support as she stumbled to the front door.

When she unlatched the door, her mother came bursting through.

"Oh my God, are you okay?" her mother asked, her face crazed with concern. She was dressed in a trench coat, her pajama pants and house slippers peeking out underneath. Lillian's ladylike Michael Kors handbag looked strangely out of sync with the rest of the outfit.

"What are you doing here?" Angela asked, shaking her head in confusion, and then stopping abruptly when the motion made the dull ache in her head worse.

Lillian approached Angela, offered her arm and guided her daughter to the couch.

"Soren called me. He said he was on the phone with you and then suddenly you weren't there. He tried calling you repeatedly but said that it wouldn't go through or you wouldn't pick up, or something. I don't know. When he called I just raced over here." Her mother's face was pink with worry. "Good thing I'm only ten minutes away." She stroked Angela's hair soothingly.

Angela exhaled. "I'm okay mom. I'm fine."

The corner of Lillian's lips pulled down. "If you are fine, why are you squinting your eyes and clutching your head like that."

Angela shook her head slowly—wary of inciting any more pain—uncertain what to tell her mother. She didn't feel comfortable telling her she'd gotten a headache having an orgasm during phone sex.

Awkward.

Angela bit her lip as her mother rubbed her back soothingly.

"Let me get you some water, honey." Her mom stood up, placed her purse on the coffee table, and walked to the kitchen. She returned with a full glass and held it gingerly to Angela's lips. "Drink this."

Angela drank the cool water thirstily, feeling the pain in her head ebb slightly with the refreshing liquid. "Thanks mom. That helps."

Her mother pursed her lips. "Can you tell me what happened?"

Angela bit her lip. "I'm not sure exactly. All I know is that I was on the phone when I got this excruciating headache. There was a buzzing in my ear, bright lights and a searing pain that started at my temples and seemed to wrap around my head like a crown. I must have passed out from the pain."

Her mother clucked her tongue. "Has this happened before?"

Angela thought back to the two times during her trip to England when she had similar experiences. She nodded apprehensively.

Although she and Lillian spoke almost every day, relationships and sex were not *ever* discussed. Her family was great at talking about concrete topics like school, business, world affairs, food, and travel; ephemeral things like feelings were not part of their repertoire. That's what friends were for.

"Honey, you need to see a doctor tomorrow. I'll call Dr. Thom for you in the morning. For now, just go back to sleep. But before you do, you better let Soren know you are okay."

The next afternoon Angela's mom drove her to an imaging center after a quick call to their family doctor who got a partnering neurologist to order an MRI.

When she was changing into a hospital gown, Angela gave her mother a nervous grin. "Funny how I wasn't really concerned before, but now that I'm here I'm kind of freaking out. What if something's wrong with my brain?" Tears pricked up in the corner of her eyes.

Her mother wrapped her up in her arms, the feeling of her light, cashmere cardigan soothing to the touch. "Shhhh. No point in speculating. I'll be in the waiting room when you come out."

Angela nodded, inhaling the gardenia scent that lingered on her mother for strength. She entered the imaging area, which was all white, the cylindrical MRI machine like some sort of futuristic space pod. The room was bathed in a dim, fluorescent blue light and the hum of the HVAC reverberated through the sterile space.

A thirty-something blond woman with a pixie cut and purple glasses approached Angela and held out her hand. "Hi, I'm Carrie. I'll be the technician on your exam today. Have you ever had an MRI before?" Carrie was wearing standard blue hospital scrubs covered by a long, white lab coat.

Angela shook her head, rubbing her arms.

"Are you cold?"

Angela nodded. "The AC is pretty intense in here."

Carrie smiled. "I'll put a blanket over you when you lie down. Go ahead and get up on the table."

Angela lay back on the padded table, arranging her hospital gown around her legs. She took a deep breath and let it out slowly.

It's going to be okay. I'm not going to worry until there is something to worry about.

"I'm going to put this helmet looking thing around your skull to stabilize your neck and head. It's important that you stay as still as possible during the test in order to get a clear image. Here are some earplugs. The machine makes a loud pounding sound," Carrie said simply.

Angela found Carrie's matter-of-fact tone calming.

"Ok. Thanks." Angela took the plastic bag with the orange foam earplugs.

Carry smiled. "The test will take about an hour, so try and relax. The machine is loud, but some people find it soothing in a weird sort of way. If you pay attention to the rhythm, you can sort of make a game out of it and the time passes faster. You can put in the earplugs now."

Relax? With my brain on the line? Right.

Angela put in the earplugs, then Carrie snapped a lattice-like structure around her head. When the table started sliding into the machine, it was so smooth it felt like she was floating. Angela took a deep breath and tried to relax, waiting for the rhythmic pounding to begin.

It's all going to be okay. It's all going to be okay.

An hour later, Angela awoke as her table emerged from the MRI machine. Carrie smiled at her as she unlatched the helmet.

"All done," she said evenly, as she rolled back the blanket. "You did great. You barely moved a muscle."

Angela was surprised at how relaxed she felt. The jackhammering sounds of the machine had made any sort of worrying or thinking impossible. The MRI had actually felt meditative.

"Thanks. You were right; the pounding sound is weirdly soothing."

Carrie laughed.

Angela studied Carrie's face, looking for some clue indicating whether there was a problem with her brain, but her face was inscrutable.

"When will I get my results?" Angela asked.

Carrie's head swung back toward the computer monitor. "I can't tell you for sure. A radiologist needs to write up a report for your doctor. It's really in his or her court now. You'll have to check with your doctor."

Angela kept her eyes on Carrie's face as she asked, "Did you notice anything unusual?"

Carrie gave Angela a neutral smile. "I'm not qualified to say anything. Sorry Angela."

Her heart sank. *I'm not going to worry until there is something to worry about.* She thought to herself firmly, willing herself to be upbeat. She smiled big, hoping that would make her feel better. "I get it. Thanks."

She went to the changing room, changed her clothes, and then walked out into the waiting room where her mom was reading a book titled *Life of Pi.*

Her mom snapped her book shut as soon as she saw Angela. "How did it go?"

She shrugged. "No idea. The technician said she's not qualified to say anything."

"I'll call the doctor and find out when we can expect results. I'm sure you don't want to have this hanging over your head…" Her mom's eyes got wide. "Sorry hon. I didn't mean anything by that."

Angela shook her head. "It's okay mom. I'm not going to worry until there is something to worry about." She said her new mantra with more strength than she felt.

"Good idea. Let's go get some vegetable pan-fried noodles and moo shu pork," Lillian said with forced excitement.

Angela smiled. "Thanks mom. That sounds good."

Later that evening, Angela called Soren. He picked up on the first ring. "Hullo? Angela? How did it go today?"

Angela's heart clenched at the worried tone of his voice.

She walked around her living room, feeling the soothing texture of the ivory carpet under her bare feet.

"I'm fine Soren. The test went ok I guess, but I won't have results until late tomorrow at the earliest." She sighed, running her hands through her long, mahogany hair. "Thanks again for calling my mom last night."

"I was so worried when you suddenly weren't on the phone." He paused and then continued, "The headache you felt, it wasn't the first time, was it? You experienced this once in Bath and then again in London, didn't you?"

"Yes, it was similar, but last night was way more intense. My head still hurts a little bit now actually, and I can't really read or watch TV. Bright light bothers me a little bit too. But I feel loads better than I did last night, so I guess that's progress." She huffed, trying to make the situation lighter than it felt.

But inside, Angela felt like she was teetering on a precipice not knowing if life as she knew it would continue as usual, or if a serious medical diagnosis would alter the course of her life. She squeezed her eyes tight, not wanting to think about the what-ifs.

"I'm not going to worry until there is something to worry about." She sighed heavily.

"Very wise. Darling. I'm so sorry I can't be there for you." Soren cursed the ocean and continent between then. He felt so helpless, sitting in his bed in Barcelona, with nothing but a mobile phone connecting them.

The way he felt tonight was in stark contrast to when they had been having phone sex. He felt so close to her then. The effect her words had on his body were visceral. It was as though the phone had melted away and she was in the room with him. And then suddenly, his worst nightmare. Complete silence. He'd been manic when she didn't respond to him.

His heart started beating rapidly at the memory. He took a deep breath, trying to bring himself back to the present.

"But you feel okay now?" He absentmindedly smoothed the abstract, navy-blue grid pattern of his duvet with his fingertips, wishing it was her body that he was running his hands over.

She sighed heavily. "I don't feel normal, but I feel a lot better than last night. It's been a long day, and I just want to go to sleep. I'll call you as soon as I hear something, okay?"

He nodded. "Okay. Please take care."

"I will. Goodnight Soren."

He hesitated before saying, "Goodnight Angela."

I love you.

Those were the words he really wanted to say

His heart sank as he imagined the woman he loved going to bed alone. He wished he could be there, tucking her in, holding her in his arms, driving her to the doctor.

He took a deep breath. Tomorrow couldn't come soon enough.

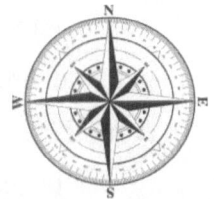

Chapter 7: Doctor's Orders

Angela sat on the black, vinyl examination table, her red cardigan thrown over the flimsy, paper gown.

"It's so cold in here. Why don't they make these things out of real fabric?" she asked her mom as she fingered the paper gown.

"Beats me."

Angela gazed out the large, black-framed windows at the world below as Lillian flipped casually through a magazine. As usual, it was just her and her mom. Her father rarely deigned to be a part of anything beyond the bare minimum of family interactions, leaving the heavy lifting of parenting to her mom.

Angela sighed looking at the people and cars below, going about their day, completely oblivious to her situation. Who knew what Dr. Thom would say when he came through that door? Her entire future could shift in a moment.

"Mom. Do you think I might have what Kelly had?" she asked, referring to her cousin, her mother's niece.

Lillian sighed heavily, putting the magazine down on the seat next to her. She gave Angela a measured look. After a brief pause, she said, "I don't know honey. I've been wondering the same thing. But what she had was a brain aneurysm and the pain she was feeling was more inside her head than around it. I spoke with her yesterday and she specifically said the pain was located behind her eyes and that her vision was affected."

Angela pursed her lips. Her older cousin Kelly had always been a vibrant, fun-loving woman. The brain aneurysm struck in her late 20's—about the age Angela was now—and required grueling years of physical therapy as well as a complete loss of independence for two years. Even now, five years later, Kelly said that she still felt less than her old self. She joked that she went from Kelly 8.0 to Kelly 3.0 overnight, and that now she was around Kelly 6.0.

The door swung open, and a somber Dr. Thom, internist, entered the room.

Dr. Thom was tall and broad; a physically fit 60-year-old man with thinning, white hair and rectangular, metal-rim glasses.

He squinted his eyes as he looked over Angela's file. Clearing his throat he said, "Good afternoon ladies. Sorry for the delay. We had to squeeze you in today between existing appointments, but I didn't want to keep you waiting. I'm sure you're anxious for the results." He nodded his head at Lillian and Angela. His gaze landed on Angela heavily.

The serious look on his face knocked the wind out of her.

It had been almost two days since Angela got her MRI, and it was as if she had been living in some alternate reality where time crawled like molasses. Life was on hold until she knew the cause of her headaches.

Dr. Thom smiled kindly. "Angela dear. I have some good news. There's nothing wrong with your brain."

Angela stared at Dr. Thom in shock, her eyes wide, and then crumpled forward, holding her head in her hands as she sobbed tears of relief.

"There isn't?" Lillian asked, surprise and relief mingled in her voice. She stood up and wrapped an arm around Angela, who leaned her head against her mother's shoulder.

Dr. Thom nodded. "Nope. Nothing wrong." He gave Lillian a sideways look before turning to Angela and saying gently, "Angela dear, could you tell me a little more about what brings the headaches on?"

Angela sniffed, blotting at her tears with the sleeve of her paper gown. She glanced at her mother hesitantly.

Dr. Thom caught the glance. He turned to Lillian, laying a hand on her forearm. "Would you give Angela and me a moment to talk privately? Doctor, patient confidentiality and all."

Lillian looked at Angela questioningly.

"It's okay mom," Angela said encouragingly.

Lillian nodded as she stood up. "I'll be in the waiting room if you need me." She closed the door behind her.

Angela sighed heavily.

"So tell me about these headaches." Dr. Thom sat in a chair, crossed his legs, and folded his arms over his lap.

Without going into any embarrassing detail, Angela told him about the three headaches she'd had that were all induced by orgasm.

He nodded his head. "Angela, these are basically tension or exertion headaches, and they aren't common but they aren't unheard of."

"They aren't? But I've never heard of them before." She shifted her weight, smoothing out her paper gown over her knees.

He smiled kindly. "Of course not. Who wants to talk about a headache brought on by orgasm? But I can assure you that I've treated patients with them before, and all of them had normal MRIs just like you. There is no medical condition behind your headache. Your brain is fine."

Angela smiled for what felt like the first time in days. *Nothing to worry about.*

Well, *almost* nothing. "Is there anything I can do to avoid them in the future?"

He shrugged his shoulders, cocking his head to the side. "From my experience, these types of headaches are more common after extremely long periods of foreplay. Was this true in your situation?"

Angela shrugged. Really, everything she and Soren did was foreplay at this point and yes, sometimes it went on for an extremely long time. The afternoon in the tub in Bath had followed a full day of ongoing sexual stimulation. Being with Soren was like one, long—delicious—tease. She had never been sexually aroused for such an extended period of time before.

Slowly, she nodded her head. "Yes, there is definitely extended foreplay involved."

He nodded, his lips pursed. "See if there is a pattern to what brings on your headaches, and adjust your sexual activity accordingly. Unfortunately—in your case—less might be more."

Angela laced up her sneakers, closed the door on her aging Volvo, and began walking slowly toward the trailhead, the satisfying crunch of decomposed granite under her feet like music to her ears. She planted her feet, twisted her arms and torso and stretched, waiting for her friend Therese to join her for their weekly hike. She inhaled deeply and looked around, feeling as light as a bird as she took in the expansive views of the fire-trail-cum-hiking-path.

The wide, clear-cut swaths that snaked throughout the Santa Monica mountains were rigorously maintained in order to ensure access for the fire department in case of a brush fire, however, most days the fire department was nowhere in sight and it was hikers and bikers that could be found enjoying these broad, gravelly paths.

Even though Angela was just minutes from the loud bustle of Ventura Boulevard to the north and Sunset Boulevard to the south, it felt like she was worlds away. After the past few days of anxious waiting, this was exactly what she needed.

At least once a week Angela and Therese—they met on the first day of college and bonded hard over their shared passion for Jane Austen—would meet for a rigorous hike somewhere in the vast Santa Monica mountain range. Today—in celebration of the news from Dr. Thom—they would do Angela's favorite stretch, a trail above Encino that paralleled the 405 freeway. She and Therese had agreed yesterday that if her doctor gave her the all clear, they would meet for a hike to celebrate.

Therese had practically squealed into the phone when Angela told her the good news an hour ago.

"See you at the trailhead Ange!" Therese yelled, her voice full of relief.

Therese Hartley was a native of Orange County—an area about an hour south of Los Angeles. She and Angela had been assigned to the same dormitory and met on "Move In Day."

After the first few weeks of school, the two women had become so close that they asked their respective roommates if they could switch dorm rooms so they could live together. Their roommates agreed as long as Angela and Therese did all the physical labor, which they happily agreed to. After undergrad, Therese went on to law school out of state, matriculating with honors and then returned to Los Angeles to live and practice law. The two had stayed close over the years—except for an 18-month stint when they barely spoke—and their weekly hike was a way to ensure that they saw each other regularly.

They had been through a lot together.

Angela buttoned up her oversized, white shirt and threw on her large sun hat. The September sun in Los Angeles was brutal, and she liked to keep the heat off her skin.

She looked at her watch. It was just after 12. Therese always left work at noon and it would take her at least fifteen minutes to get here from her office in Sherman Oaks. She had just enough time to give Soren a quick update. He had seemed almost as anxious for the news as she was.

She dialed his number. He picked up on the first ring.

"What happened?" Soren's voice was tense and full of anticipation.

Angela burst out into relieved laughter. "My brain is fine," she said loudly, her smile generating enough watts to supply many power plants. She glanced around quickly, grateful that there was no one around to see her yelling into the phone like a maniac.

"What? That's fantastic. That's amazing!" Soren said, his own voice many decibels louder than usual. "What did the doctor say?"

She smiled mischievously as she kicked a large pebble. "Well, apparently, when I accuse you of torturing me with your teasing ways I am not far off. Medically speaking that is. Apparently, it's all of the tension that's built up before my orgasms that gives me headaches. My doctor basically said that you need to make me orgasm *faster*."

"Really? Well, if that's what the doctor orders, who am I to say no?" His tone was comical, and the mix of relief and joy in his voice made Angela's heart tighten.

God I love him.

She sighed. "But other than that, my brain is totally fine."

"That's such a relief." He exhaled heavily.

Angela turned as she heard crunching footsteps behind her. Her friend Therese approached, her shoulder-length blonde hair pulled through her baseball cap in a ponytail. Therese was about an inch taller than Angela, and slim on top but with a tiny waist, and voluptuous hips accentuated by the bright blue tank top and tight, black yoga pants she was wearing. Angela held up her index finger and mouthed, "Just a second," to her friend.

Therese nodded.

"Darling, I have to go. My friend Therese just arrived. She and I are going on a celebratory hike." Angela turned away, cupping her hand over her mouth. ""I miss you so much. We are still on for our date night call this week, right?" A thrill of anticipation shot up her spine.

"Of course darling, only this time I'm under doctor's orders to make you come sooner, so you better be ready." His tone was dark and lascivious.

Angela could picture him licking his lips, his eyes full of predatory lust. A delicious ache blossomed in her gut.

"Mmmm. I can't wait."

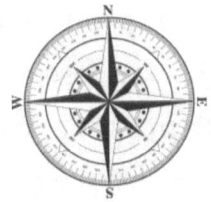

Chapter 8: Good News

"Girlfriend, have I got some good news for you," Charlene said excitedly, reverting from her usual flawless, professional register into the casual-girlfriend tone she used with Angela.

It always amazed Angela how different her MBA friends sounded when she talked to them at work—many of them at high-powered, corporate office jobs—versus how they spoke when no one from work was around.

Angela and Charlene Nelson had met as exchange students at BIN, August of last year. A native of Tennessee, she now resided in Minneapolis, Minnesota where she was an up-and-coming executive pulling down six-figures for a major medical technology corporation. At thirty-three, Charlene was one of the younger executives; she had been working for the same company ever since she was twenty-two. Her two years at MBA school had been paid for by her employer who was grooming her for upper management.

Angela sat up straighter. "Really? What is it?"

Charlene paused before gushing dramatically, "I have to go to Barcelona for a work conference."

"Oh you are too lucky. I'm so jealous, but how is that good for me? Are you going to bring me back some *jamón ibérico de bellota*?" Angela asked, referring to her favorite Spanish ham.

Sometimes Angela wished that she had gone the corporate route; the money that some of her friends were making was mind-boggling. But whenever she thought about working in an office, she got a tight, suffocating feeling in her chest; she was just not worker bee material.

Freedom was the value she held above all others.

"I'm going to do much better than that. Since the company is paying for me and hubby to fly out there, I thought I would give you an early Christmas present and use some of my miles to fly you out!"

Angela stood up from her couch in shock. "What! Are you serious? Oh my gosh, you are the best friend in the world. Are you sure?" she asked, pacing around her large, rectangular, koa wood coffee table with excitement.

"Of course I'm sure girlfriend! What's the point of me working my butt off, flying all over the planet, if I don't put some of these work miles to good use. Barcelona wouldn't be the same without you. I've missed it and I've missed you and what better way to visit? Besides, we still know so many people there, and I thought it would be fun to see everyone," Charlene assured.

Soren! She'd get to see Soren so much sooner than they had planned. He had promised to visit her in Los Angeles over the upcoming Christmas break, but that was still over two months away.

Angela's head began to spin as she thought of going to Barcelona again. The food, the sounds, the sights. She could work on *The Festival* too. Now that she knew what she was writing, being in Barcelona would help to flesh out the details of her locations.

What an amazing turn of events, she couldn't wait to tell Soren.

Angela squealed into the phone, "You've just made me the happiest girl in the world. When are we leaving?"

After Angela hung up with Charlene, she checked her watch. It was only 9pm in Spain, so Soren would still be up. He picked up her call on the first ring.

"Hullo darling Angela, what a nice surprise. I didn't expect to hear from you today. Did you want to have another phone date?" Soren asked in a deep voice filled with promise.

At his words, the serpent in Angela's abdomen began to coil up into a pleasurable knot remembering their conversation yesterday when Soren had described in graphic detail how he wanted to go down on her. Her nipples tightened at the memory.

Even though their physical relationship had not yet been consummated, their phone dates had given them free rein to explore all manner of physical pleasures. She hadn't known how satisfying phone sex could be until Soren had initiated her into it. The last few weeks had been quite an education; fortunately, Angela was a fast learner. And by following Dr. Thom's suggestion of not drawing out the foreplay as long, Angela had been able to avoid any more orgasm-induced migraines.

"Mmmmm," she purred into the phone, closing her eyes momentarily. "Round 2 *would* be nice, but darling, I have some really good news, that's why I'm calling." She pushed aside the vinyl blinds of her apartment and looked out into the interior courtyard. One of the children in the building was running around, smelling the roses that her downstairs neighbor grew.

"What is it?"

"I'm coming to Barcelona in two weeks," she practically yelled into the phone with excitement.

"What?" Soren exclaimed with uncharacteristic enthusiasm.

"Charlene has a work conference in Barcelona and she offered to fly me out."

"Wow, that *is* good news. When do you arrive?"

"Monday, October 22nd, then we fly out on Friday. I know it's not a long trip, but I can't wait to see you." She leaned against the window frame, imagining Soren's strong, warm arms around her.

"I can't wait to see you," he said, his voice low and husky.

"And feel you…" she added suggestively.

He murmured his agreement with a low growl in his voice. "Yes, I can't wait for that either."

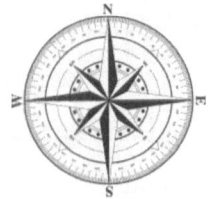

Chapter 9: Jabberwocky

Angela cursed as she balanced the *Thomas Guide* map book on her legs, scanning the building fronts trying to find the address for the bookstore she was looking for while keeping one eye on the road in front of her.

She had spent the last couple of weeks visiting small, independent bookstores to take the pulse of store owners and see where her books would fit best while trying to glean as much information about the children's book industry as possible.

Despite years of predicted bankruptcy, the internet retailer Amazon was finally starting to gain some traction in the book market and had recently begun adding other offerings to its lineup. However, Amazon's success was still not threatening small, independent bookstores—who had already managed to survive the competition of megastores like Borders and Barnes & Noble. These indie bookstores tended to be in high-traffic retail areas, with loyal neighbors who supported small businesses. The store Angela was looking for now was in one of those areas: Melrose Avenue.

Melrose—as locals called it—was one of Los Angeles' premier shopping streets and had a reputation for being the rebellious kid sister to Rodeo Drive's debutante. If Rodeo Drive was carats and stilettos, then Melrose was piercings and fishnets. The offerings on the eclectic street ranged from luxurious to funky to trashy, and the area was as well known for its burger joints as its fancy, Italian restaurants.

Angela kept scanning the storefronts in search of the name and address she was looking for. After visiting almost twenty small bookstores, she was feeling a bit jaded and road weary. While some of the stores had expressed interest in carrying her book, no one had any advice on how to find an illustrator or publisher. However, one of the stores she visited had recommended that she check out Jabberwocky because it focused on children's books exclusively.

"Why can't people put up damn address numbers and help a girl out," she burst out as she struggled to find her destination. Fortunately, the slow-moving traffic of Melrose allowed her to gawk without inciting the ire of other drivers.

Finally, she spotted the large, bubble-shaped, purple-black letters she'd been looking for: Jabberwocky. "It's about time," she said, relieved. She looked over her right shoulder as she pulled to the side, preparing to park.

"Damn." She cursed as she watched a man on a vintage Triumph motorcycle snag the prime, unicorn parking spot right in front of the store. There were no other spots available on the block. She saw a sign on the side of the building that read "Park in Rear."

As she pulled past the beautiful, sleek machine she watched as its rider got off, unzipped his well-worn, black leather jacket, exposing his black t-shirt beneath. He took off his helmet and shook out his curly, dark hair like a model in a shampoo commercial. Angela slowly turned right into the store's driveway, craning her neck to scowl at the motorcycle rider who stole her parking spot when she caught a glimpse of a handsome, tanned face with a 5-o'clock shadow and a jaw like Superman.

She sucked her breath in, surprised.

Hello Tall-Dark-and-Dangerous.

She shook her head—momentarily caught off guard by the distractingly handsome face she'd just seen—and turned her eyes back to the front to find a space for her aging Volvo sedan.

After getting out of the car, she swept her long hair over her shoulder and smoothed out the front of her knee-length, A-line dress with its abstract pattern of black, white and red. She walked to the store's back door. The words "Jabberwocky" spelled out the store's name in puffy-looking 3D letters covered with glittering black bits of obsidian that managed to be both fanciful and slightly foreboding at the same time. The sign was a smaller scale version of the one she had just seen on the front of the building.

She pulled open the heavy door and heard a bell chime. The interior of the upscale, children's bookstore was equal parts Cirque du Soleil, Tim Burton, and *The Little Prince*. There was an edgy, creative vibe to it, which fit its location on Melrose perfectly.

Soren would trip out at this place, she mused, guessing that there was probably nothing like Jabberwocky in Denmark.

The carpet had a whimsically-psychedelic vibe with a Barney-purple background and acid-green blobs scattered about like misshapen polka dots. The furniture in the space was an eclectic mix including chairs from every era and style, but unified by glossy white paint and upholstered in a rich jewel-toned velvet stripe. Starburst-shaped light fixtures completed the exuberantly funky look. The ceiling was covered with words projected by some unseen source. "'Twas brillig, and the slithy toves," the words flashed and were replaced, "Did gyre and gimble in the wabe." Angela recognized the words of Lewis Carroll's famous *Jabberwocky* poem.

She sauntered slowly around the store, savoring the ambiance like a fine meal. The air smelled of fresh ink and cardstock.

Tracing her hand along the lacquered bookshelves, she delighted in the rows upon rows of children's books, which included many unique and exotic titles that she had never seen before. This was exactly the kind of place that she could see her books doing well. She allowed her fingers to drift over the book spines, pulling out titles and covers that appealed to her.

There were books with entire landscapes that had been built from random objects like paper clips and pushpins that were then painted and photographed into intricate scenes of railroad stations and train tracks. Then there were others with sophisticated black and white photography that told the story of a boy and his hobbyhorse, but with layouts and composition worthy of the finest coffee table books.

After scouring the shelves for thirty minutes, she grabbed a couple of dozen books and set them down on a table next to a club chair that felt like a broken-in baseball mitt. She grabbed the first book and lost herself in its pages.

Two hours later, Angela flipped through the books she had read. There was one about a little, blond boy learning to sail that reminded her of Soren. She smiled. *It will be a cute gift.* She flipped through the other books and selected nine that she wanted to purchase before walking up to the register. A mom with a young child was being rung up by a petite woman with a nose-ring, and funky orange dreadlocks who caught Angela's eye and said, "I'll be with you in a sec."

"Take your time," Angela replied.

Angela flipped open the cover of the top book she was holding when out of the corner of her eye a movement caught her attention. It was Mr. Tall-Dark-and-Dangerous carrying a huge stack of books and he was walking toward the register, his well-sculpted biceps bulging under the weight of his cargo. He caught Angela looking at him and flashed a luminous smile, complete with deep dimples, as a thick curl of black hair fell into his eyes.

Her eyes widened and her heart started beating faster.

Wow, he's hot. She was momentarily mesmerized by how extraordinarily good-looking Mr. TDD was. Angela was not usually distracted by looks—after all L.A. was the land of pretty people—but on a scale of 1 to 10, Mr. TDD was off the charts. There was also something vaguely familiar about him.

He broke her reverie by laughing as he attempted to blow the stray tendril of hair out of his face with no success. Angela took a deep breath and looked down at the books in her hands to keep herself from making eye contact as he drew closer to the register.

He put the stack of books down on the counter with a thud. "Why don't you take your break now Hannah, I got it here." He nodded at the woman behind the register as he smiled kindly at Angela.

"Cool." Hannah nodded and walked away.

Mr. TDD looked at Angela's stack of books and whistled. "Wow, you've got quite a haul here. Are you stocking up for Christmas?" he asked, a mischievous twinkle in his dark chocolate eyes.

Angela paused, caught off guard by his overly familiar tone. She looked at him hesitantly. "Um, no…it's research actually," she said, feeling uncharacteristically shy under the warmth of his penetrating gaze.

Pull it together girl. It's just a pretty face.

She couldn't remember the last time she'd felt this flustered and tongue-tied.

"Research?" He cocked his head to the side.

"Yeah, I write children's books." Usually she would have taken his question as the perfect opening to pitch him her books, but instead she shifted uncomfortably under his gaze.

"Really? What kind of books?" he asked with genuine interest. He started ringing her up as he waited for her answer.

She squared her shoulders and took a deep breath, preparing to deliver the spiel she'd developed over the last couple of weeks.

Mr. TDD looked up at her, an amused look on his face.

She narrowed her eyes, and began speaking quickly. "Books about other places and other cultures. The one I'm finishing up is set in Barcelona and tells the story of the city's largest festival, called La Mercè. The text will be in English and Spanish."

His eyes widened and the corners of his mouth twitched upwards. "Go on." He continued to scan her purchases.

She continued, "I want the books to be entertaining and educational. The Barcelona book has a young girl and boy as the main characters. I want to illustrate the story with drawings superimposed over real photographs that I've taken."

His eyebrows arched dramatically. "In-ter-res-ting," he said, drawing out the single word.

She looked away from his face and stared at the cork-covered top of the register counter like it was the most fascinating thing in the world. She drummed her fingers lightly, looking for a distraction from the face in front of her. She could hear her heart beating loudly in her ears.

"You know, that sounds really cool. We don't have anything like that here. You should bring the rough draft by, and some of your photos. It sounds like something we might be interested in carrying." He grabbed her last book, scanned it and put it in a purple bag that said "Jabberwocky" in black, iridescent letters.

Angela looked up and gave him a big smile. "You think the owner would be interested in it?" she asked excitedly, forgetting her recent discomfort quickly. It was the first time someone she wasn't related to had shown real interest in her idea.

He chuckled lightly, the rogue curl on his forehead bouncing loosely. "Yes, I definitely think *he* would be interested in it. That will be $215.74."

Angela winced at the amount, handing him her business credit card. *You gotta spend money to make money.* "Great, I'd love to bring my rough draft by. How can I get in touch with him?"

Mr. TDD gave her a sly smile as he smoothly handed her a business card and pointed to the email address at the bottom. "Send an email here. And your name is…" he looked at the business card she handed him, "Angela. Hey that's pretty."

She couldn't stop the blush that came with his compliment. *Damn it.* She took a calming breath. "You'll tell him to expect my email?" she asked hopefully, trying to get the conversation back on track.

He gave her a strange smile. "Yes, he'll know why you are emailing."

"Thanks so much, I really appreciate it. I'll send an email later today." She averted her eyes from his warm gaze as she rushed to grab her purchases and raced for the safety of her car.

When she put her hands on the steering wheel, she noticed that they were visibly shaking. She took a few deep breaths.

It's just a face!

Back in the safety of her apartment, she looked at the thick, white cardstock of the business card. The font on it was dark black and looked like the lettering from an old-fashioned typewriter. It was edgy, just like the store. The card read, "Kieran O'Connell, Owner, JABBERWOCKY."

She opened up her email program and began writing. After a few edits she settled on.

Dear Mr. O'Connell,

I was in your fantastic store today and the cashier told me I should reach out to you. I'm writing a children's book set in Barcelona that will be both educational and entertaining. I'm planning to illustrate with drawings superimposed over photographs that I took personally. Please let me know a good time to meet.

Best,
Angela Holguín, MBA

She couldn't decide if the "MBA" after her name gave her gravitas or seemed braggy, but she decided that as a young woman she wanted to err on the side of looking like she had some life experience, so she kept it.

She hit send and began flipping through one of the new books she had purchased at Jabberwocky when she heard a ping from her email program.

Hello Ms. Holguín,

I'd love to see your book. There is a coffee shop on the same block as Jabberwocky. Are you available tomorrow at 11am?

Cheers,
Kieran
P.S. MBA, huh? Impressive.

She smiled, glad that she had included her degree. She wondered what Mr. Kieran O'Connell looked like. She imagined a petite, well-dressed man in his fifties with red hair and green eyes. He probably had a background in theatre or design, given the funky interior of Jabberwocky.

Dear Mr. O'Connell,

I would love to meet you tomorrow, but I'm heading to Barcelona for a week. Can we meet the week after next?

Thanks,
Angela

Her email program pinged almost immediately.

Dear Ms. Holguín,

That's too bad. I was looking forward to our meeting. Week after next is fine. How's Monday at 11? In the meantime I'd love to see whatever you feel comfortable sending me: manuscript, outline, mini-bible. I'll sign any NDA you like.

Travel safe and enjoy some jamón ibérico for me.
-Kieran

Angela pursed her lips. Kieran O'Connell clearly knew his Spanish ham since he referenced the more expensive and less well-known *jamón ibérico*—preferred by all foodies—rather than the more common *jamón serrano*. If *serrano* was a BMW 7 series, *ibérico* was a Rolls Royce.

She typed a brief reply, attached her outline and first two chapters, and hit send. She smiled big, throwing herself onto her couch with glee.

Having her books in a store like Jabberwocky would be a huge coup. She couldn't wait to hear what Kieran O'Connell thought of her book.

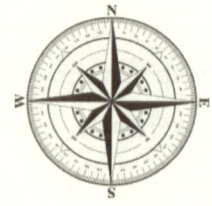

Chapter 10: Barcelona

Angela stowed her tray table in preparation for landing and smoothed out the front of her jeans. She looked out her window with excitement as the ground of Spain approached quickly in greeting. Pulling on the sleeves of her raspberry-colored cotton top, she took off her colorful cotton scarf, stowing it in her beautiful canvas and leather carry on that Soren had gifted her back in London.

The last two weeks had been a whirlwind of activity. Up until Charlene had called her, Angela had been working simultaneously on five different book ideas. However, the unexpected trip to Spain was an opportunity to really flesh out the Barcelona book, so she had concentrated on that one in earnest the last two weeks filling in as much of her manuscript as possible. She had made many notes pointing out knowledge gaps in her book that she wanted to plug during this trip.

Of course, she'd have to fill those knowledge gaps during any time not spent with Soren.

Soren!

In just a couple of hours she'd been in his arms again where she belonged. The thought sent a warm lance of desire through her pelvis. She could almost taste his lips as she closed her eyes, imagining the cool, woodsy scent of his cologne. This time when they parted, she would be sure to take a memento with her. She missed his scent almost as much as she missed his body.

However, part of her was also looking forward to getting back to LA next week. Kieran O'Connell had written her back late last night, and his email had been so encouraging she had practically wept with relief.

Dear Ms. Holguín,

Thank you for sharing your work product with me. I really like how spunky Jorge and Estel are. I think Jorge might not be the right name for your hero though. Don't they speak Catalan in Barcelona? Jorge seems like too Spanish a name. My two cents.

In your outline, you mention that Jorge overcomes his fear of heights in the book. Why don't you open with a scene that illustrates this fear? Maybe there's a cat that's stuck in a tree, or something like that. I think it would really pull in the reader and make them sympathize with him right away.

I'm attaching links to a couple of books on the craft and business of children's books. I think you will find them very helpful.

I look forward to our meeting. Travel safe.

-Kieran

Finally, she had found her badly-needed mentor. Her business was moving forward slowly but surely.

She could feel her stomach drop as the plane approached the runway quickly and made contact, bouncing along the tarmac before settling into a smooth roll.

I'm here! A thrill of excitement rushed through her body, starting at her feet and working its way out through her scalp. She couldn't wait to—once again—taste the colorful cuisine, smell the briny air, and feast her eyes upon the whimsical architecture of Barcelona. The love she had for this magical city by the sea felt almost romantic.

She gave thanks once more for Charlene's generosity, and for her own situation, which allowed her to pack up and leave town for the week without causing any waves. She only had two outside commitments that she had to worry about. The first was her freelance job transcribing dictation. But since it was freelance, she didn't have a boss that she had to clear her vacation with. She just wrapped up any projects she was working on, and wouldn't take on anything new until she returned.

The second commitment had been a little tougher. She was taking a make-up class at the MBA school she just graduated from. Professor Colburn's class was considered a "must take" for entrepreneurial students, but it was only offered once a year in the fall. Since Angela had been on exchange in Barcelona last fall, she had missed her opportunity to take it. Fortunately, Professor Colburn always held five spaces in the class for new graduates for this very reason.

The entire class of sixty-eight students was divided up into teams of four. Although missing class was frowned upon, her teammates had understood when she told them about the trip. One of them said, "Just send an email telling the TA's that you are sick. We'll back up your story."

Fortunately, the class only met once a week, so she would only be missing a single session.

As the plane taxied to her gate, she gathered her belongings. She couldn't wait to see Charlene and her husband Rodney. They had coordinated their flights so they would land within an hour of each other and could share a cab on the 25-minute ride into town.

Angela exited the baggage claim and spotted her two friends. She and Charlene squealed loudly as they ran to each other, embracing in a big hug.

"It's so good to see you," Charlene said. She was wearing a white eyelet blouse and dark jeans. Her long, thin braids were as perfect as always, and her thick, black glasses gave her a professorial look.

"You too. Thanks again for this. It is really one of the nicest, most generous things anyone has ever done for me," Angela gushed, a giant grin plastered across her face.

"Don't mention it girl. I'm just happy we get to be in Spain together again, even if it's just for five days. Come say 'hi' to Rodney," she motioned to her husband who was sitting about twenty feet away, his legs propped up on their luggage. He stood as they approached.

Rodney was a compact and muscular man with skin the color of dark chocolate, a bald head and just the slightest whisper of a mustache. An athlete all his life he still bulged as though he was about to enter a wrestling match at any moment.

He had become a dear friend to Angela during the times he had visited Charlene in Spain during their semester abroad, and he gave Angela a big bear hug when he saw her.

"It's good to see you Angel," he said teasingly. He was wearing a black t-shirt with the name of a sports team Angela didn't recognize, along with his trademark tan cargo pants. A pair of sports sandals completed Rodney's extreme-sports-meets-MacGyver look.

"I still can't believe we are here, together," Angela said with gratitude and wonder in her voice.

"My back believes it after that horrible overnight flight," Charlene said, massaging her lower back. "And I'm starving! Should we get a cab into town?"

"Yes please!" Angela marveled at how foreign the airport felt to her after ten months away. She had practically lived at the airport during her months in Barcelona, with her travels to Paris, Rome, Madrid and Morocco. But somehow it seemed different; she felt like a visitor to Barcelona instead of a citizen. The thought made her sad.

God I love this place.

On the cab ride into town, Angela and Charlene fell back into their habit of chit-chatting in Spanglish, as they waxed poetic about their adopted city and the places they wanted to visit.

"How was your flight?" Charlene asked.

"Crazy. I had to leave my apartment five hours before in order to allow enough time to get through security. This was my first time flying since September 11th. It's amazing how different things are…and it's only been a month."

The radically increased restrictions on air travel served to keep the memory of the September 11th terrorist attacks fresh on everyone's mind. No one knew what the "new normal" would look like yet.

"We had to leave really early too. I was in New York for work a couple of weeks ago and the mood is still very somber there. I don't think anyone knows yet the full impact of that day," Charlene said presciently.

As they began their approach to the city center, the unmistakable landmark of Montjuic rose up on their right-hand side. The majestic stone promontory lent an air of gravitas to the lighthearted city, and stood like a watchtower granting admission to all who passed.

Angela's eyes stole a wistful glance to the west, toward the neighborhood of Les Corts, where she had lived during her time in the city. Her tiny apartment with its sun-drenched balcony had been such a welcome home for her that part of her yearned to return to it. However, on this trip she would be staying with Charlene and Rodney in the central—more touristy—part of the city to the east, in a fancy hotel paid for by Charlene's work.

Angela said a silent prayer of gratitude for Charlene's employer, growing more grateful by the second that her friend worked a well-paying corporate job with all the benefits. The entrepreneurial life had its own rewards, unfortunately, fancy hotels and flights to Barcelona were not yet a part of them.

Soren had been surprisingly silent about the sleeping arrangements when Angela mentioned staying with Charlene. She figured this was—yet another—of his ways of keeping the brakes on their physical relationship. She no longer cared if or when they would have sex; she just wanted to feel his arms around her again. That would be enough.

It was still too early to check in at the hotel, so the trio decided to head straight to the heart of the city: Plaça de Catalunya. The famous plaza—referred to as Plaça Catalunya—was not at the exact center of the city, although it was close. It stood at the top of La Rambla— one of Europe's most famous, and ancient, promenades—and formed a bridge between the old and new parts of the city.

"Let's go find somewhere to eat, I'm starvin'," Rodney said, a bit of his Tennessee accent coming out.

"Let me text Soren where we are. Let's stay above the Liceu so he can find us easily," she said, referring to the grand opera house that marked the halfway point of La Rambla; the old theater—which opened in 1847—stood almost exactly halfway between Plaça Catalunya at its north end and the pedestaled statue of Christopher Columbus at its south end. Angela grabbed her European mobile and sent a quick SMS to Soren.

As they started walking southeast, Angela pocketed her prepaid phone and scanned La Rambla, one of Barcelona's oldest and most well-traveled streets for both locals and tourists. She inhaled deeply as she admired the wide avenue, its leafy plane trees shading the Mediterranean sun from the beautiful people of the city; it was one of her favorite vistas in the whole world. Citizens and visitors of all ages and sizes bustled about, on their way to the shore, or the market, or the café. Angela wondered what secret magic was at work that allowed La Rambla to feel busy while also maintaining a sense of elegant serenity; the street was full of activity without feeling frenetic.

The air was beginning to turn crisp and the leaves on La Rambla were in harmony with the weather and just beginning to show the tinges of gold that signaled fall's arrival. Angela breathed in the clean, briny air and closed her eyes, enjoying the feeling of the dappled light falling on her face, created by the thick canopy of trees overhead.

It felt so good to be in Spain again. So much had happened in the ten months since she had last been here: she had graduated from her MBA program, she was laying the foundation for her children's book business, and she was in love with Soren Lund.

Not that he knew that...yet.

She hoped that this trip would be a big turning point for their relationship both emotionally and physically. She was ready to demonstrate the depth of her feelings for Soren with both her words and her actions. Her heart began beating faster in anticipation.

Rodney's voice cut into her reverie. "This looks good. Let's eat here." Rodney gestured to one of La Rambla's many sidewalk cafés. He sighed as he parked the two roller bags he'd been dragging behind him—as well as the large duffel bag that had been slung across his back—and sat down with a loud thud in the closest aluminum café chair.

The sidewalk cafés were 100% about location and 0% about quality, but the look on Rodney's face made it clear that he wasn't moving. "Now my vacation can begin," he said, locking his hands behind his head and leaning back in his chair.

Angela and Charlene traded eye rolls and followed his lead. "Okay Rodney, we see that you are tired of walking," Charlene said as she pulled her crossbody purse over her head and placed it on the table.

His eyes widened, full of mock innocence. "Now whatever gave you that idea?"

Angela smirked and pulled up another chair, wincing as the cold aluminum worked through the back of her thin shirt. She texted Soren their exact location and began scanning the crowds, looking for the stormy-blue eyes she loved so much.

"Look, they have that black rice here," Charlene said, pointing to a menu item.

"Yum. I had that once at tragaluz," she said, remembering the amazing meal she had on her first date with Thomas. *Was that only a year ago?* She shook her head in disbelief. So much had happened since then. "The time I had it, it was amazing. But I'm not sure I want to try it here." Angela pursed her lips, as she continued to look over the menu.

Just then, a pair of large hands covered Angela's eyes.

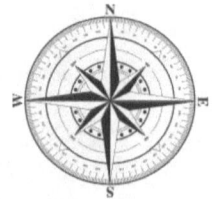

Chapter 11: Three Little Words

Recognizing Soren's cool, woodsy scent, Angela jumped up from her chair and flung herself into his waiting arms, squealing madly.

He pressed his lips against the top of her head. "Hullo beautiful."

Leaning into his chest she murmured, "Hello yourself." She pulled him to her tightly, reveling in the feeling of him pressed against her. It was so nice to feel him in her arms again: real, solid, present.

When she pulled away, she took in his beautiful ocean-blue eyes—thrilled to see them twinkling back at her.

A serious look came over him as he searched her face with an almost sad look. "I've missed you so much," he said quietly, leaning in to kiss her on the lips.

Peck, peck, passion.

Their sweet, chaste hello kiss dissolved into a deeper one full of longing, desire, and something else. Angela couldn't quite place it, but her head became foggy as a delicious warmth unfurled inside her, starting at her chest and reaching down through her legs like long, smoky tendrils. She pulled Soren to her with an urgency that spoke of how much more her feelings for him had developed during their three months apart.

Soren responded by clasping her tighter still and moaning lowly, a sound that vibrated through her.

Clearly, he was enjoying their reunion as much as she was.

Rodney cleared his throat loudly. "Are you going to introduce me Ange?"

Angela and Soren separated abruptly, sheepish. "Yes, sorry, excuse us," she said, wiping the side of her mouth with her middle finger. "Soren this is Charlene's husband Rodney. Rodney, Soren." She motioned between the two men.

Soren stood up straight and looked at Rodney with his usual polite seriousness as he stuck out his hand in greeting. "Hullo, so nice to meet you."

Soren was wearing his usual student-life attire of jeans, button-down shirt, and V-neck sweater, although Angela noticed that his jeans were smooth and dark, not his usual rumpled, faded pair; his sweater was a beautiful robin's egg blue instead of his usual gray; and his hair was noticeably tamer than his usual mane. She smiled, recognizing he had put a little more effort into his appearance for her.

Rodney ignored Soren's proffered hand and stood up to his full height. He was shorter than Soren by at least four inches, but so powerfully built that they occupied the same amount of physical space. He walked around Soren slowly, looking him up and down, blatantly sizing him up.

Soren lowered his hand and shot a quizzical look at Angela who shrugged her shoulders and shook her head.

A bit of tension was just beginning to build when Rodney started chuckling softly, slapping his hands together. "I'm just messing with you Soren. But you better be good to our little Angie here. She's a gem." He extended his hand to Soren. "Put 'er there."

Soren exhaled and shook his head as he took Rodney's hand. "I'll do my best." After he released Rodney's hand, he walked over to Charlene, bent down, and kissed her on both cheeks. "Hullo Charlene. Thanks for bringing Angela to me."

"No problemo Soren. Just be sure to return her in one piece," Charlene said, giving Soren a playful wink.

What's that about? Angela narrowed her eyes at Charlene who gave her a mysterious shrug.

Soren turned to Angela and with pleading eyes asked, "Are you ready?"

"Ready for what?"

"Ready to go? I have a surprise for you. Nice luggage by the way," he said pointing to the matching roller bag and carry on that he had gifted her in July.

She smiled slyly. "Thanks. A male admirer gave them to me."

Soren narrowed his eyes threateningly. "A male admirer, huh?" He slung her carry on over his shoulder, grabbed her roller bag with one hand, and reached for her hand with his other. "We'll see you for dinner. SMS us the address," he said to Charlene authoritatively as he started to walk away from the café with purposeful strides, Angela in tow.

Angela looked back toward Charlene who smirked as she waved at them. "Have fun kids."

Angela looked down at their clasped hands. She loved how tight and strong Soren's hand felt in hers; their fingers laced together snugly. He led her north, back toward Plaça Catalunya as he walked briskly, pulling Angela along insistently. There was an urgency to Soren's actions—to his need to be alone with her—that sent an erotic thrill through her. Angela felt like one of those women in the caveman cartoons; the only thing Soren *wasn't* doing was pulling her by the hair.

She glanced at Soren's face. His lips were moving as though he was rehearsing something to say. She was just about to open her mouth when they arrived at the plaza.

Soren stopped abruptly, put down her luggage, and gripped her face between his hands. "I want a proper kiss. I've been thinking about this moment all week," he said, desperation filling his voice.

He pulled her face to his and kissed her passionately, devouring her with his mouth; his tongue lacing itself around hers, exploring her lips, mouth, and tongue with a fervent need.

He couldn't get enough of her.

One hand snaked itself through her hair and the other planted itself on the small of her back, pulling her close. *Jesus.* The feeling of her body pressed up against his was like plugging himself into a socket; electricity pulsed up and down his body. The faint scent of roses wafted up to his nose, causing his heart to beat faster. *She's really here.*

He had missed her so much in their time apart and he still felt horrible about how they parted at Heathrow. This kiss was an apology wrapped up in a welcome—alternating between happiness and desperation in its frenzied energy—as he tried to close the distance he had felt the last three months with this single embrace.

They separated with great gasps, coming up for air, neither of them wanting the moment to end.

Soren pulled Angela close and hugged her tightly. "I missed you so much..." His tone a mix of relief and disquiet.

"I missed you too..."

"And I'm so sorry," he said with a heavy sigh.

Her brows arched and she cocked her head. "For what?"

His gaze shifted between her hazel eyes, momentarily surprised by their vibrancy. It was always like this when he saw her after they'd been apart. His memory could never do justice to the aura of kinetic energy surrounding her. He shook his head. "I'm sorry for Heathrow," he choked out, full of emotion.

She furrowed her eyebrows. "Still? Forget about it. I have." She waved her hand dismissively.

But for Soren it was as though it happened yesterday. It was as if he was made of stone and his memories were etched into rock and not easily erased. And while rock carvings might not last forever, they certainly lasted much longer than the shifting winds of Angela's temperament.

For Soren, the image of her retreating back—walking toward the plane—still haunted him. He tried for weeks to replay the scenario differently than how it actually happened, hoping for some relief from his guilt. But he never seemed to be able to make the creative leap required to remember the situation in any other way than how it happened.

And each time he remembered it, it wasn't a memory; it was like he was reliving the event all over again, in all of its painful glory.

The frigidness that he had exhibited to her that day still gutted him. How idiotic could he be, thinking he could let his sun walk away and not feel anything but cold despair?

He had kept her in the dark about just how badly he still felt as the phone wasn't a personal enough form of communication for an apology of this magnitude. But now that she was here he felt as though a dam was going to break and the flood of regret he had been carrying with him—regret over the many things he wished he said and done differently in London—would cascade over them both.

He sighed, shaking his head. "That's just it. I can't forget about it. I'm not like you, I don't just 'move on.' I've relived that morning hundreds of times, and each time it has added to the pain I felt that day. What may have begun as a hill has grown into a mountain because without you physically here, it didn't really feel as though we had put it behind us. It took you being here, touching me, kissing me, embracing me for me to really believe that you forgave me and to fully let it go." He ran his hand through his hair, his eyes pleading.

Angela's eyes widened. Soren's apologetic outpouring was completely unexpected.

She looked at his face, sincere anguish etched on it. It was clear this reunion held a meaning for him she hadn't anticipated. She didn't notice it before, but upon closer inspection, he looked tired; his eyes ringed with purple, his shoulders slumped—like he was carrying a burden that had been keeping him up at night.

Her heart clenched. She stepped forward and embraced him.

They had apologized about Heathrow on the phone so many times that she thought they had put the incident behind them. She would never have believed that he had not moved on as she had.

Her temper might run hot and fast, but it burned out just as quickly; forgive and forget.

But it seemed like he still needed something from her so that he could have his own relief.

Pulling him tighter she whispered quietly, "I forgive you Soren. I might not understand why things went the way they did that day at Heathrow, but I feel that our phone conversations since then have demonstrated to me the depth of your feelings, and helped to heal the wounds of that day."

They had always been more inclined to express their feelings physically rather than verbally, although the months apart had begun to narrow the gap.

Immediately Soren's body relaxed; he sighed deeply.

His relief tugged at her heart viscerally. She was falling even more in love with him as they stood there. A thrill of fear ran up Angela's spine as she wondered if Soren could ever love her as much as she loved him.

They continued to cling to each other in the crowded plaza; completely oblivious to the busy throngs surrounding them. Bird sellers and mimes hocking their wares. Taxis honking as they sped through the crowded intersection. Pedestrians glancing over at the striking couple, so clearly in the midst of an emotional exchange.

When they finally separated, Soren had a relieved look on his face, as though a weight had been lifted. "I can't tell you how much better I feel now that I've apologized in person."

Expressing his emotions verbally had never been his strong suit. He was too much like his father, stoic and reserved.

"I had been contemplating flying out to Los Angeles just to apologize in person when you called to tell me about this trip." He leaned in and kissed her sweetly.

"Really?"

"Yes, really. If my school schedule allowed for it, I would have done it ages ago." He smiled warmly at Angela, his blue eyes sparkling happily like a sunset reflected off calm ocean ripples. He grabbed her hand and kissed the back of it. "And now I have a surprise for you."

"What?" She smiled broadly. It was nice to see him so light and happy.

"You'll see." He held out his arm to flag down a cab.

They hopped into one of Barcelona's omnipresent black and yellow taxis—that covered the city like a swarm of friendly bees—and headed north into the Eixample.

The Eixample, which meant "extension" in the area's native language of Catalan, was the heart of Barcelona, even though it ironically began life simply as a way to connect the original, small, isolated towns that now added up to modern day Barcelona.

Angela looked out the window, taking in the vibrant art deco architecture that personified this part of the city, which had been constructed in the late 1800's and early 1900's.

The cab drove up the flamboyantly-luxurious Passeig de Gracia, which was the prettier and more petite love child of Los Angeles' Rodeo Drive and Paris' Champs-Elysées, and had originally been constructed to connect the original city of Barcelona, now known as the *Ciutat Vella* or "Old City", with the small town of Gracia to the north.

They drove past the famous *La Manzana de la Discòrdia,* The Apple of Discord, which was a block of houses built by four of Barcelona's most famous architects that sang with color and texture.

Angela craned her neck to see her favorite, Casa Batlló, whose undulating roof of iridescent peacock-colored tiles and hilt-like chimney was a literal homage to St. George—the patron saint of the region—and his dragon slaying.

After a few more blocks, the cab turned right and pulled up to a stunning 19th-century, stone façade with an ultra-modern glass addition crowning it like the headdress of an Egyptian pharaoh.

Angela turned to Soren. "Why are we at a hotel?"

"Because I have flat mates, and I wanted to be alone with you," he said, leaning forward for a quick kiss.

Charlene must have been in on this plan. Clearly Soren was calling her friend for more than just emergencies.

Angela studied the imposing building. "Of course you have to pick someplace über expensive," she said, trying—and failing—to keep the exasperation out of her voice.

His face fell. "I didn't pick it because it was expensive. I picked it because I thought that the adaptive reuse of a historic building would interest you. Was I wrong?"

Her face flushed. "No, you weren't," she said quickly, suddenly feeling ungrateful. She wasn't sure she would ever feel completely comfortable with his extravagant gifts. She wanted to be his equal in all ways, and money was the one area where she just couldn't compete. She didn't like the feeling.

A good-looking young man opened the cab door and gave them a friendly smile. "Hello, my name is Carlos. Welcome to the Hotel Claris," he said with a quick bow. He offered a hand to Angela and helped her out of the cab. "Won't you follow me this way?"

Soren quickly came around the cab and offered Angela his arm. They followed Carlos through the antiquities-filled lobby that was starkly-decorated with minimalist, contemporary furniture, echoing the contrast of old and new seen in the building's exterior.

Angela looked around the vast, open space unsure if she was in a hotel or a museum. On display were ancient mosaics from Rome, statues from China, and art objects from other far-flung corners of the earth. The modern feel of the honed white marble that composed the walls, floors, and columns was softened by creamy swirls of white and caramel running throughout the stone, reminiscent of a frothy cappuccino.

While Soren checked in, Angela wandered about, taking in the surroundings. She ran her hand along the back of the supple leather of an Arne Jacobsen egg chair and studied a headless, robe-wearing statue nestled in the embrace of a curving, marble staircase edged by a ribbon-like, chrome handrail. Just behind the staircase was a sunlight-filled atrium, where a collection of gray and black stones—ranging in size from a foot high to eight-feet tall—was surrounded by a shallow sheet of water. Angela closed her eyes and could just make out the burbling sound and faint, fecund scent of running water.

The hotel was a feast for the eyes, a beautiful blend of old and new, simple and fanciful, precious and playful. Angela could see why Soren had picked this exact hotel for her and the knowledge sent a lovely flush through her.

She couldn't wait to take some pictures of this place and sketch the rock fountain. Her grandfather—the man who had taught her to draw and her true father figure—encouraged her to draw at least once a day. She wasn't as disciplined as that, but she did manage to draw at least twice a week. He would love the atrium with its slightly Asian feel, reminiscent of a Japanese block print.

She was admiring a whimsical display of intricately cut paper leaves—masquerading as a floral arrangement—when Soren approached.

"Shall we?" He looped her arm through his and pulled her toward the bellhop who led them to the elevator.

They walked into the glass-walled elevator, and Angela looked down on the watery, stone-filled atrium. She could now see that the stones rested on a transparent, glass floor, allowing light to penetrate to whatever lay below.

The elevator doors slid closed and then opened quickly at the second floor.

The bellhop smiled at them. "Short ride. Many of our best rooms are on this floor," he said mysteriously. He led them down a hallway, opened their hotel room door and stepped back, gesturing for Angela and Soren to walk in.

Angela smiled as a familiar aroma reached her nose. She immediately recognized the significance of the scent remembering the virtual wall of roses Soren had gifted her back in London. A delicious warmth swept through her.

Soren tipped the bellhop and closed the door.

She shot him a look of mock anger. "Please tell me you didn't buy thirty dozen again."

He smiled. "No, this time I only bought three dozen, since we were apart for three months…"

"One dozen for each month?"

"Precisely," he said, a gigantic grin plastered on his face. "Besides you were so annoyed by the thirty dozen that I figured I should tone it down a little bit," he said with a small smile.

She leaned in and gave him a kiss, relieved that he was learning to moderate his gifts. It made her feel *slightly* less financially inadequate. "Thank you for that. I love them…and I love how exacting you are. It's adorable."

He seemed to grow taller at her praise.

They walked deeper into the room, the entryway surprisingly dark, past a full bath and into the luxuriously furnished, double-height living room. A diamond-tufted, armless sofa dominated the space, upholstered in a muted mauve velvet; throws of faux fur draped over its thick back. Across from the sofa were two caned armchairs, lacquered a glossy black and topped with ivory cushions. Adjacent to the sitting area was a massive, wood cabinet that felt faintly Asian and was topped by a gaggle of white and blue Chinese porcelain and flanked by colorful African masks mounted on high columns. A shuttered spotlight on a tripod stood in the corner giving the whole area the feel of a movie set. A massive, turquoise Murano glass chandelier hung decadently over the entire scene.

Sitting on the low, black trunk-cum-coffee-table were three dozen roses, but instead of the rainbow of colors Soren had given her in London, this time all thirty-six were a deep red color, and they stood out dramatically against the ivory-colored walls and neutral-toned furniture of the space. A bottle of champagne in a standing silver ice bucket, and a plate of chocolate truffles, completed the romantic *mise-en-scène*.

"Champagne? Nice touch," she said with an arched eyebrow, running a hand along the silky velvet of the sofa as she turned back toward the entryway noticing for the first time the lofted bedroom space above it. *So that's why the entry was so dark.*

"It's better than champagne," he said. He then caught her gaze. "This entire floor is comprised of two story suites. They are all decorated differently, but when I saw this one, it said your name."

Her heart fluttered at his words; the bellhop's comment—about the hotel's best rooms—now making sense.

"The only bad thing about this room is that there's no view." He pointed to the windows, which were covered with long, sheer curtains. "But there's a gorgeous view from the rooftop pool. I thought we could have breakfast there in the morning."

She smiled and shook her head. "Always such a planner."

The light of the chandelier twinkled off the walls, reflected off mirrored paneling decorated with an intricate pattern of white trim that mirrored the design of the chamfered streets below.

Angela's eyes followed Soren like lasers on a target as he took off his sweater, laid it on the sofa, and walked over to the ice bucket.

Now that they were alone in the hotel room, she could feel the energy between them pinging like electricity between two poles. She bit her lip, her anticipation building.

Could this finally be it? She felt faintly nauseous, the butterflies in her belly beating out of formation in a combination of desire and nerves. She had thought about the moment when they would consummate their relationship for so long, now that it might be upon them, she was anxious. Could the reality ever live up to the expectation?

Then again, maybe this wasn't it. Soren had held her at bay for so long, maybe this was just another moment of foreplay in his long, drawn-out plan. She turned toward the windows and took a deep breath. *Relax. Enjoy!* She closed her eyes, listening to the pleasant melody of Soren pulling the champagne out of its ice bath, popping the cork, and pouring her a glass.

She turned as he approached her. Handing her the delicate, crystal flute he said, "I hope you like it."

Angela lifted the ivory-colored bubbles to her mouth; her eyes lit up. "Is this sparkling sake?"

Soren nodded his head and smiled. "Do you like it?"

"I love it. I didn't know such a thing even existed. How did you find it?" She took another luxurious sip, enjoying the feeling of the slightly-sweet carbonation.

"When I asked for the bucket of ice the concierge said they would include a bottle of champagne. I mentioned wanting sake and he said he had the perfect alternative." He raised his glass toward her and took another sip.

Angela lifted the flute to her nose and inhaled. "It's so light and refreshing, and the flavor is so fruity." She paused, rolling her fingers around the glass as she struggled to place the aroma. "It tastes like lychee," she said, referring to the sweet, gelatinous tropical fruit that was a favorite of her mother's. "I love it."

The corners of Soren's mouth twitched. He leaned forward and gently stroked her silky hair, tucking a vibrant mahogany lock behind her ear. Caressing her face tenderly with the back of his hand, he savored the softness of her skin. Angela closed her eyes and leaned into his hand. He matched her movement, leaning forward, kissing her gently, savoring the sweetness of the sake mixed with the sweetness of Angela.

A wonderful contentment washed over him, followed quickly by a wave of desire. He'd been planning this exact moment ever since Angela told him about her trip; spending hours searching for exactly the right hotel room in exactly the right hotel. Thank God the concierge had saved him the many hours he might have spent searching for exactly the right sake. He wanted everything to be right for this moment. But now that it was here, he hesitated.

The moment wasn't *exactly* right…yet.

He took her hand, lacing their fingers together, and led her to the sofa. They sat down simultaneously on the silky sofa that was the muted violet of a Chinese magnolia. Their knees touched, sending a tingling sensation up his thighs. He put down their glasses, took her hands, and looked into her eyes.

He studied Angela's face. Eyes wide. Brows arched. Mouth slightly parted. He wished that he could memorize her expression; preserving it for future recall with accurate clarity. The mixture of hope, love, and desire was intoxicating.

"Angela, you bewitched me from the moment I watched you put your red lipstick on while sitting on the steps of The Temple." He took a deep breath, a pleasurable ache in his stomach.

Her eyes narrowed, confused.

He answered her implied question. "I saw you sitting there one day with Charlene, and you pulled out your lipstick. I was mesmerized watching you put it on. I had to remind myself to start breathing again."

She smiled at him, her eyes filled with mirth. He'd never mentioned this before. The picture he painted was so romantic; she didn't want him to stop.

He continued. "And even though that's the day you cast your spell, the truth is my feelings for you have never stopped growing. Despite the challenges we had in London, and the challenges we've faced being apart, I am extremely hopeful about the future." He dragged his thumb along her lower lip, down her cheek, and along her chin.

A lump developed in Angela's throat.

Soren inhaled a double breath. "I never feel more alive than when I am with you. When we're apart, it's like the sun has set. If it were up to me, we'd be together always. I guess what I'm trying to say is that I love you Angela Holguín, with all my heart." He squeezed her hand as he said the last sentence sending tiny goosebumps up her arms.

Angela gasped softly, her lips widening further, her chest tight with emotion. She shook her head, uncertain what to say.

She decided to keep it simple. "I love you too."

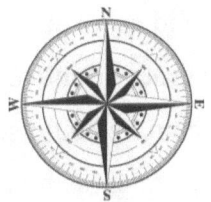

Chapter 12: Bonding

Soren's eyes widened as his gaze traveled over her face, stopping at her mouth, staring at the enticing pink of her tongue framed by her lush, rosy lips. *Those lips.* His heart started beating faster.

His eyes flicked upwards toward the bedroom loft unconsciously, but Angela smiled and nodded, squeezing his hand.

They stood up slowly, Soren wrapping his arm around her shoulders as he led her to the floating staircase and guided her up the stairs to the bedroom loft, which was a study in white and gold.

A fluffy, king-sized bed took up most of the cozy space, with a petite, Roman-style scrolled bench at the foot, and gold ceramic nightstands crowned with pineapple-shaped lamps on either side. A huge chandelier, with gold leaves and vines, hung over the bed as though it had sprouted from the ceiling, part of an enchanted forest.

He stood by the side of the bed and pulled her to him, caressing her cheek with the back of his hand and then slowly dragging his fingers down her arm.

Angela inhaled quickly at his touch.

"Mmmmm, that feels good." She closed her eyes as her head lolled to the side.

"You're so lovely," he said as he quickly scooped her up and laid her down on the bed in one graceful move.

Her eyes fluttered open and he could see the desire he felt mirrored in her eyes. They were crossing over a point of no return and he could not be happier. His stomach ached with pleasurable anticipation.

He lay beside her on the bed and studied her face seriously. "It feels like I've been waiting for this moment for years," he said as he ran his hand over her abdomen and down her right leg.

She sighed, her eyes following his hand. "Me too," she whispered quietly.

Her silky voice was like oxygen to his desire. He leaned forward, kissing her gently with small, rosebud kisses. But when her tongue snaked out to meet his open mouth, his urgency grew quickly; his body alive with a desperation he had never experienced.

He had promised her that when the time was right he would make her his own, and tonight was finally that night. He had missed her acutely during their time apart, and he wanted to close the distance between them completely, to lose himself in her.

She met his growing passion equally, matching him in urgency and desperation.

His hands moved over her body, caressing her through her blouse and jeans, kneading her with the sensual probing of his strong fingers. He dug into her hip bones with his thumbs, as his tongue lapped at her neck, causing her to buck and moan loudly.

"God woman, that moan. It drives me crazy." Tired of the thousands of miles that had separated them—as well as the millimeters that were separating them now—he removed her clothing, unpeeling her jeans and top impatiently, wanting there to be no boundaries between them any longer.

He stopped momentarily to admire her near nakedness: long toes, delicate feet, strong legs, shapely hips, smooth stomach, voluptuous chest, graceful arms. She was glorious. He ran his fingertips up and down the length of her body, drinking her in.

Angela stared at Soren, watching the look of loving concentration on his face as he traced trails of fire all over her body. She writhed almost imperceptibly, trying to stay motionless so that she could keep watching him. He was mesmerizing.

Finally she couldn't hold back any more and she moaned loudly as his hand absentmindedly brushed across the top of her thighs, cascading over her mons temptingly.

"Soren, you are driving me crazy," she said with breathless agony. "And you are wearing too much clothing." She arched her brow, raising herself up on her arms.

He smirked as he turned to her, lifting his arms. She kneeled on the bed as she unbuttoned his shirt, pushing it off his shoulders impatiently.

He looped his arm around her bare waist and pulled her to him. "Come here you."

Angela inhaled sharply as their bare skin collided, sending a hot pulse of desire straight to her clit.

A low growl escaped his throat. "God that feels so good." He pulled her head to the side and gently licked and bit her neck. Reaching behind her, he unhooked her bra, gently pulling the right strap to the side. His tongue followed the trail of the satin strap as it slipped off her shoulder.

Angela moaned as she tilted her head further, while Soren's fingertips traced down her shoulder, over her latissimus, and then along her waistline leaving a path of goosebumps in their wake. She shivered slightly when his hot palm came to rest on her hip.

His eyes glanced across her collarbone, following his hands as he repeated the same movement on her left side, his tongue leaving a hot, wet trail of fire across her left shoulder. Her nipples puckered tightly as her bra fell to the bed, the cool air of the room whisking across their surface.

"Lovely." Soren licked his lip as he smiled at her, sending a warm flush down her torso.

He put his arm in the small of her back and lay her back on the white comforter. Looping his fingers through the waist of her satiny, nude panties, he shimmied them down her legs, his hands cupping her shapely calves on the way down.

She laughed spontaneously. He'd found her ticklish spot. He smiled at the sound of her laughter. Of all the things he loved about her, he loved her carefree laughter most. It epitomized everything he admired about her: her passion, her spontaneity, her excitement for life.

When she was completely naked, he raked his hot gaze over her entire body. She followed his eyes, feeling almost shy. She had never felt so bare in her entire life; his hot look of lust burning her flesh with his lascivious intentions.

Soren ran his hands down her thighs, squeezing them tightly as he caressed her strong legs. He wanted nothing more than to have these legs wrapped around his waist and be buried deep within her. He moved his hands to the space betwixt, allowing his fingers to dance between her inner thighs, feeling the hot slickness of her desire painting her skin. His penis throbbed at this discovery. God how he wanted to slide into her, feel her wetness as he ground himself deep inside her.

But not yet.

He tried to clear his head, wanting to draw their lovemaking out as long as possible. He knew that the months of anticipation were not working in his favor, but he wanted to pleasure Angela first. He felt her hands, loosening his buckle. He put out a hand to stop her. "Not yet Angela." His pants were a necessary barrier to keep his desire in check.

"But I want to feel you completely naked," she protested, her voice heavy with desire.

His penis bobbed in frustration. "I want that too. Too much in fact. I want this to last…I want to please you."

She bent her leg and placed her foot on his chest, squeezing his nipple with her long, dexterous toes. "You do please me."

The movement of her foot gave Soren a glimpse at her smooth lips, plump, and creamy below a crown of midnight curls. The salty musk of her sex snaked its way up to his nose and sent a shower of heat down his shoulders and back. He grabbed her foot and began sucking on her big toe, alternating between lolling his tongue around it lazily and sucking with brutal intensity.

Angela's head fell back in response. "Fuck that feels good," she said breathlessly, caught off guard by his passionate sucking.

As he pulled on her leg to suck and lick on her foot and toes, he inadvertently opened and closed her inner lips, sending teasing claps of stimulation to her clit.

She pressed down into the mattress with her free foot, trying to increase the stimulation by clenching her thighs together, but she couldn't get the leverage. She slapped her hands against the bed, frustrated.

Angela reached up, grabbed his belt and threw it to the floor with a loud clank. She gently ran her fingertips over his visible bulge. Soren jerked away slightly—as though her touch burned—but continued sucking.

"Oh God," Angela cried, jerking her head from side to side as he slid his tongue down the skin between her toes, sending delicious, tickling spirals up her legs and pelvis.

Soren watched Angela's thrashing, his cock throbbing with desire. Between the sounds of her cries, the scent of her sex, and watching her buck under his sucking, he felt like he was going to orgasm right then.

He pulled her toe out of his mouth and closed his eyes with concentration. Angela—sensing his need—reached out with her hand and gently tapped his package from below; giving him a tiny whack.

Soren groaned lowly, an unusual sound that was half pain and half pleasure. It turned her on immensely.

"Again darling, harder," he begged through tight lips.

Using slightly more force, she was rewarded with more of his pleasurably-painful groaning. "Yes, uhhhh…" He shuddered slightly, his head dropping back; lost in his ingasm. Through closed lips, he mumbled, holding his breath for a few moments as he twisted his head to the side and then exhaled loudly. "Oh God," he said in a voice much lower than usual.

Angela smiled knowingly. "That was fun to watch."

He chuckled, taking a moment to study his love. Angela's hair was arranged around her head and shoulders in a look of sensual debauchery, her honey-colored skin set off by the snowy white of the bedding. She narrowed her eyes at him as she caught him watching her. Her lusty gaze sent hot flames licking up his arms.

"You. Naked. Now." She said forcefully.

This time when her hands went to his jeans, he didn't protest. She quickly undid his fly, pushing them down with her hands.

"Wait, condoms." He dug into his pocket, placing the foil-wrapped squares on the metallic nightstand.

He lowered himself down, placing his mouth gently on hers, enjoying the fullness of her lips as their kiss intensified. He felt Angela's hands on his jeans, pushing them down first with her hands and then with her feet. Then she looped her toes under the waistband of his boxers and pulled them off as well.

His penis bobbed, thick—although only semi-hard—recovering from the dry orgasm he'd just had. She'd never seen him less than fully erect, and she noticed that his member looked different from any she had seen before. It had a soft fold of loose skin, inching forward from the base.

Realization dawned. *He's not circumcised.*

She reached down and wrapped her long fingers around his firm shaft, running her soft palm against the sensitive skin. The silky, not-quite-loose flesh felt warm and lush in her hand as though Soren's member had its own kid glove.

He closed his eyes and inhaled quickly, leaning forward into her touch.

She kneaded gently, feeling him come alive in her hand. Thick. Hard. Demanding. As he lengthened, his built-in glove disappeared, adding even more length. She couldn't wait to feel him fill her up.

Soren moaned. The feeling of her hands on his most sensitive skin felt so good that it made him sway, suddenly dizzy. He leaned down and kissed her, laying his body on top of hers.

Fully naked, their bodies skimmed together, lighting a fire along the multiple points of contact between them: nipples, abdomen, thighs, feet. But none matched the heat in his pelvis as his penis brushed up against the smooth skin of her inner thighs.

She groaned and then whispered into his ear, "God that feels so good." She leaned away, looking him in the eyes. "Soren, I want you so much."

Soren looked into her hazel eyes, glassy with desire. A pleasurable pain building up in his lower abdomen at her words. "I want you too," he said breathlessly.

She pulled him back down, wrapped her legs around his, and whispered urgently in his ear, "Please be inside me."

Her hot, breathy words were like a match. He could feel every nerve in his body tingle as he reached over to grab a condom.

Tear. Pinch. Roll.

Angela attacked his neck with her mouth, as she dragged her nails up and down his back, sending shivers along his spine.

He rolled her onto her back and hovered over her. With his middle finger, he gently spread her naked lips, ensuring that she was ready for him. From the feel of her swollen slickness, she had been ready for some time. He lingered at the entrance to her sex, gently probing it and teasing her clit with his thumb. Her moans kept climbing, growing louder with each rub.

"Soren, you are driving me fucking crazy."

He removed his finger and slid it in his mouth. His brow arched. "You taste so good."

Her eyes widened. She couldn't wait any longer. She took matters into her own hand, literally, and grabbed his penis, holding it tight at the base. "You. Inside me. Now."

This time Soren's eyes widened, the sensation of her grip on his penis making him lightheaded. Her squeezing pushed the pleasurable tingling out to the head of his erection, while simultaneously sending a slightly painful and restraining sensation down the length.

He positioned himself between her legs and allowed her to guide him into her. The heat of her sex was intense, engulfing his own so that he was lost inside her, all boundaries between them erased. He began to glide in and out slowly, once, twice, three times.

He felt her pulsing on his penis, milking him with her hidden muscles. "Oh God that feels good," he cried gutturally, as he pushed through her squeeze.

She ran her fingertips down the front of his chest and stomach; squeezing his nipples gently. Her eyes fluttered closed and she rocked her ass from side to side, his length touching every inch of her inside.

"Mmmm," she moaned. "Roll us over. I want to ride you."

He wrapped his arms around her waist and rolled them both over so that Angela was straddling him. She took his hands and placed them on her breasts. "Hold these."

"With pleasure." He loved the firm doughiness of her large breasts.

She leaned back and steadied herself with her arms against his chest. Closing her eyes, she began to slowly rock back and forth, finding her rhythm, riding him.

He watched her face as she slowly began to pick up speed, enjoying the combination of sounds and facial expressions flickering across her face as her desire built. Faster and faster, he could feel her wetness on his own thighs as she ground her swollen sex into his pelvis.

"Uh, uh, uh," she moaned over and over again her groans matching the rhythm of her hips.

Soren's entire world contracted to just the places where their bodies were touching; a universe of sensation in an intensely confined area, too concentrated to last; soon they would have to explode back out.

She opened her eyes and gave him a wicked smirk as she leaned forward slightly, adjusting her legs so that her feet were on the bed and she was squatting over him. She raised herself almost all the way off his penis and then bounced gently on the tip, bobbing almost playfully on the head and then just when he thought he was going to cry out from frustration she impaled herself on his full length with a single, hard stroke.

"Fuck," the word was ripped involuntarily out of him as the blood rushed from his head to his cock.

She lifted herself back up and bobbed again on the tip, gyrating her hips slowly to the left and the right, twisting while she bounced and then just when he thought he couldn't take anymore, she thrust herself down again.

He groaned throatily. "Oh God."

A huge smile broke out on Angela's face; she was clearly enjoying being in control. He moved her breasts together, holding them both lightly with one hand as he snaked his thumb down and began stroking her clit with long, loving movements.

"Mmmm," she purred in response, narrowing her eyes in a feline expression.

She continued bobbing and thrusting, bobbing and thrusting as she twisted his nipples and ran her fingertips over his abs. She loved feeling his nipples grow tight and erect under her attention, and then watch his torso undulate as she dragged her nails over him. Her body wound up with each deep thrust; tightening both inside and outside; inching them both closer to their release.

They writhed together synchronously, creating a melody of groans, grunts, and moans accompanied by a harmony of sharp slapping as skin smacked against skin.

Their rhythm picked up speed as they crescendoed toward their inevitable climax, perfectly in tune.

She tucked her legs back behind her and lowered herself down, rocking slowly, back and forth, back and forth; grinding her clit into his pelvis with each forward movement. Leaning over, she kissed him.

Soren moved his hands to her ass and pulled her closer to him as she rocked. Her nipples tightened rubbing against his chest and the air grew hot between them; blurring the boundaries between their bodies further. Conscious thought left them both and they became a single knot of nerves, sensation, and chemistry.

Each rock of their hips was like a lasso loop around Angela's heart, binding them closer and closer together: heart, body, and soul. Breath synchronized, moans rhythmic, rocking faster as they climbed higher.

Angela braced her arms against his chest again as she looked him in the eyes and increased her rhythm to a harsh, relentless speed, her breasts pinched together by her biceps, bulging like ripe berries. Her breathing growing labored as her motions grew shorter until she was no longer riding him, but desperately grinding on him until in a final spasmodic spring of motions they lunged together to the edge and screamed, "Ah, yes, yes, fuuuuuck, uhhhhh…" Crashing over to the other side, their orgasm shook them, causing them to shudder violently as one.

Angela rocked one, two, three more times before collapsing onto Soren's chest, both of them slick with sweat. As his arms wound around her, the lasso tightened, squeezing her heart painfully as tears threatened to flow. She snuggled into his chest and inhaled his musky odor.

She wound herself around him, holding firm, feeling her heart squeeze tighter and tighter as she tried to fight back her tears. Soren lazily caressed her shoulder sending chills up her arms and down her back, causing the floodgates to open.

She was out of control, pure emotion, she started weeping softly.

"Ssshhh, ssshhh. Is something wrong? Did I hurt you?" he asked, his voice cracking.

She laughed and cried harder at his words, as she tasted the salty tears in her mouth. "No, nothing's wrong." She shook her head and wiped at the tears with the back of her hand. "I think I'm just overwhelmed. I couldn't be happier, really. That was the most beautiful thing I've ever experienced."

He pulled her tight and sighed. "For me as well," he whispered, gently wiping the tears from her eyes. He kissed her forehead inhaling the familiar rose scent of her skin. "I've never had a simultaneous orgasm before."

"You neither? I thought it might have just been new to me." She traced heart shapes on his skin.

He chuckled. "No darling, we did that to each other." He kissed her again reassuringly, sweetly, and then passionately, feeling at last the freedom he had desired to feel with her ever since that night at his flat in London when he watched her pleasure herself.

She was finally *his*, he was finally *hers*. This was what he had wanted. His heart ached with relief. "You are mine."

"I was already yours," she tsked gently.

"But now it's official." He caressed her shoulder with his fingertips and she wound her leg between his. He loved the feeling of being naked with her.

"Always so fastidious," she teased.

She looked into his blue eyes and felt her heart clench again. She wanted to cling to him and never let go. Putting her head on his chest, she tightened her grip around him like a koala hugging a tree, craving the feeling of oneness that she had felt during their lovemaking.

"I love you Soren," she choked, barely getting the words out before the tears started flowing again.

"Ssshhh, darling. Don't cry." He kissed her, tasting the sweetness of the sake and the salt of her tears mixing in their mouths.

"I...don't...know...why...I'm...crying," her words came out between sobs, "I...just...love...you...so...much."

He pulled away just enough so he could look into her hazel eyes, which the crying had made an even brighter shade of green. "I love you Angela darling. I've loved you ever since our time in Barcelona. I love you so much that I promise you, I will always do what's right for you. Your happiness is the most important thing in the world to me. I consider it my duty to protect it for you." He pulled her hand to his mouth and kissed the back of it tenderly.

She studied his face, his eyes blazing. She knew he meant his words. He had always demonstrated that he would never let his own desires get in the way of what was best for her. He was so selfless in that way. She was sure that she had never been loved by anyone like this before.

She could feel her eyelids getting droopy as the combination of passion, emotion, and jetlag overtook her. She snuggled into Soren's chest and began to drift off as she heard Soren's voice in the distance, "Sweet dreams my love."

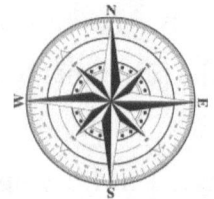

Chapter 13: Amplified

"*Ciao guapa*, it's so good to see you. How have you been?" Marco leaned in and kissed Angela on each cheek, and then added a third one unexpectedly.

When Angela gave him a confused look, he laughed and said, "Remember? Three for the pretty ones."

She laughed, remembering how annoyed she had been when Enzo had pulled that same stunt, but with Marco it was somehow charming. "Is that the Italian custom?" she asked with an arched brow.

"No, no. The Italian custom is as many as you can get away with if the woman is pretty," he said with an ironic wink.

She laughed loudly.

Marco Lucian was a native of Rome and he was as lively as one would expect given his birthplace. His vivid green eyes danced almost as merrily as his hands, which were as important as his words in expressing himself.

A classmate of Soren's at BIN, Angela had met him last year during her semester abroad and they had quickly established a rapport that had only strengthened during their time apart. Whenever Marco made the long drive from Barcelona to Rome—in his beat-up, silver Mercedes—he would call Angela and they would speak for one or two hours about everything from politics to food to philosophy.

The two friends were meeting for a late brunch at a crepe place near Angela's old apartment in the Les Corts district of Barcelona. Angela only had two more days in Barcelona and she didn't want to leave without a visit to her old hangout.

The small bakery-café was plain and industrial, with big, glass windows in the front, white subway tile on the walls, and sturdy aluminum chairs and tables to sit at. The one bit of frivolity were giant, yellow utensils that hung on the wall in lieu of art. Despite the lack of decor, its small size, the bustling activity within, and the delicious aroma of baking bread managed to give it a cozy feel.

Angela smiled at her friend. He was wearing black jeans, a brown leather belt, and a white, button-down David Saddler shirt with a stiff collar that always seemed to be standing up. Angela had long ago remarked on his perma-popped collars, and he shared with her that it was this feature that made David Saddler his favorite shirt maker in Rome.

Her friendship with Marco was one of the dearest relationships she had in her life. It was hard for her to believe that someone who had such a different upbringing from her could understand her so thoroughly. She felt that they must have known each other in a former life since that was the only explanation that made sense. Time simply flew when she was with him, and their conversations were always full of laughter *and* wisdom.

"How have you been?" Angela asked, as she unbuttoned her blazer. She had chosen fitted, black corduroy pants that were tucked into brown, equestrian-style boots. A thin black turtleneck and a brown and black hounds tooth blazer completed her stylishly preppy look. Her long hair was pulled back into a neat ponytail.

"Pretty good. Just doing a lot of interviewing for jobs next year. It looks like I'll be returning to London." His tone was indifferent.

"Isn't that what you want?" She blew gingerly on her steaming cup of hot chocolate sprinkled with cinnamon.

He shrugged his shoulders animatedly, the way he did everything. If there was a rating system for shoulder shrugging with 1 being "barely perceptible" and 10 being "shoulders touch the ears" then he was a 12. Marco used everything from his forehead to his knees to communicate, as though a single gesture couldn't possibly explain everything he needed to say.

"It's not ideal. I don't love London, but at least it isn't Italy. I don't want to go home yet," he said as he smoothed out the front of his jeans.

"How come?"

Marco ran his hand over his bald head as he thought. "It's not big enough for me. I like places with different types of people. Rome doesn't attract people from all over the world the way London does. Plus there's just more opportunity," he said with another ear-touching shrug.

"Well I hope you can afford a nicer place than where you were living this past summer," she said, raising her eyebrows meaningfully as she remembered his dodgy neighborhood near Canary Wharf.

"Yes, yes," he said as he rolled his eyes. "So, how is it going with Soren? You seem quite serious." He lifted his cappuccino to his mouth. After lunch he would switch to espresso; he had a strict rule about drinking cappuccinos only before lunch.

"It definitely feels serious." She nodded her head, smiling. "I'm crazy about him. But this long distance thing…" she trailed off uncertainly. "I mean, it's fine for now. He's already planned a trip to come out to L.A. the day after Christmas, but I don't really know how it's going to work moving forward. Who knows when we'll see each other after that?"

The truth was, she had no idea where her relationship with Soren was going. When she spontaneously decided to kiss a sleeping Soren in London last July, she never would have guessed they would be declaring their love for each other three months later while attempting to maintain a relationship with 6,000 miles of land and sea between them. It felt simultaneously wonderful and overwhelming; like jumping out of an airplane.

Marco gave her a knowing look. "It's not easy. It was a big mess with me and Carolina," he said, referring to his girlfriend of many years with whom he parted ways last month after a year of long-distance. "And we weren't as far apart as you and Soren. She was in Rome and I was here in Barcelona, not a big deal. But the distance…" he said, shaking his hand as though he had just burned it. "The distance amplifies everything."

Angela took a bite of her crepe filled with banana and chocolate-hazelnut spread. She felt momentarily guilty about enjoying something with GMO-ingredients in it, but justified it by thinking that she didn't eat this way usually. "Don't you mean the distance *diminished* everything?" she asked, confused how distance could amplify anything.

"No, I mean amplified." He leaned forward as he continued, "Every misunderstanding, every missed phone call, every canceled trip home became a bigger deal than it was just because of the distance. I think the distance inserts a level of distrust into a relationship by its very existence. You really have to *over* communicate to make it work." He arched his brow, taking another sip of his cappuccino. "When you live in the same city with a person you can easily catch when they are not happy about something. There are subtle clues in their face or body language, but over the phone…eh." Like a magician pulling flowers out of a hat, he flipped his palm upward and pursed his fingers together for emphasis. "It's hard *guapa*, it's hard."

"Well, I haven't seen that yet." She shrugged, not wanting to think about anything that could come between her and Soren.

Marco harrumphed as he chewed on his ham and egg crepe. "It's only a matter of time."

She scowled at him. "Thanks a lot. Are you trying to curse me?"

"Of course not. I'm just a realist, that's all," he said with a final, ear-touching shrug.

Angela narrowed her eyes at Marco as she chewed.

He leaned forward and pointed at her with his index finger. "I would be happy for you to prove me wrong, but this has nothing to do with you and Soren. This is about human nature. You *can't change* human nature."

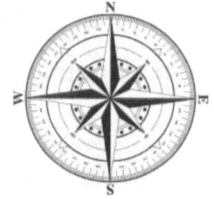

Chapter 14: Last Night

"So you been having fun?" Charlene asked Angela over lunch at one of their favorite old haunts: an all-you-can-eat sushi bar with a conveyer belt of dishes located in the heart of the Eixample.

"Yes Charlene, oh my gosh. Thank you again for the plane ticket," Angela answered as she bit into a caterpillar roll made of cooked eel and sliced avocado, covered with stripes of *kabayaki* sauce and sprinkled with sesame seeds. Angela closed her eyes, enjoying the combination of vinegary rice, fatty avocado, and sweet *kabayaki* in her mouth. She wiped a spot of sauce from her mouth and said, "You are the best. And I'm glad you could sneak away for lunch, I've barely gotten to see you."

The two friends had not seen each other as much as they would have liked this trip. Soren had lived up to his promise of bringing Angela to meet Charlene and Rodney for dinner Monday evening, but in the afterglow of their lovemaking the two of them were distracted throughout the meal; anxious to get back to their hotel room for another round of hot and heavy.

Looking back, Angela couldn't even remember what they ate that night, her focus had been so completely taken up by how sensual Soren's just-kissed lips looked, all pink and pillowy, and the lingering red of the bite marks she'd made to his neck on the cab ride over. She had practically jumped when his hand worked its way up her thigh over dessert. It was surreal to watch the contrast between Soren carrying on an everyday conversation with Rodney—all Nordic sensibility above the table—and his teasing, erotic fingers below.

However, as distracting as wrestling beneath the sheets with Soren was—who would have believed what amazing foreplay *that* could be—it was Charlene's full work schedule that had kept her and Angela apart the rest of the time.

"These conference schedules are brutal, but I just couldn't take being locked up in a cold hotel ballroom for lunch again. I can't stay long though." Charlene slurped a bit of bright green seaweed salad from her chopsticks, covered in sweet rice vinegar and sesame seeds. She looked chic and professional in her well-cut slacks and blazer, a pearl brooch pinned to her lapel.

As a marketing executive, Charlene was expected to attend every conference event in order to schmooze and see to the needs of the attendees. The only other time the two friends had seen each other was for dinner last night, Wednesday, a designated "free night" for Charlene's conference attendees. The two couples had spent the evening at a seafood restaurant in Port Olímpic, an area that—as the name implies—was built for the 1992 Olympic Games.

In reality, Angela had spent more time with Rodney on this trip than anyone else. Charlene's husband had become her sight-seeing buddy while Charlene was working and Soren was in class, and they had become very efficient tourists conducting quick-strike missions so that Angela could run back to the hotel room whenever Soren *wasn't* in class.

They had managed to see the Picasso museum, which featured none of his most famous works but was worth it to see examples from when the great master was a child; visit Santa Maria del Mar, no longer as close to the sea as the name would imply but with an amazing stained glass rosette worth visiting; and visit the hauntingly-beautiful garden of the Parc del Laberint d'Horta, Angela couldn't believe how magnificent this labyrinth park was and how few people even knew it existed.

"So how was dancing last night?" Charlene raised her eyebrows, referring to the plan discussed at dinner to go dancing with some of the students from BIN. Charlene had decided not to go, too tired to meet for midnight dancing with a 6am wake-up call looming over her.

Angela deflated at her friend's question. "We didn't go."

"*¿Por que?*" Charlene asked, pushing her long braids behind her shoulder.

Angela shrugged mildly. "Don't you remember? Soren hates to dance." She popped another piece of caterpillar roll into her mouth with her wooden chopsticks, realizing too late that it was too big. Her mother would have rolled her eyes at her stuffed mouth; she frequently reprimanded Angela for her less-than-dainty ways. She chewed carefully.

Charlene furrowed her brow. "Oh right, I do remember that. So getting to dance with you isn't incentive enough for him to go out?"

Angela shook her head, holding up her index finger as she continued to chew. She swallowed and took a sip of tea. "Apparently not. You know, I thought things would be different now that we are together, but he still prefers to be with me one-on-one. This morning I went to campus to meet him for coffee and I could feel him staring at me when I talked to Marco or any other man. It's like laser beams in the back of my head. Rodney is the only man who doesn't get me in trouble."

Charlene laughed as she shook her head. "Men."

Angela continued. "Anyway, after we had dinner with you two, he convinced me to return to the hotel."

A hot flush crept up her face as she remembered just *how* he had convinced her. It had involved a dark corner, her short skirt, and Soren on his knees. Soren's tongue could be very compelling.

She shook her head and took a deep breath, returning to the present. "But he promised me that we could go to the party at Marco's flat tonight. You are coming to that, right?"

Charlene nodded. "You bet, I wouldn't miss it. The conference officially ends at 5pm tonight, and then I'm free. It's my last chance to have some fun in this town!" Charlene said with a wink.

Soren pulled Angela into his arms and held her tightly. "Wouldn't you rather stay here and take a bath?" he asked enticingly.

They were lying in their downy, white bed, basking in the afterglow of their orgasms.

Angela kissed him deeply. When she broke away, she looked him in the eyes. "Soren, you know I would love that. But this is my last chance to see my friends here. I haven't danced a single night since I've been here and I've only spoken to Marco twice. Don't get me wrong, I've loved being cooped up with you here at the hotel. It's been very *hygge*."

He smiled. "I can tell you've been practicing. You've almost got the pronunciation right," he teased lightly.

He knew he was being unfair keeping Angela all to himself, but he just didn't enjoy competing for her attention among her bevy of friends—especially the male ones.

Angela rolled her eyes at Soren. "Except for dinner, we've stayed in all three nights I've been here, and it's been wonderful…but you promised that we could go to the party tonight. After all, I'm leaving tomorrow and I'd like to see some of my friends one last time."

Soren pulled Angela toward him. "About that…"

"About what?"

"Why don't you stay a bit longer? I can buy you a new plane ticket."

Angela pulled away and looked at Soren, her heart speeding up uncomfortably. It bothered her that Soren thought that money could solve a problem that he didn't really understand. "Soren, I have to get back. First of all I have that finance class that I can't miss and—more importantly—you see that manuscript over there?" She pointed to the table where she had been working on her book. "Well it isn't going to publish itself. I'm almost done with the first draft and I want to have someone with more experience help me get it published. I have an appointment scheduled for Monday that I don't want to miss."

She looked at Soren's crestfallen face. Her words had taken him from hopeful to deflated in just a few seconds. She caressed his brow, running her finger down his strong cheek and sculpted chin. In a softer tone she continued, "Besides, you'll be out to visit soon. You are still coming to L.A. after Christmas, right? That's only two months away."

"It's actually nine weeks away, which sounds much longer," he said with a long face.

Angela giggled at his expression. It looked like Soren was almost pouting, except that a pout on him looked a lot like constipation. "Soren, I have *work* to do. I spent too much money on my education to not use it. I want to publish my books as quickly as possible. The clock is ticking."

She hoped he understood. It was important for her to accomplish her goals. Personal motivation was the hardest part about being an entrepreneur and she knew that extending her stay in Barcelona would be the exact opposite of what she needed at this time…professionally at least. Besides, it irked her that Soren didn't ask her if she was available to stay longer before offering to buy her a new ticket. It's as if he thought she didn't have a life in L.A.

He sighed loudly. "Alright then. Back to Los Angeles you go." He pronounced the last syllable of her hometown as though it was a long vowel: Los Angeleeze. She found it endearing. He continued, "I do admire how motivated you are. It's quite a turn-on actually." He slid his hands down the bare skin of her back tenderly.

Angela sighed, happy to hear that he understood. Relieved, she mewled at his sensual touches. With a suggestively-raised eyebrow she said, "We still have an hour before we have to leave. But I'm not. Missing. Marco's party." She narrowed her eyes, walking the line of forceful and seductive, daring him to contradict her.

Soren raised an eyebrow in response. "I can do a lot in an hour."

Angela closed her eyes, sighing heavily as Soren began planting hot kisses on her throat and chest, working his way down her naked body, leaving a wet trail of desire in his wake.

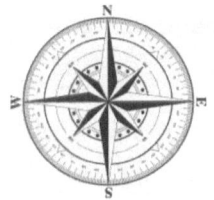

Chapter 15: Through The Looking Glass

Angela grabbed her black leather art folio, tucking it under her arm as she closed her car door, and headed to her meeting with Kieran O'Connell.

She'd barely been back in L.A. for three days, but she felt great. In actuality, she couldn't tell if she had adjusted to Pacific Time yet or if she was just running on pure adrenaline. She'd worked on her manuscript nonstop all weekend—needing to remind herself to eat and sleep—wanting her story to look its best.

She dressed up for the meeting today and was wearing a red pencil skirt with a white blouse and a lightweight silk cardigan with a black and cream leopard print. A necklace of creamy, faux, baroque pearls around her neck was juxtaposed with knee-high, black leather boots—with a short Louis heel—adorning her feet. Her long hair was collected at the nape of her neck in a messy bun. The overall effect was professional but hip, very "sexy librarian," which she figured would be a good vibe for the owner of a bookstore. She smiled, thinking that Soren would probably like this outfit as well.

She smoothed out her cardigan as she walked into the dimly-lit coffee shop, admiring the iron and tile work of the old building. A handful of large pumpkins and decorative squashes were sprinkled about the space. Halloween was only two days away.

She took off her sunglasses and surveyed the room. She hadn't been able to find a picture of Kieran O'Connell on the Jabberwocky website, but she imagined that he would be fortyish, bookish, and fair. No one in the shop fit that description.

She put her folio and black handbag down at a table and went to the counter to order some tea. After ordering, she looked at the young man's name tag and asked the goateed barista, "Carlos, right? Do you know Kieran O'Connell?"

He nodded, chin turned up. "Oh yeah, Kieran comes in here all the time."

"I'm supposed to meet him here, but I don't know what he looks like. Is he here now?"

Carlos looked around and shook his head, lips pursed. "Nope, he's not here. Hold on a second, let me get you your tea." He came back with a steaming mug and put it on the counter. He looked up at her. "Be careful it's hot."

"Thanks, I will."

Angela grabbed her mug and was turning away from the counter when the barista said, "Oh wait, there he is," and pointed toward the door.

Angela followed the direction of Carlos' hand—smiling in anticipation of finally meeting Kieran O'Connell—when she locked eyes with a familiar face. The shock of recognition hit her and she fumbled with her mug. "Ouch!" she yelled, scalding her hand with the boiling-hot tea.

She unconsciously stuck her finger in her mouth as Mr. TDD approached her with outstretched arm, a mischievous smile on his face, and a black tendril blocking one eye.

"Hello Ms. Holguín, Kieran O'Connell. Nice to meet you." He smiled widely, flashing his deep dimples at her.

She scowled at him as she put down her tea and offered her unburned hand. She pulled her burned fingers out of her mouth. "Nice to *meet* you," she said, accentuating the word "meet" sarcastically.

He laughed loudly with the booming resonance of a stage actor. "Are you mad at me?"

She narrowed her eyes. *Oh no he didn't.*

She gazed angrily at Mr. TDD. No wait, Kieran, taking in his faded black jeans, black t-shirt, and loose black cardigan. He was more James Dean than Barnes & Noble. Even without his motorcycle jacket, he still looked like a bad boy, and he was very different from what she had been expecting.

She pulled her finger out of her mouth. "Is this some sort of joke?" Her heart was beating rapidly in her chest.

"Joke, no why?" His expression became concerned as it flicked from her face to her hand. "Is your hand okay? Let me take a look at it." He gently reached for her wrist.

She attempted to pull it away from him, uncomfortable with the charge that laced through her arm when he touched her, but he held it firmly. He turned her hand over tenderly in his own, studying her burn intently.

She scowled at him.

He didn't notice her reaction. "This is pretty bad. You need to put some aloe on it right away or it will blister," he said sincerely.

She yanked her hand out of his grasp and gazed at him haughtily. "Great, I'll just go cut a leaf off the aloe in my car." The bite of her words surprised her. She wasn't sure why she was antagonizing this man, but something about him bugged her.

This was not how she had envisioned her meeting with "Kieran O'Connell, Bookstore Owner" going, but then again, Kieran O'Connell was not the man she had imagined him to be. The one upside of her temper was that she didn't feel embarrassed or tongue-tied around him today. Her anger had sharpened her tongue to a point.

His eyes widened in surprise, a bemused smile dancing on his face. "You're a feisty one, aren't you?"

She cocked her head at him, her eyes like slits. No one had called her feisty since college; it always struck Angela as a politely-condescending way of telling someone you annoyed them. But the would-be embarrassment of his comment bounced off the shield of her white-hot anger as she hissed at him, "Why didn't you tell me *you* were the owner of Jabberwocky when I met you the other day?"

Kieran looked momentarily chagrined. He swiped at a wayward tendril of hair. "I guess I thought it would be a laugh since you clearly didn't consider me 'children's bookstore owner' material," he said with air quotes.

She arched one brow in agreement. He definitely was not the typical children's bookstore owner, but then again Jabberwocky, with its cutting-edge vibe in this funky neighborhood, did have a sense of his edgy, leather-clad, motorcycle-riding self.

She took a deep breath. "Okay, you got me. I was expecting Kieran O'Connell to be a middle-aged blond man who spoke with an Irish accent."

He threw his head back and boomed with laughter once more. "No, that's my uncle Paddy in Jersey." He paused a second to consider her carefully. When he spoke again, his expression softened along with his voice. "Hey, I'm sorry if I caught you off guard. I really am interested in your book. I didn't mean to embarrass you. Am I forgiven?" he asked earnestly, his dark brown eyes turning serious for the first time since they had met.

It was annoying that he could read her so effortlessly. She liked to think that she could hide her discomfort from a complete stranger. But she recognized the sincerity of his apology. Besides, she needed to forgive him; she *needed* him...for her book.

She met his gaze and found herself taken aback once again by his good looks.

She couldn't tell how old he was. His longish, bouncy curls and smiling expression gave him a youthful appearance, but he had a touch of gray in his stubble and the subtlest hint of wrinkles around his eyes. She guessed he was somewhere between 33 and 39. He was easily the best-looking man she had ever spoken to in her life, and it was very, very distracting.

Kieran O'Connell was like a traffic accident; you couldn't help but gawk.

She was mildly aghast at her reaction. Not only was she already in love with the man of her dreams, but she was a professional. She closed her eyes, shaking her head to clear her thoughts. *This is a business meeting. Let's get down to business.*

She gave him an office-appropriate smile. "Yes, I forgive you. I guess I shouldn't be so narrow-minded about what a children's bookstore owner can look like." She hoped she was managing a light tone, but her fingers were starting to throb. She shook her hand, trying to fan the pain away.

Kieran searched her face for something, but if he found what he wanted, she couldn't tell.

He pointed to her hand. "You really should put something on that. Look, I have an aloe in my office. Let's move this meeting to Jabberwocky and we can bandage you up," he said authoritatively.

Before she could protest, he had picked up all of her things and gave her an expectant look.

"Hey Carlos, can you throw her drink in a to-go cup?" He threw out the light command to the barista who stood up straighter at the sound of Kieran's voice.

"Sure Kieran, no prob."

Carlos ran over with a cardboard cup and poured her tea into it. He handed the cup to Angela.

"Thanks," she said as she followed Kieran out of the coffee shop and toward Jabberwocky.

The glare off the street was powerful. Even though it was November, the afternoon sun in Los Angeles was still strong. Angela squinted at the bright light bouncing off the cars, not used to facing it without her dark sunglasses. The loud parade of vehicles, on the eternally busy street, added their own heat to the thick, dry air. Angela looked out of place in her pencil skirt and cardigan amid the human crush of jeans and leather. She blocked the sun with her bad hand as she caught up to Kieran.

"Follow me," he said lightly, that mischievous smile back in residence on his lips.

She couldn't tell if he was mocking her, or if he just always looked that way at people, but she found him very hard to read and that unsettled her.

Maybe this isn't a good idea. The unsolicited thought flashed across her mind quickly. She brushed it away, remembering that Kieran was an influential bookstore owner, and exactly the person she needed to help her move her business forward.

He shot her an inquisitive sideways glance. "So what made you want to write children's books?"

She paused thoughtfully. No one had ever asked her that question. "Well…I've always loved to read, but when I was growing up there were very few books that had kids who looked like me, and I want to change that."

His eyebrows shot up at her answer.

She continued, "There was this one author though, Leo Politi, who wrote books about kids from all over the world, and illustrated them himself too. I met him one day when I was in Chinatown with my mom. He said I looked just like his character Moy Moy, and he autographed his book for me. I guess he kind of set the course of my life that day. *Moy Moy* was my favorite book because it was the only one where the character looked anything like me. I still have it."

He inhaled deeply, his eyes softening. "You know, I ask every author I meet that question, and you just gave the best answer I've ever heard. That's sweet Angela. I get where you are coming from."

Her eyes widened. "You do? How?"

He smiled, hesitating for a second and then leaned forward as though sharing an important secret. "Well, my name might be Kieran O'Connell, but that's only half of the story. My mother is from South America. My middle name is Alphonso…"

"Kieran Alphonso?" She wrinkled up her nose, wondering how any parent would choose such a random combination of names.

"Yes, Alphonso," he said with a stern look that immediately silenced her. "Obviously I think Kieran suits me much better." He gave her a look daring her to mention his middle name again.

She shook her head. Relaxing she gave Kieran a rueful smile. "Don't worry; your secret is safe with me. Kieran it is."

He smiled big, his dimples shining through.

For the first time this afternoon, Angela felt like she was on even keel. She breathed a bit easier.

Kieran continued, "Yeah, so I know what it's like to not quite fit in. My dad's family is as fair as my name implies, but I got my mother's coloring, and as a child, I always felt more Latin than Irish. Besides, my dad was born in Ireland but grew up in New York, so except for his love of soccer and Guinness, his Irish culture is kind of nonexistent."

"That's exactly like me. My name is completely Spanish, but—"

"Let me guess. You have Asian blood too," Kieran said, cutting her off, his eyes twinkling.

She took a closer look at him and blinked a few times. He didn't look *happa*—the Hawaiian slang for someone who was half-Asian like herself. Usually only other *happas* noticed that she had Asian blood. Most people heard her name and just assumed she was Latina. "Yes, how did you guess?"

Kieran shrugged. "My mom's family is from Lima, and there is a community of Peruvians with Japanese ancestry. In fact, the last president of Peru was the son of Japanese immigrants. I have some cousins who are half-Japanese and they kind of look like you."

She nodded her head. "My mother is Chinese and I've always identified with my Asian side more than my Latin side. She was a stay-at-home mom and dad was...*is* a workaholic, so I guess it's natural to feel closer to the culture of the parent that you spend more time with."

Kieran's frank admission of their shared mixed heritage made her relax considerably. It was yet another reason why he was the perfect person to help her with her books. He *got* her.

They had arrived at Jabberwocky, and Kieran held the door open for Angela. The moderately-lit and quiet interior was a relief from the noise of the street. Although there was no policy against talking in the store, there was a library-like hush to the space.

The store was decorated for Halloween, with elaborate paper masks—in the style of *Dia de los Muertos*—filling the front window with their hollow-eyed gazes and various sizes of round dots in all the colors of the rainbow attached to the walls and dangling from the ceiling like oversize confetti. It was very festive, colorful, and edgy, just like Jabberwocky.

"I love the decorations," Angela said, admiring the crafty, but sophisticated paper artwork.

Kieran followed her eyes. "My mom does all of them. She changes it every year. She's got a great eye." A look of pride glanced across his face.

She followed him to the back to a small office with glass walls covered on the inside with privacy blinds. He put her bags down, closed the door, and grabbed a first aid kit hanging on the wall. He removed a small pocketknife from his pocket and cut a two-inch section from a plump aloe plant sitting in his window.

"I always have an aloe plant at home and where I work," he said offhand.

"You do?"

"Yeah, they are hard to kill and if you ever get burned there is nothing better than its juice. I learned that from my mom. It's the perfect plant: hardy and useful."

She watched as he expertly ran the edge of the knife down the sides of the aloe leaf, removing its prickly spines, and then sliced it down its fleshy middle revealing its sticky juice within.

He looked into her eyes as he asked, "Where does it hurt?"

She pointed to the fingers that were aching and he cut a piece of aloe to fit, placed it on her hand and wrapped the two fingers together with gauze and tape. He took her bandaged hand and raised it to his lips. "A kiss to make it heal," he said as he briefly brushed his lips against the bandage while he locked eyes with her.

She pulled her hand back quickly, caught off guard by the kiss and the intensity of his gaze.

A dark look passed over Kieran's face. "I'm sorry, that was awkward. I'm not sure what came over me. Please accept my apology," he said, his voice full of regret. He hesitated briefly and then turned his back on her as he packed up the first aid supplies, leaving her free to contemplate his actions.

While kissing her hand seemed at odds with the professional nature of their meeting, there was something about Kieran that made it non-threatening.

When Kieran turned back to her, his face was unreadable. He gave her a look as if he expected her to say something.

Angela didn't know what to say, her heart racing once again. Her only clear thought was that Soren would be outraged if he had witnessed the exchange.

She couldn't tell him.

Her heart clenched at the traitorous thought.

He cleared his throat. "May I?" he asked, gesturing to her folio.

She nodded, holding her bandaged hand as he picked up her book layout, and spread it out on his desk. She watched him closely.

Clearly in his element, he examined her pages with rapt concentration and peppered her with questions. "Why La Mercè as a subject?"

Grateful for the neutral territory, she started speaking of her own experience with Barcelona's most important festival. "It's such a magical experience. The whole city practically shuts down. There are concerts, parades, and fireworks around every corner, but the Catalan people are also very proud of their culture and they do some things that are uniquely their own."

"Such as," he said brusquely, suddenly all-business.

"Such as the parade of the giants. They have these bizarre-looking, *papier-mâché* heads that are gigantic. They are kind of like a cross between a float and a puppet.

"The Barcelonese treat them like they are real people and they dance down the street and everyone fawns over them. And then there are the human pyramids. Towers formed by men and women standing on each other's shoulders. The highest are eight or nine levels high and they balance a little kid at the very top. It's just crazy. You would never see that in the States. And the whole event is just so full of joy and good fun. It's a really special experience." She felt giddy reliving the vivid memories of her time in Barcelona.

Angela held her breath, waiting for Kieran to say something. She could see now that he was a serious businessperson, despite the bad-boy bravado of his motorcycle attire. Her MBA experience had taught her what a person looks like when they are doing an internal cost-benefit analysis, and she could see that he was in the middle of one.

"I like it," he said quietly, his arms crossed, his hand on his chin.

Angela inhaled sharply. "You do?"

He looked up, suddenly. "Yes, I do. It's unique, it's vibrant, it's contemporary. You have a voice all your own, I've never seen anything like what you are doing." He studied her face seriously before he continued, "You paint a very compelling picture: a unique book idea with an absorbing story that lends itself to great visuals. I also think the public will like you. Authors who can promote their own work have an advantage over those who can't. You are well-spoken and intelligent, and you have a great personal story that will be a fantastic hook when it comes time to promote your book, especially here in L.A."

She felt herself flush with excitement. "Really?"

He nodded. "I do have a comment though."

She nodded for him to continue.

"Readers want to connect with a specific person, not a vague idea. So while I love the idea of the festival, you need to find one or two central characters that readers can focus on and experience the festival through that person's eyes." He paused and studied her thoughtfully, like he was judging her.

She looked away as she considered his words. She hadn't thought of it that way before, but now that he pointed it out, it seemed so obvious. "Of course, you're right. Well, it looks like I have some rewriting in my near future."

He chuckled loudly. "There will be lots of opportunity for rewriting. It's the nature of the beast." He stood up straighter, and opened his arms, palms up. "I'd love to help you however I can, whether it's finding a graphic designer, an editor or even a publisher. Of course, once it's complete I will happily carry it here at Jabberwocky, and of course we should have the launch party here…that is, if you want that." He leaned against his desk and clasped his hands together in front of him.

Angela blinked, stunned. *Did he just say what I think he said?* She repeated his words in her mind, realizing what he'd just offered her. Her eyes widened. "Oh my God," she screamed with excitement and flashed Kieran her biggest smile before knocking him off balance by throwing her arms around him and hugging him tightly, her effusive nature getting the better of her professionalism.

Kieran hugged her back, but then loosened his grip considerably.

Angela pulled away from Kieran, and shook his hand with her good hand. "Sorry, thank you so much. I'm not sure what came over me, but you don't know how happy you've made me. I didn't mean to just grab you."

She put her bandaged hand to her forehead, embarrassed by her exuberance and overwhelmed by his show of faith in her idea.

Kieran stared back at her, an unreadable look on his face. Suddenly he stood up, wrapped his arm around her waist, and pulled her to him, crushing his lips against hers.

Angela cringed as Kieran's lips sent an unwanted thrill of desire through her body aided equally by the twin thrills of recklessness and guilt.

Angela pulled away from the short kiss as though coming up for air. Her good hand flew to her mouth in disbelief, her eyes horrified. She backed quickly away from Kieran and bumped into a chair. "Damn."

Kieran's face was ashen. "Oh my God, I'm so sorry Angela…"

She turned swiftly, gathering her things; not listening as she rushed out his office door. She ran through the back door to the parking lot, yanked open the heavy door of her aged Volvo, threw her stuff on the passenger seat, and got into her car. She buckled her seat belt, pulling out of the driveway recklessly fast. Her heart was racing like a thoroughbred at the Kentucky Derby.

Get away, get away, that single thought was compelling her to flee Jabberwocky as though it was a disease whose affliction she could outrun. Once she had driven a few blocks, she let out a deep sigh and inhaled for what seemed like the first time since rushing out of the store.

She pulled over onto a leafy residential street, stopped the car, and crumpled over her steering wheel. Her hands were shaking.

What the hell was that?

Her mind raced as she struggled to understand the kiss that she had not anticipated, nor wanted, but had enjoyed all the same. Kieran's dark, inscrutable face, with its mischievous eyes, invaded her thoughts unbidden.

"Fucking stupid." She slammed her good hand into her steering wheel.

She racked her brain for the mistake that caused this to happen. The hug had been as much of a surprise to her as to him; the spontaneous act of unexpected joy unleashed on the nearest human. And then he kissed her.

The thought of Kieran's tongue in her mouth sent a pleasurable lance through her stomach.

"No," she shouted as she gripped the wheel. "No, no, no, no, no," she continued, yanking the wheel as though she could rip it off.

She closed her eyes and concentrated on thoughts of Soren, hoping to burn Kieran from her mind with an angelic visage of the Dane. Images of happy moments flicked through her mind before she picked one to focus on.

She thought of the time he held her as they watched the sun rise over the majesty of Prior Park and the city of Bath was spread below them like something out of a fairy tale. She remembered the warmth of his arms around her, and the pleasure of nestling her head on his chest as the liquid gold of the morning sun shone upon them. The morning air had been cool that day compared to warmth of his body, and the feeling of the sun on her face—as he kissed her in the early morning light—had been heavenly. A warm glow spread over her chest as she remembered the perfection of the scene and her pulse slowed to a more normal rhythm.

She'd only spent an hour with Kieran and already she had two secrets to keep from Soren.

Not good.

She breathed evenly a few more times before opening her eyes, starting the car, and pulling away from the curb.

She merged into the stream of cars that was constant on L.A.'s major streets; a never-ending parade of multi-hued, metal insects buzzing to and fro that made many wonder out loud, "Doesn't anyone ever go to work in this town?"

Deep in autopilot mode, she made her way onto the freeway thinking about everything and nothing at the same time, a jumble of disconnected thoughts and images running through her mind. *Gravel crunching underfoot, Soren's stormy eyes, mango salsa, NPV, SMART cars, truth or dare, loose tendril, hug, book, Jabberwocky.* The randomness kept her from spiraling out of control by focusing on any single thing for too long. She didn't want to consider the reality that she needed to close the door of opportunity presented by Kieran O'Connell.

The price was just too high.

She jumped at the sound of her cell phone ringing, the digital jingle breaking into her non-thoughts. Rifling through the items on her passenger seat, she cursed, attempting to find her phone; but it was buried deep below the tangle of bags that she created when she left Jabberwocky in a rush.

"Voicemail it is."

Her heartbeat had returned to normal, as she thought with perfect clarity that Soren could never know about today. If his jealous rages about Rolfe and Marco were any indication of his reaction, he would never understand.

The kiss meant nothing and she was not going to let something as dumb as that ruin what she had with Soren.

Kieran sighed, staring at the space that just moments ago Angela's luminous presence had filled.

What the fuck was I thinking?

He walked over to the small refrigerator in his office, grabbed himself an IPA, and sunk down into the well-worn leather of his club chair. He took a deep swig from the bottle as he pondered the surprising turn of events of the last hour.

He had to admit now that he had been intrigued by Angela Holguín ever since the day he saw her standing at his register counter with a stack of books half her size that included many of his favorites. When they spoke, her unique book idea had only stoked his interest, and then when he realized that she didn't know he was Jabberwocky's owner, he couldn't resist misleading her. It had been refreshing how she hadn't tried to sell herself to him.

During their email correspondence, he found himself wanting to see her as soon as possible, and once they had set a date, he began counting down the days. He had chalked his enthusiasm up to professional curiosity…but now he knew better.

He could pinpoint the exact moment he realized he was attracted to her. It was when he had finished bandaging her hand and looked into her eyes.

She is lovely.

The rogue thought had flitted across his conscious mind much to his dismay. Until that second, he hadn't really noticed Angela as a woman. Of course she was attractive, not in a hyper-feminine "pretty" way, but like Jane Russell, a "dame" in the best sense of the word. She had an almost masculine energy to her; her yin and yang were well-balanced. The most he had thought about her looks was that they would be a great asset when it came time to market her book and do media interviews, launch parties, and signings.

That was, until that unbidden thought beckoned his attention.

And then he had to go and fucking kiss her hand.

He swore, taking another deep pull from his beer. As a potential business partner Angela was off-limits; not that he was dating anyway. Kieran was the master of not mixing business with pleasure; he had learned that lesson the hard way. Of course, truth be told, there weren't many children's book authors that had the charms of the one who just ran out of his office.

He had tried to hold her at arm's length by throwing out the comment about needing to narrow down her characters; call it a test of sorts, but he was curious to see how she would take his feedback. It was important to know if they would work well together in the many months ahead.

Book publishing was not a short-term project.

Part of him had hoped she'd take the note poorly and not want to work with him. But she'd taken his comment like a champ, only raising her in his regard.

And then he had to go and fucking kiss her.

He had forgotten how sweet a woman could feel in his arms—his many years of monk-like entrepreneurship had beaten it out of him—and he had drank thirstily from Angela like a man lost in the desert; surprised at how his body responded to her, completely losing his hard-earned self-control. It seemed like his lips were on hers before he'd even had the conscious thought to embrace her.

He closed his eyes, remembering the scent of roses wafting off her and how soft and lush she felt pressed against him. She felt so much smaller in his arms than he had expected. When she broke the kiss, it was only the look of horror on her face that kept him from pulling her back and crushing her to him once again.

He shook his head and laughed. It had been years since Kieran had done anything reckless. He had forgotten how thrilling a clandestine kiss could feel. He couldn't deny now that he was attracted to Angela.

"Damn, stupid idiot," he slammed his bottle down on his desk, rattling its contents and spraying himself with a rain of beer. "Crap!" He kicked his club chair with the toe of his motorcycle boot.

He stood there stewing momentarily; trying to figure out what he should do.

Finally, he swung around to his computer, sat down in his office chair, and opened one of her emails, looking for her phone number. He jabbed the buttons on his cell phone and waited for her to pick up. "This is Angela, leave me a message," her voicemail taunted.

"Angela, it's Kieran. I'm so sorry, that was completely unprofessional, I don't know what came over me, but I promise it won't happen again. I hope you can forgive me. Please call me back."

He hoped his message had struck the right tone, because a faint feeling of desperation had come over him. Angela's bright light had awakened something in him that had been dormant for too long.

Whether or not he was willing to admit it to himself, he needed to see her again.

Almost an hour after leaving Jabberwocky, Angela pulled into the parking garage of her apartment building. The stairs seemed steep today as she carried the weight of her physical and emotional baggage up the many steps to her second floor apartment.

The door creaked quietly as she opened it. She took off her shoes and put her keys into the iridescent Murano glass bowl—in the shape of a butterfly—that sat on her entryway table. Throwing her bags on one of the lounge chairs, she headed to the bathroom to shower, thinking that a clean start might lead to a fresh start.

She emerged from her shower feeling refreshed, and unpacked her folio. The meeting with Kieran had forced her to make quick progress on her book, but now that she was almost done with it, she wasn't quite sure what the next step was. Of course, she still needed to narrow her characters down, as Kieran so wisely suggested, but she already knew how she wanted to handle this, and felt confident she would have a solid first draft ready quickly.

But what to do then?

"Damn kiss," she said glowering at her manuscript. She grabbed her cell phone. She needed to talk to someone. Maybe Therese could meet her for a hike.

When she looked at her phone, she saw the voicemail from earlier. Not recognizing the number, she hit play. A shiver went up her spine as she heard Kieran's deep, resonant voice. *"Angela it's Kieran. I'm so sorry, that was completely unprofessional, I don't know what came over me, but I promise it won't happen again. I hope you can forgive me. Please call me back."*

His voice created a confusing mix of emotions in her; a combination of tenderness, guilt, and regret. She could practically see his deep-dimpled smile and his wayward, black tendril, taunting her.

She dialed Therese immediately. It was early afternoon, and her stomach was rumbling with hunger pains. She walked over to the kitchen and opened the refrigerator as she waited for Therese to pick up.

"Hey Ange, what's up? I can't talk long, I'm at work. I have a trial tomorrow," Therese said pointedly.

Angela groaned. "No hike then?" She pulled out some leftover green curry and brown rice from the weekend.

"Not today, but what's up?"

She dumped the leftovers into a glass container and threw it in the toaster oven. "Therese, the craziest thing just happened and I don't know what to do."

"Give me the short version."

She leaned back against the counter, waiting for her food to warm up. "There is this really cool children's bookstore on Melrose that would be perfect for my books. I met the owner today, who by the way is a leather-wearing, motorcycle-riding hottie with a capital 'h.' Anyway, he said he loved my idea and that he definitely wants to carry my books. When he said that I got *really* excited and I threw my arms around him…" Angela trailed off, embarrassed.

"Uh-huh…"

Angela could tell from the tone in her voice that Therese already disproved. Her extremely corporate work experience would never have tolerated that kind of display of emotion.

"And I gave him a hug. I was just so excited I couldn't help it. And then suddenly he kissed me."

Therese coughed. "What?"

Angela put a closed fist to her forehead. "I know, I know. I'm such an idiot. I don't know why I hugged him. It wasn't a conscious thing. I was just really happy and he was the person standing right in front of me."

"And then what happened?" Therese sounded like a detective collecting witness statements.

"After the kiss? I freaked out! I grabbed my stuff, ran out the door and drove away as fast as I could."

"Why?"

"Because I didn't know what to do," she said flatly. "When we stopped kissing I was flustered and embarrassed, and I just ran out of there." Angela's face flushed just thinking about it.

"Okay, well, it doesn't sound like you are angry about the kiss, so tell me this. Did you like it?" Therese asked calmly.

The question surprised Angela. She paused, ashamed to admit the truth. "I did. I can't believe I just said that, but it's true. I did. But it was wrong, it was a mistake, and now I don't know what to do, because the truth is, I *need* him."

"What do you mean 'you need him?'"

"I mean, I'm at the point with my book where I don't know what to do next. I need advice, a mentor, someone to guide me through the publishing process. And Kieran is absolutely perfect for that, in so many ways."

"Hhhhmmm. Interesting conundrum." Therese clucked her tongue as she thought.

"And he called me to apologize. While I was driving home, he left me a voicemail. He said he was sorry, it was unprofessional and that it would never happen again."

"Do you believe him?" Therese was such a jaded lawyer, always second-guessing everyone's motives.

"Why wouldn't I?"

"Angela, you can be *so* naïve sometimes. For such a smart person, you can be really dumb. What I *mean* is: do you think his apology was sincere, or is it a maneuver to get into your pants?"

"What? No, come on, really? A maneuver?" Angela shook her head in disbelief. She doubted Kieran needed to maneuver to get into anyone's pants. Most women in the world, and probably quite a few men, would happily disrobe for a specimen like him.

She shook her head.

This was not a helpful train of thought.

Her toaster oven pinged, indicating her food was ready. She grabbed an oven mitt and carried it to the dining side of her dining table, the other side functioning as a makeshift computer desk.

Therese sighed. "Yes, a maneuver. Maybe he's trying to get you back into his office so he can finish the job."

"I don't know him well enough to say for sure, but I don't think so. Kieran doesn't strike me as desperate or manipulative. But I'm thinking that after this afternoon I shouldn't go back."

"Whoa, whoa, whoa. I'm not saying you need to do anything that drastic...*yet*. Look, you said you needed him, why not see if he can help you out? It was just a kiss, and he apologized. Frankly, I'm glad to see you getting so much action. You know, it's been a long time since you let anyone close, ever since Rai—"

"Therese..." Angela cut her off threateningly, cold chills cascading down her back. Therese knew better than to bring up that subject.

"Okay, I withdraw that statement." Therese sighed. "But maybe you should just talk to this guy on the phone for now. Avoid meeting him in person, try and suss him out; see if you can trust him."

"That sounds like a good idea," Angela felt relieved that she didn't have to do away with Kieran completely. "But what about Soren? Don't I owe it to him to tell him?"

"Owe it to him to drive him insane with jealously when he's thousands of miles away and can't do anything about it?" The tone of Therese's voice made it clear that this was a rhetorical question.

Angela paused. "I see your point, but, I feel bad about it. I feel like I need to confess." She blew on a forkful of curry, a knot of guilt mixing with her hunger pains in her stomach.

Therese blew out her breath loudly. "Then confess, by all means, to me, to your mom, to the church. But leave Soren out of this. You did nothing wrong, why do you feel bad?"

The color rose in her cheeks as embarrassment flushed her face. Angela said quietly, "Because I liked it." Angela moved the phone away from her ear as her friend's cackling laughter exploded through the earpiece.

"Angela, that just means you are alive. If a good-looking man kissed me, I'd enjoy it too. You can't help how you feel. Honestly, what happened between the two of you is like ice cream compared to my stalking trial tomorrow. I'd say that you are clear on all charges honey."

Angela sighed, relief flooding her body. "Thanks Therese, you are the best."

"Love you Ange. Now I have to go. Let me know what happens."

"I will. I'll see you for our hike this weekend, right?"

"Wouldn't miss it."

Angela looked at her phone and considered calling Kieran back, but she still didn't know what to say to him. She needed some time to collect her thoughts.

She took another bite of food and pulled her manuscript over to her. "Might as well finish this guy off."

A couple more days of serious work and her first draft would be done. Maybe then she would know what to say to the mysterious Kieran O' Connell.

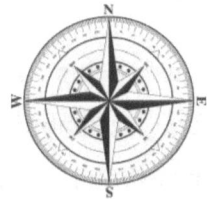

Chapter 16: Amplification

"So would you do it? Would you take the loan from the bank or the money from the angel investor?" Professor Colburn looked over his glasses at the students, his question hanging in the air like a guillotine.

It had been a week since her trip to Barcelona, and Angela was back at her business school for a class called "Finance for Entrepreneurs." Her trip already seemed like a dim memory as she focused all of her attention on the distinguished-looking man at the front of the room.

Nervous anticipation flooded the space as the students waited to see whom Professor Colburn would call on. He looked down at his seating chart, studying it like it held the meaning of life. When he looked back up he said, "Ms. Holguín."

A rush of relieved sighs filled the room.

Angela took an imperceptible breath to calm her nerves.

Looking like you knew what you were talking about was as important as the words you said in MBA school, and she wasn't about to look flustered.

In Professor Colburn's class, being called on to answer a question was a potentially fatal inevitability. In this class, forty-percent of one's grade was based on participation, except the professor had engineered a unique sort of peer pressure to ensure that students performed.

The entire class of sixty-eight students was divided up into teams of four, and each student's participation grade was the accumulation of points earned by all four people on their team. Every student would be called on exactly twice over the quarter, and each answer was scored on a scale of 0 to 5 for a total possible score of forty points by each 4-person team. A single 0-point answer meant your overall course score just dropped half a letter grade.

Every. Answer. Mattered.

Even though Angela wouldn't be getting a grade for this class, all of her team members would and she wasn't about to let them down. This was the only reason Professor Colburn allowed a handful of already-graduated students back in his class. He knew they wouldn't take the class lightly.

Angela stared back at Professor Colburn calmly. He was peering at her over the top of his black frame glasses in his tweed sport coat and tie. Hiding her nerves she said, "It depends Professor Colburn. This case is about the classic struggle between money and control. If you take the money from the bank, you are getting less capital and you will be required to make monthly payments on the debt, but you also are not giving up any control. If you go with the money from the angel you get more capital, and have no monthly payments, but you give up majority ownership."

This question was full of pitfalls for Angela. In her mind the answer was clear: take the bank money. Angela hated the thought of building something and not having total ownership over it. That's just how she was wired. However, she also knew that wasn't necessarily what the teacher wanted to hear…but maybe if she framed it just the right way…

"At this stage of *this* entrepreneur's journey, I would take the bank money."

Silence descended over the classroom as Angela, and all the students, waited for Professor Colburn to say something.

Entrepreneurial finance questions were rarely straightforward, and students earned the full five points by providing the analysis behind the answers, as well as the answer itself.

"And why is that Ms. Holguín?" Professor Colburn asked with just the slightest hint of a smile playing upon his lips.

Angela wasn't sure if the smile was because she was falling into some sort of trap or because she was correct. She took a deep breath and continued, "Because in this case, the entrepreneur has a long road ahead of him or her. Medical products are not something that you can get to market quickly. If the entrepreneur gives up majority ownership at this point, how will she or he raise money in the future? And if the entrepreneur can't raise money in the future, then the product might never even make it to market. The angel investor in this scenario is really cobbling the entrepreneur by asking for majority ownership. I understand the idea about taking on investors and getting a smaller slice of a bigger pie, but there are too many unknowns at this point. The entrepreneur could end up with no pie if he or she takes the equity deal at this point."

A hush fell over the classroom as everyone waited for Professor Colburn's verdict. Angela turned to look at the teaching assistants seated in back, whose hands were poised over their notebooks, ready to write down whatever he said.

After a pregnant pause he replied, "Very good Ms. Holguín. Full marks. Five points."

A huge smile broke out on Angela's face as her team members slapped her on the back in congratulations. She just raised all their grades with her thorough analysis, and in this class that was no small feat.

"I'll see you all next Friday. Enjoy your weekend. Class dismissed," Professor Colburn said with his usual wry smile.

Angela caught his eye and he raised an eyebrow, giving her a wink of approval. Angela felt her chest expand with pride at the non-verbal compliment from the mercurial instructor.

Angela had often felt like an outsider at business school. Her interest in small and socially-responsible businesses placed her in a very small minority, but tonight she felt like she belonged.

It was 7pm on a Friday night and all Angela wanted to do was go home, eat, and shower before her regularly-scheduled phone call with Soren at ten. She started packing up her bag when she was accosted by her friends RJ and Dalia.

RJ, whose real name was Rasheed Jasiyah, was a hilarious, beautiful man who was raised in Los Angeles to Pakistani parents. He had the brightest smile of any person Angela had ever known, which was made even more brilliant by the contrast against his dark chocolate skin.

Dalia Dolorosa was one of Angela's best friends from the MBA program and she was drop-dead gorgeous in a "don't-hate-me-because-I'm-beautiful" sort of way. She had straight, jet-black hair that hung to her shoulders, and dark brown eyes that flashed black when she was mad; tall and slender, Dalia had an elegance to her that made her immediately intimidating to most people.

Back when Dalia and Angela first met—the summer before business school at a luncheon welcoming Latino-students to the MBA program—Angela never would have guessed what good friends they would become. At first, Angela found Dalia to be aloof and cold. But over the course of their two years in business school, they had become inseparable and were now like the sisters each had never had, speaking at least once a day if not more.

Dalia and RJ were in the same boat as Angela, having also gone abroad last fall, and returning to campus post-graduation to take Professor Colburn's class.

Like Angela, Dalia got a lot of attention at business school with the 1-woman to every 10-men ratio and the fact that many of the straight, female students were already married. The ratio of men to women also meant that each team of four in Professor Colburn's class had only one woman on it, and some had none. Fortunately, the teams were made up by the teaching assistants, so there was no feeling like the kid on the playground that no one wants on their kickball team. However, Dalia was a "quant jock", the business school term for someone with a numbers background, and would have been in high demand anyway.

"Our team is going out for drinks at the Liquid Kitty. It's karaoke night. You want to come?" Dalia asked, her eyes shining.

The Liquid Kitty was a dive bar by West L.A. standards, but in most cities, it probably would have been one of the nicer places on the block. It was famous for its ridiculously-strong martinis and its ridiculously-dark interior.

You could make out with a stranger in there and have no idea what the person looked like.

Angela glanced at the way Dalia had her arm looped through RJ's. Any other person might have misunderstood the affectionate gesture. But RJ was not one of the men who admired Angela and Dalia because of their gender. He played for the other team.

Angela sighed. "I can't. I need to get home. It's date night with Soren." Angela started packing up her laptop and papers. She pretended to ignore Dalia rolling her eyes in her direction. "Besides, I'm hardly dressed for a night at a bar." She motioned to her business casual knee-length, gray skirt, long-sleeved, white pullover and red wrap she was wearing. Of course Dalia always looked ready to go out in her skintight jeans, a sheer purple and black top and black, knee-high boots with a three-inch heel. Not that she needed the height.

"Oh come on. It's one time...and you never come out..." Dalia replied in a tone that vacillated between pouting and whining. "And we should celebrate. You are the queen of the night. You got your answer right!"

Just then, Angela's team started gathering around her to congratulate her for earning them five points.

"Way to go Angela," said Patrick, the dark, curly-haired former accountant.

"Yes, *excelente* Angela," said Francisco, the Argentinian with a heart of gold, who pronounced her name Spanish-style with a combination hard "g" and breathy "h" in place of the American style soft "g": Ang-hell-a.

"Hey guys, don't you think you should take Angela out to celebrate? After all, she just moved you that much closer to earning an 'A' in this class..." Dalia trailed off meaningfully.

"I'm in," Patrick said immediately. He was always game to celebrate.

"Sure, why not," said Francisco who was young, single, and went out every single night whether or not he had something to celebrate.

The lone holdout on Angela's team was Nathan, who was married and had two kids.

"Come on Nathan," Dalia said, fluttering her eyelashes at him. "Let's celebrate."

Angela shook her head as she zipped up her bag. She could tell Dalia was not going to let up.

Nathan shook his head from side-to-side in classic "aw shucks" form. "Okay, let's go before I change my mind."

Dalia whooped and turned back to Angela. "What do you say Ange?"

Angela slung her bag over her shoulders. Liquid Kitty was less than thirty minutes from her apartment. If they went right away, she could hang out for an hour or two and still make it home in time for her phone call. "Fine. Let's go."

At around 7:30pm the large group of MBA students invaded the small, dark bar that reeked of alcohol from the countless martinis that had been spilled on the perennially-sticky floor.

The Liquid Kitty was a narrow rectangular space lined on the right with a red vinyl bench that traced the outline of the wall down the entire length of the room like a gash of garish lipstick. In front of the bench were small tables and low stools. Along the left side of the space was a standing-height bar that took up about three-quarters of the wall. Directly behind the bar was the small stage area where karaoke equipment was set up for the night.

Dalia had succeeded in recruiting almost twenty people from their class. Of course, her job was made easier by the fact that everyone always wanted to celebrate when Professor Colburn's class was over because of the intense preparation required all week for the three-hour class. The weekend was that much sweeter because it meant the students had two days to not think about his class.

It was still early for a Friday night, and the Kitty was fairly empty, allowing Angela and her friends to claim the bench and tables directly in front of the karaoke space. Martinis began to flow almost immediately, as though the bar had been waiting for them to walk through the door. The only person not drinking was RJ, who abstained for religious reasons, but always looked like he was having the best time of all of them.

"Here you go Angela, congratulations," Patrick said, as he placed a martini glass sloshing with chartreuse-green liquid into her hand.

"Thank you…but I can't. I have to go home soon; I can only stay for an hour, tops." Angela scooted the glass across the table toward Dalia.

Dalia pushed the green drink back toward Angela. "Oh come on Ange, you can stay for one drink. If you leave at 9:15 you'll make it home with time to spare."

"You forget, I can't drink the way you can." Angela raised an eyebrow at Dalia, who was known to drink many of their male classmates under the table.

"Come on. Let's have fun!" Dalia lifted her glass to her lips and downed it.

Angela scowled at her friend. Maybe she could just have half a drink…

The sun blared through the windows, waking Angela as it lit up the beige bedroom.

Beige? My bedroom isn't beige, Angela thought groggily as she struggled to wake up. Her eyes were still not fully-opened as she smacked her dry—yet sticky—lips, realizing that she felt incredibly parched. Still half-asleep, she rolled to her side and saw Dalia fast asleep, her black hair covering half her face.

She looked at her watch; it was almost 10am.

Her eyes shot open as the night started to come back to her. She remembered going to The Liquid Kitty. All three members of her team had the same *original* idea to buy her a martini to thank her for her five-point answer. She remembered not wanting to offend anyone and sipping from each of the cocktails.

The rest of the night was fuzzy, but she vaguely remembered sitting in the passenger seat of her own car while someone else was driving.

Dalia must have driven my car.

The thought triggered her memory as she remembered Dalia leaning over and opening the car door as Angela threw up on the side of the street.

Suddenly the sticky feeling in her mouth became disgusting.

Quickly, she went to the bathroom and stuck a bit of toothpaste in her mouth to rinse out the aftertaste of vomit and martini.

Yuck. I am never drinking another fucking martini in my entire life.

The one upside of throwing up was that at least she didn't have a hangover. She studied her reflection in the mirror. She was still wearing her clothes from last night's class. There was a spot of something—*Vomit?*—on her wrap. She grabbed a wet washcloth and scrubbed at it furiously.

She walked to the kitchen, poured herself a glass of water and drank it thirstily. As she was refilling the glass she heard, "Hey, you're awake. Good morning."

"Fuck Dalia, I missed my phone call with Soren. Where's my phone?"

Dalia yawned, scratching her head as she entered the kitchen. She made her cut-off t-shirt and cotton pajama bottoms look like the latest thing from the runway. "Um, I left your stuff by the front door. It must be in there somewhere."

Angela walked to the front door, grabbed her laptop bag, and shoved her feet into her red, patent leather flats. Stuffed in the side pocket of her bag was her cell phone, dead. "Damn it. My phone is dead. I have to go."

Dalia held up an index finger as she finished drinking her water. "What's your hurry? Why don't we go have breakfast?"

Angela scowled. "You don't understand. Soren is going to be worried sick. He always overreacts when he can't get in touch with me." She thought back to the emails he sent when he couldn't reach her after her flight home from London; a chill went up her spine.

Dalia rolled her eyes. "Seriously, he acts like your mother."

"Thanks Dal, that really helps. I'll call you later."

Angela charged her phone in her car on the twenty-minute drive home. When she got to her apartment, she sat on her couch, looking at her phone as if it was a coiled viper ready to strike. She sighed loudly and powered it up. She waited half-a-minute for the gadget to go through its cycle and then she frowned as she read the screen: 7 MISSED CALLS, 3 VOICEMAIL MESSAGES.

Crap.

This was going to be 10-times worse than the emails after her London flight. She closed her eyes and pressed the phone to her forehead.

She was not looking forward to this call.

She dialed his number.

The phone didn't even complete a full ring when he answered. "Oh my God, Angela, are you okay?" Soren asked in a frantic rush of words.

The sincere concern in his voice made Angela wince. Her words came out in a torrent, "Yes, Soren, I'm fine. I'm so sorry, but last night did not go as planned. Some friends talked me into going out, everyone was buying me drinks, and I got much more intoxicated than I planned. I couldn't drive and ended up sleeping over at my friend Dalia's place. I just woke up half-an-hour ago and my phone was dead. I called you as soon as I got home." Angela felt pretty good about her explanation. It was reasonable enough.

"Do you have any idea how concerned I was?" His voice was angry-quiet. "I've been trying to reach you for over twelve hours. I already called Charlene twice and was on the verge of calling your parents. I've been out of my mind with worry and all this time you were passed out drunk somewhere?" By the end of the sentence, he was no longer calm, his voice seething with emotion.

Angela didn't appreciate the accusatory tone in his voice. How could he be angry with her over something so innocent? It's not like she was Thomas and this was a reoccurring issue. "It wasn't planned Soren, it just happened. I had every intention of being home by 10pm, but my classmates wanted to celebrate because I answered a question in class correctly..." she realized immediately how lame that sounded, but before she could explain, he started speaking.

"Really Angela? That's your explanation? You got drunk because you answered a question correctly?" His voice was heavy with icy sarcasm.

His tone surprised her. "Is that what you think of me?" she asked, throwing his sarcasm back at him. "You know what Soren? The only thing I did wrong was miss our 10pm phone call. I would have called you earlier to give you a heads up when I decided to go out with my friends, but that would have meant calling you at 3 or 4 in the morning your time, and I didn't *plan* on missing our call."

Soren's overreaction was only affirming her decision not to tell him about the other day with Kieran. Any residual guilt she might have felt about that vanished with his accusatory tone.

She shrugged off her wrap. She couldn't believe how hot and angry she was getting over this minor thing. If they had lived in the same city, this never would have happened.

Marco's words suddenly made sense to her: amplification.

On the other end of the line, Soren stewed in his own anger. Even without her missing a phone call, he couldn't shake the concern that there were men in Los Angeles trying to steal her away from him. When he wasn't able to get in touch with her last night, all of his worst fears flooded back to him. *Maybe she was on a date. Maybe she was kissing some other man right now. Maybe she was smiling and flirting with a group full of men around her.*

He closed his eyes and twisted his fist into his forehead, hoping for some clarity.

"Soren, are you still there?" The heat of her previous tone was already gone.

As usual, he couldn't keep up with her mood swings. It took him time to transition between emotions, not that he was ready for that yet. He was still incredibly angry.

"Seriously Soren, I've already apologized. I'm having a hard time understanding why you are making such a big deal out of this."

He sighed. She was right; she had not done anything technically wrong. But Soren just couldn't shake how he felt. On top of that, he found it incredibly frustrating that Angela was so far away. Nothing was simple with this much distance between them. He stewed quietly, unable to let it go.

Finally, Angela broke the silence. "Soren?"

"I'm here," he answered petulantly, struggling not to say anything that would make the situation worse. He ran his hand through his hair as they sat in silence for a few more seconds. "I don't have anything else to say right now. Why don't I just call you in a few days?"

She sighed heavily. After a long pause she said, "Okay...I love you."

He echoed her sigh and squeezed his eyes hard. "I love you too." He put down the phone and slammed his hand on the table causing his water glass to slosh about.

He leaned back in his desk chair.

How could such an innocent incident become such a big issue?

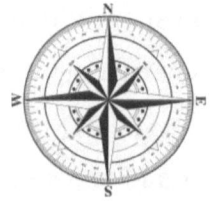

Chapter 17: Progress

Angela looked over at her manuscript taunting her from where it lay on the dining table. She felt as though she had read those fifty-four pages at least a hundred times, looking for corrections or improvements that she could make.

Corrections? More like procrastinating from calling Kieran.

She scowled knowing that there was nothing left for her to do but to call him. He had left two other voicemails over the last week. The final one had really piqued her interest since he mentioned finding a book on his shelves that he thought would be a good model for her, and that the publisher was a company he worked closely with.

She dialed his number quickly before she could chicken out.

He answered on the first ring. "Hi Angela, what's up?"

His casual tone gave Angela no clue on how to proceed; it was the ultimate poker face. She decided to follow his lead. "Hey Kieran. I've been working on finishing my book, and I've edited it about a million times, so I was hoping we could go over it in more detail."

"That's great. I look forward to reading it again. I'm pretty much always at the store. Do you want to bring it by the next couple of days?"

Angela paused remembering Therese's advice about keeping their interactions to the phone. "Um, well, maybe we could just talk over the phone?"

Kieran chuckled lightly. "We could try, but unfortunately I don't have a photographic memory."

She could tell by his tone that he was smiling now. She wasn't sure if he was mocking her or trying to put her at ease, but her sense was it was the latter.

He continued, "I didn't get to go over it as closely as I would if I was giving it an edit, but I can certainly give you a couple of general pointers that you could incorporate before we meet in person."

"Okay, that sounds great. Like what?"

"Well, it's important that you grab your reader from the first line. Two of the best ways to do that are either to surprise your reader by placing your protagonist in a challenging situation right away or by writing the prose in a way that is so poetically clever that you are drawn in immediately."

Angela thought about what he said. "Okay, I get your first example, but can you give me an example of a poetically clever line?"

"Sure, that's easy. The first line of *Pride and Prejudice* is a perfect example. 'It is a truth universally acknowledged, that a single man in possession of a good fortune—"

Angela finished the line for him, "Must be in want of a wife." A warmth blossomed in her torso.

"Exactly. That line is amazing. It captures your attention immediately and draws you in. So my recommendation to you would be that you rework your beginning to be more captivating using one of those two scenarios. In children's books, rhyming and rhythmic language are also great tools, so maybe you can work that in as well."

"Okay, great points. Anything else?" Their conversation was inspiring her.

"Yes. Your text should enhance your photographs, not explain them. Don't repeat in words what the photograph clearly illustrates; add text to explain what isn't visible."

Wow, he's good. "Thanks Kieran, that's very helpful."

"Any time…and of course, incorporate the tip I gave you about a lead character."

Angela smiled. "Already done. It helped a lot, and I already have an idea for how I can incorporate your idea about putting my character in a challenging situation in order to draw the reader in immediately. Can I take a couple of days to incorporate these comments and then we can meet in person later in the week?"

"Absolutely. Anytime, let me know. Bye Angela."

"Bye Kieran."

"And Angela?"

"Yes?"

"I'm glad you called," he said as he hung-up.

Angela hung-up and then smiled as she thought about their conversation. Kieran O'Connell was certainly a complex man; between quoting Jane Austen, giving her amazing editing feedback and then bringing up the awkwardness between them without really bringing it up…well, she wasn't exactly sure how to classify him, but he was certainly intriguing.

Angela looked at her watch; it was almost 8pm, which meant that freeway traffic would finally be dying down. The sun had set a couple of hours ago, and the winter sky was as black as coal, although Melrose Avenue was still bustling with pedestrians and car traffic.

Angela stifled a yawn. She twisted in her chair, stretching her back, and gazed through the window of Kieran's private office into the store space beyond. The privacy blinds were fully open and she could see the Thanksgiving decorations fluttering; a collection of leaves in fall colors suspended from the ceiling.

She and Kieran had been looking over her manuscript for almost five hours, ordering greasy Indian delivery for dinner, and she was exhausted. Editing was a completely different skill set than writing, and she felt like she was in English grammar boot camp. Who knew there were so many different ways to use a hyphen? Kieran, however, still looked full of energy. She felt bad to be the one breaking up this incredibly productive meeting, especially since Kieran was being so generous with his time.

"Tired?" Kieran asked.

"Yeah, sorry. I've read the book so many times that I feel like I'm getting cross-eyed."

"It happens. Look, why don't you leave this with me and let me spend a few days with it. It will be good for you to not look at it for a bit so that you can have fresh eyes on your next edit."

Perking up, Angela said, "Oh, okay. That makes sense."

Angela started to pack up her things as Kieran flipped close the manuscript and looked up at her.

"Angela, it's been great working with you today, but I would like to clear the air before you go home."

Angela stiffened, unsure what was coming.

Kieran leaned forward, resting his arms on his knees and looked at Angela intensely with his soulful, brown eyes. "I just wanted to apologize again in person. I don't have any excuse or explanation, I just want you to know it will never happen again. Okay?"

Angela relaxed her shoulders feeling the tension drain away. Almost three weeks had passed since "the incident" and she had completely gotten over it. Even this conversation was actually very easy…so why did part of her feel disappointed?

"Thanks Kieran, that's very big of you, but I don't think you were completely to blame. I was so excited by your generous support of my idea that I let myself get carried away. I should *not* have thrown my arms around you, so I'm pretty sure we're even." She gave him her biggest smile and offered her hand as a peace offering.

He shook her hand and smiled back at her. "Great. Look, why don't you plan to come back here the same time next week. Mondays are always somewhat slow anyway. See you at 3pm?"

Angela hesitated. "Are you sure? I don't want to take advantage of—"

He cut in. "You're not taking advantage of anything. Angela, everyone needs help. I didn't open Jabberwocky without the help of many people, and I would be honored to help you realize your dream. So, 3pm okay?"

She sighed, grateful for his generosity. "Sure, that's perfect." She stood up, grabbed her bag, and headed to the door. "See you next week."

"Yeah, see you." He watched her through the back window as she got into her green Volvo and pulled away.

He sighed, slumping into his chair.

It had been hard, but not impossible, to maintain a completely professional demeanor around Angela. He kept finding himself wanting to reach out and touch her or ask her personal questions; studying her profile when she wasn't looking. All issues he'd never faced with the many authors he'd worked with before her; and now he'd gone and invited her back on one of his busier days of the week. He rolled his eyes, recalling the charge he'd felt when he shook her hand, wondering if she'd felt something similar.

He hadn't yet worked up the courage to ask her if she was seeing anyone, but he could guess at the answer. It would explain why she had run out of his office that day a few weeks ago; then again, maybe she was single but just not interested in him, or maybe she just wanted to keep things professional—she had never offered a single detail about her personal life, other than those he'd asked her about directly.

He spent a few minutes trying to divine which of the three options was most likely before he found himself reliving their kiss again, as he had every day since it happened.

He couldn't remember the last time a woman had infected his thoughts the way Angela did.

He shook his head, trying to clear his mind of the rose-scented Angela Holguín. Maybe with enough practice it would get easier.

It had to.

"Hullo darling."

Just the sound of Soren's voice over the phone was enough to light up Angela's body like an incandescent bulb. She was practically vibrating with pent-up sexual energy. It had been too long since she'd felt Soren's arms around her; she could no longer remember exactly what they felt like. Her once visceral memories were now hollow shells and soon they would be no more than dust as the passing of time eroded them away completely.

For some strange reason she could remember Kieran's single kiss more easily than Soren's last one. She frowned; swatting that unwanted thought away and forced a smile into her voice, not wanting to bring Soren down. "Hello yourself. I miss you." She stood up from her desk chair and stretched. She'd been transcribing for the last few hours and hadn't moved the whole time.

"Hhhhmmm, I miss you too. It's so good to hear your voice."

She walked to her picture window. Thanksgiving was in a couple of days, and the weather was getting colder. She had started sleeping with her ultrathin Merino pajamas, and today the sky was gray and overcast. "Yours as well. How have your interviews been going?"

"Oh bollocks they are so tedious, but I did get one offer, so I suppose I won't be unemployed when I graduate."

"An offer? Congratulations. Where to? I'm sending you a huge hug and a kiss over the phone, can you feel it?" She turned back to her living room, and started sauntering around her coffee table.

"Almost," he said in a sweetly forlorn sort of way.

Angela could imagine his sad smile.

"To a smaller bank than the one I was at this summer, also in London. It's not what I'm looking for though."

She wondered what part he wasn't looking for. Smaller bank? London? Something else? There was so much uncertainty in their lives right now; it made it hard to feel secure. Before she could ask him what he meant, he asked, "How about you, what did you get up to this week?"

She ignored the nervous feeling in her stomach that his question initiated. "Remember the meeting I had with a bookstore right when I got back from Barcelona?"

"Yes."

"Well the owner of that store really likes my manuscript and has been helping me refine it. His feedback has completely transformed my book. It's been exciting."

"Congratulations darling, that's wonderful. I'm so happy for you." His tone was reserved but positive.

"Thanks. We have a weekly appointment to keep me moving forward. He said that a realistic goal would be to finish the book by May or June and get it published over the summer just in time for the holiday shopping season next year."

"That sounds reasonable."

She sighed. "Yes, but honestly, I want to get it published tomorrow. However, I also want it to be as good as it can be, so I guess I'm just going to have to take it slow. It seems I'll need to keep my transcription gig for another year."

Angela was looking forward to the day when she could support herself financially off her entrepreneurial endeavors and not need side gigs to supplement.

"I think that's wise. I look forward to reading your book when I'm there for the holidays," Soren said wistfully.

Angela smothered a squeal. "Yes! I can't wait to see you in person; only thirty-six more days to go." She'd been marking off the days on her calendar with a red Sharpie.

"It seems like an eternity before I can touch you again," Soren said with the subtlest groan in his voice.

"I know; it's torture being apart. I miss running my hands through your hair and kissing those beautiful lips of yours."

"Hhhmmm, don't stop. Tell me more."

"So how did you get into children's books?" Angela asked as she devoured another amazing chicken and mushroom lettuce wrap.

There was something about the umami of shitake mushrooms combined with the subtle nuttiness of water chestnuts and the sweetness of plum sauce that Angela found heavenly. Even the iceberg lettuce, something she normally avoided like the plague, was an important component, its watery-crispness cutting through the fat and sweet. She closed her eyes and allowed herself to fully enjoy the flavor combination. It tasted even better since it wasn't turkey. After four days of Thanksgiving leftovers, she was done.

"I don't think I've ever seen anyone enjoy food as much as you do." Kieran's eyes were scrunched up and sparkling, his lips twitching up at the corners.

Angela nodded, not wanting to speak until she finished chewing. "Yum, that was delicious." She cocked her head at him. "Don't change the subject. I asked how you got into children's books."

Angela and Kieran were taking their 6pm dinner break, as was their custom on their long Monday afternoon work sessions. Her book was improving tremendously under Kieran's inspired direction, and they had settled into an easy and comfortable working relationship, despite their rocky start.

Kieran never brought up the kiss again and neither did she. Their relationship was professional, but casual and friendly. Angela found herself looking forward to the end of the weekend because it meant she would get to see Kieran soon, although she told herself she was just excited about getting his feedback on her latest revisions.

And his feedback had been overwhelmingly positive. Angela was like a flower in the sun, growing and thriving under his professional tutelage. It felt so good to share her passion for literature with someone, and to receive the praise of someone she admired both as an entrepreneur and as a reader.

"What? You mean I don't look like a lover of children's literature?" he joked, dark eyes flashing.

She narrowed her eyes, taking in his black on black attire. His wardrobe seemed to consist of only a handful of items, all black. "Not exactly."

He laughed. "Your honesty is refreshing, if painful."

"Painfully honest, that's my middle name."

"Do you have a middle name?" He furrowed his brow as he took a bite of lettuce wrap.

"Are you changing the subject again?" She scowled.

Kieran arched a brow. "Maybe."

"Then the answer is maybe."

"Maybe you have a middle name?"

"Yes. And maybe I'll tell it to you if you tell me why you started Jabberwocky." She crossed her arms over her chest.

At the mention of Jabberwocky, his face turned serious again. He paused a few moments. "As tempting an offer as that is, it's not something I like to talk about," he said with finality as he took a bite of fried, brown rice.

Angela's curiosity was piqued. Kieran had always seemed like an open book. Over the last month, they had spoken about a wide range of topics and issues, and he was always incredibly forthcoming. She knew how he loved his mom to pieces, what it was like growing up with three, older sisters, his passion for soccer, his dual degree in English Literature and Philosophy. Seeing him clam-up like this was a first. "Wow Kieran. So mysterious. You are making me very curious."

Kieran gave her a stern look. His implied warning was clear. This topic was off limits.

He sighed heavily. "Allow me to summarize by saying: something good came out of something bad, and let's leave it at that."

"Leave it at that?"

"Yes, leave it," he said in a final tone.

Clearly this was one story that he didn't want to tell.

What could have happened to make Mr. TDD so secretive?

"So what do you think?" Soren asked excitedly.

Angela was annoyed; but she didn't want to sound ungrateful so she answered noncommittally, "It sounds nice."

Her tone must have given her away.

Soren sighed. "You don't sound excited about it. Won't it be nice to go away together? The pictures of Santa Barbara look beautiful. I thought it would be fun to take a little trip while I'm there."

Soren's 5-day visit was in a little over three weeks and he seemed determined to spend as little time as possible in Los Angeles during his trip.

Angela sat on her off-white sofa, squirming under his questioning. Good thing he couldn't see her visible discomfort. "But I was looking forward to showing you around L.A, and introducing you to my family and friends."

"But I'm coming to L.A. to spend time with you, not with them," Soren said coldly.

His tone only annoyed her more. It was nice in London when he took the initiative to plan their trip to Bath, but he was on her turf now. She didn't want him thinking it was okay for him to always make the plans, especially without consideration for what she wanted. "But my friends and family are a big part of my life Soren. Don't you want to know more about my life here?"

He sighed heavily. "Just consider it, okay? I have to go; I'll call you in a couple of days?"

She exhaled. She hated it when they had a bad phone call. Fights over the phone took longer to get over than fights in person. "Okay."

"I love you Angela. Being with you is what's important to me."

"I love you too." Angela ended the call; annoyed.

She stood up and opened the door to her balcony, inhaling the cool winter air. She leaned against the doorframe, trying to imagine Soren standing next to her.

She didn't want their time together in L.A. to be like their time in Barcelona, where they barely left the bedroom. Sex was great, but if their relationship was going to have a future, they needed to get out more. She wanted to show him everything she loved about her hometown. Part of her even hoped that he might fall in love with it since she wasn't sure she wanted to live anywhere else.

She didn't want to push him away, but what future could they have if they were just a vacation romance?

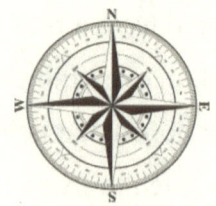

Chapter 18: A Revelation

Angela paced around her apartment nervously. A few days had passed since her disagreement with Soren about Santa Barbara. She knew they needed to have a serious talk, but she was dreading it. Some things just can't be discussed over the phone.

She had been here before. Twice she had met someone while abroad and tried to keep the relationship alive while the other party resided in a different country, and twice it had failed. The most recent time was with Thomas, although that barely counted since she had not really cared about the future of that relationship.

However, she cared about Soren…deeply. He was kind, thoughtful, and loving; considerate, sexy, and mature. He had so many wonderful qualities that were important to her in a long-term relationship, but she recognized the very real challenge they faced: the lack of a foundation.

It isn't as if they were together for a year before moving apart. What they were doing was much harder: trying to build their relationship's foundation *while* they were apart, and without any notion of when they would be in the same city again for anything more than a brief trip.

With a heavy heart, she dialed his number.

"Hullo my lovely, how are you?"

The sound of his voice brought an instant smile to her face and she momentarily forgot her bad mood. "It's so good to hear your voice," she said honestly. She ached to feel his arms around her.

"What's wrong Angela?" As usual, Soren was tuned into her emotions.

The kindness in his voice immediately made her feel bad. It would be so much easier to just give in to what Soren wanted and go away to Santa Barbara with him, but part of her knew that wasn't what their relationship needed.

Soren waited patiently for Angela to speak.

Finally she said, "Soren, I've been thinking a lot about your Santa Barbara idea, and I think it's a lovely gesture, but…" She paused and took a deep breath before saying, "I feel like you are trying to avoid meeting my friends and family."

After a few moments of silence, Soren finally answered. "It's true Angela, I prefer having you to myself."

Angela was disarmed by his frankness. She was used to people who tried to twist the truth to make themselves look better, but she was reminded once again that Soren didn't operate that way. He was never one to deny the truth, even if it illuminated an unattractive quality about him.

"I know you've told me about how uncomfortable it was when we were in school together, the feeling that you had to compete with the other men who were around, but certainly that isn't an issue anymore. There is no competition, I've chosen you."

He sighed. "Yes I know that intellectually, but it does still *feel* like a competition when we are around others."

"Why?"

"Because, darling Angela, you may have chosen me, but that doesn't mean that they aren't still trying to win you over." His tone held the slightest flavor of condescension

Angela's throat felt hot and constricted. Part of her wanted to hang up the phone, but she needed to see this through. "Who's they?"

"They. You know, the other men. The Rolfes and Thomas' of the world. They. Just because we are together, doesn't mean that other men aren't actively trying to take you away," his tone was quiet, but accusatory. "Besides, it's not like you don't encourage it," he said, coldly.

Angela inhaled sharply; Soren's cold tone and thoughtless words were like a slap in the face. "What?" she stuttered in disbelief, a sharp chill running up her spine.

"When you have as many single men around as you do, it's not like you aren't putting yourself in a position to be hit on," he said, his tone icy.

Tears sprung up in Angela's eyes. She inhaled deeply, trying to steady her racing heart. When Angela spoke again, her voice was steely. "I have to go."

"No wait..."

"I'm going. Goodbye."

Angela was livid as she looked at her watch; it was almost 1:30. She would need to leave in the next half hour to make it to Jabberwocky on time for her weekly meeting with Kieran, but the last thing she wanted to do was work on her book.

She needed to get outside and let off some steam; a hike would do the trick. Maybe after her hike she would feel like working on her book.

She called Kieran.

He picked up on the second ring. "Hey Angela, you still coming by this afternoon?"

Angela hesitated. She didn't want to skip their weekly session, they were accomplishing so much every week, but she was in no mood to work right now. She needed to sweat. "I'm sorry Kieran, but I need to cancel."

"What's wrong, are you okay?"

Remembering the professional nature of their relationship Angela tried to recover, "I just got some bad news and I need to clear my head. I was thinking about going for a hike."

"I hear you, that really helps me too. Look, why don't I join you? We can go for a hike and I can bring your manuscript with me, so you can work on my proposed changes this week. What do you say?"

She paused briefly, surprised by his offer. "Yeah sure…that sounds good."

Angela looked out over the vast horizon below. The view from this point always filled her with wonder. It was an amazing 360-degree view.

On the far left was downtown Los Angeles with its tall skyscrapers. Center-left was Century City with its office towers and center-right stretched the California coastline with its famous broad beaches all the way down to Palos Verdes. Behind her, the San Fernando Valley was stretched out in all its glory with Lake Balboa glimmering like a large center-stone sapphire set into the heart of a necklace.

She sat down in front of a few of the short, stone cairns that previous hikers had created out of the sandstone available on the path's surface. It had been a strenuous 40-minute hike to get to this point. Kieran was probably twenty minutes behind her since he had a longer drive. She stretched her hand over her eyes to see if she could spot Catalina Island, which was usually hidden in the coastal fog.

She had told Kieran to meet her at this spot; she knew she needed to release some of her negative energy before she saw him. The hike had done its job; each huff and grunt on the steep inclines a welcome release of her anger. Her mom always criticized her for sounding like Monica Seles when she played sports, but Angela had never made any promises of being dainty to anyone. Besides, the grunting had served its purpose; she no longer felt the tension in her shoulders or the need to yell, that she had felt when she hung up with Soren.

Now that she was calm, she forced herself to consider Soren's words objectively. Did she encourage other men?

Angela had always counted men and boys among her best friends, going back to when she was eleven. She had always been something of a tomboy, and between soccer, basketball, and track-and-field, there was always a lot of male energy around. Not to mention the fact that in business school the ratio of men to women had been about 10-to-1.

It wasn't that she *chose* to surround herself with men, but that her interests forced her into environments filled with more men than women. In fact, she had made some of her best women friends in business school precisely because that environment had attracted other women who were more like Angela than the women she had met before; women like Charlene Nelson and Dalia Dolorosa.

She was starting to feel pretty good about herself—and her intentions—when a rogue memory flitted in that filled her with doubt: the kiss she shared with Kieran. She closed her eyes in frustration. Did she encourage that kiss? Did she lead Kieran on? Was she leading Kieran on now?

As if on cue, she could hear the crunch of footsteps behind her making their way up the sandy gravel path toward the peak she was sitting on. She turned around and saw Kieran approaching in his usual attire: black sweater, black jeans, black boots.

She furrowed her brow. "You don't change your clothes even when you hike?"

Kieran shook his head as he grinned broadly, his dimples on full display. "I'm a simple man, what can I say? These are boots after all. These are *my* hiking boots."

They both laughed at his joke.

He strode up next to Angela, took off his sweater and wrapped it around his waist. "Whew, that incline really gets the blood pumping, huh?"

Angela nodded.

"But what a reward. Wow, this is a spectacular view." He lifted his hand over his black Ray Ban Wayfarers and did a 360-degree turn.

"Isn't it amazing? I don't know of that many places where you can see the basin and the valley at the same time." Angela pulled her sunhat down around face.

"It's fantastic. Thanks for sharing."

He sat down cross-legged next to her and they sat together in companionable silence taking in the view; Angela not wanting to talk and Kieran sensing her desire for silence. The sound of the 405 freeway below could be mistaken for a rushing river; the roar of cars echoing up the canyon walls toward them.

Kieran was surprised to find that the 405—"the four-o-five" as locals called it—had any redeeming qualities at all. He raised and lowered his sunglasses admiring how clear the skyline was. The autumn sky was cool but bright, and recent rains had washed away the foggy haze that often clung to the horizon.

"You know, I never thought that I could find the 405 beautiful," Kieran said quietly, almost to himself.

Angela guffawed loudly, caught off guard by Kieran's random comment. The physical relief of laughing felt so good that she allowed herself to roll with it, and her laughter slowly dissolved into silly uncontrollable peals and then into full-blown giggles. Tears of mirth began pouring down her face, releasing the pressure her conversation with Soren had built up.

At first Kieran laughed along with her, but then he just gave her an amused look as he watched her double over and grab her side as her abs started cramping.

"Ouch, it hurts," she said in between her laughing sobs. "It…hurts."

He shook his head at her. "Wow, you really liked that one, huh?"

Angela nodded her head silently. "Yes, sorry," she giggled lightly. "Sometimes it just takes over." Finally, she raised her head and said, "Thanks for that. It was just what I needed."

Kieran nodded his head. "With pleasure. That was quite a laugh attack. Not sure I've ever witnessed anything like it."

Angela gave him a playful scowl. "Let's just leave it at that, shall we?"

Kieran held up his hands in surrender and took in the view once again. "Have you ever thought about writing a book set in Los Angeles?"

She paused, feeling like he was looking right into her.

After some hesitation, she finally said, "I have *one* idea," her voice breaking uncertainly.

He turned to look at her, and she was grateful for the barrier of their sunglasses so she wouldn't have to look at his soul-piercing eyes. "Tell me about it?"

She picked up a stick and fiddled with it. "Well, it's different than all the other books. It's not as cultural, it's more...philosophical."

His eyes widened. "I'm intrigued."

She hesitated before starting. This idea was by far her most personal and she had never shared it with anyone before. It felt important to her, but maybe it was just in her mind. Maybe no one else would see the significance of it. Maybe it was too abstract because it didn't have the bright colors and vivid details of other cultures to support it the way her other stories did.

She began slowly, "Every year before school started my parents and I would go on a camping trip," she paused searching his face for interest.

He smiled encouragingly. "Go on..."

She took a deep breath. "We always camped at the same place, Los Leones beach—"

"I've never been—"

"You haven't? Oh it's magical. The main beach has these amazing boulders, which are perfect for climbing. The beach is broad and clean. It's really a great place. We would spend all day on the beach, and then go back to the campsite for dinner and fall asleep to the crashing roar of the waves..." she drifted off, caught up in the vivid childhood memories.

He dusted off his knee. "It sounds beautiful."

"It is, incredibly beautiful. And that's kind of the point of the story. You see, the main beach is so beautiful that for many years— more than ten actually—we never ventured beyond it. Then one time we went camping on a low tide weekend. I think it's called a minus tide, meaning it is lower than average. In all the years we had been going to Los Leones, the tide had never been this low before.

"Well, on the other side of the rocks there was a small beach area that was too small to spend the day at because as soon as the tide came in, it would disappear completely. But on this day, the tide was so low that you could walk along the shoreline over to that small beach without getting wet, you didn't have to climb the rocks to get to it. In fact, the tide was so low that we could walk to the beach beyond that one as well which was littered with giant pebbles, great for skipping…"

Kieran smiled as he listened.

She continued, "Now mind you, this third beach, the pebbly one, we didn't even know it existed. We had no idea that there was this huge beach just north of the one we always spent our days on. But it didn't end there, beyond that beach was another, and another.

"And then we came to another huge rock outcropping, bigger than the one at the main beach, and as we turned the corner we came face-to-face with a huge gaping tunnel, 20-feet high, that had been carved out by the ocean and was usually under water. We walked through the tunnel, it's about 40-feet long, and on the other side was this tiny beautiful beach that looked like a picture postcard from Greece. It was so beautiful. I had never seen anything like that in person, and here it was in my backyard all this time."

She paused to gather her thoughts. "We spent hours exploring that tiny beach and the sharp, eroded rocks that surrounded it. There were so many cool nooks and crannies to scamper around, it was so fun. A few hours later, we decided to walk back to the main beach where we'd left our towels and umbrella. It took about twenty minutes and as we walked my joy of the day's discoveries turned into sadness."

Kieran's brows knit together. "Sadness, why?"

She smiled weakly. "Surprising, right? You see, what made me sad was *how long* it took us to discover that cave. I mean, we had been visiting Los Leones for years without any idea that just a short walk away was one of the most beautiful sites in all of Los Angeles. It made me wonder how often life is like that. How often do we become so comfortable with our own little piece of pleasant that we don't take a chance to explore what's just around the corner? What if paradise is just around the corner from pleasant? Discovering that incredible cave made me wonder how many other times I had missed out on something fantastic because I didn't make the effort to go just a little further."

Kieran smiled and shook his head. "Wow, that's deep Angela. It's like a parable. Your message is surprising, but relatable."

She laughed self-consciously. "Don't make fun of me, I've never told anyone that idea before."

He sat up straighter and leaned toward her. "I'm not making fun of you. I'm being perfectly serious. That is a deep and beautiful story. You should absolutely write that. The locals would go crazy for it."

"Really?"

"Yeah!" He threw his arms open emphatically. "It celebrates a local treasure, it would photograph beautifully, and it teaches an important lesson. You're right, pleasant can keep you from paradise. It's warning against becoming comfortably numb. That's a great lesson."

She blushed at his praise. She couldn't believe how good she felt; his words had completely changed the tone of the day.

He took off his sunglasses and looked at her seriously. "You know what?"

"What?" She furrowed her brows.

"I'd really like to see the beach myself. Why don't we go sometime?" His brown eyes sparkled.

"To Los Leones?"

"Yeah. I think your book idea is fantastic. You should start writing it now; on those days when you feel like taking a break from *The Festival*. It will be a good palette cleanser."

Angela arched a brow. "Palette cleanser, huh? I like that."

He laughed. "You would. You're such a food snob."

She narrowed her eyes. "We prefer 'foodie.'"

He shook his head. "Let's go day after tomorrow. The sun is supposed to hold this week, but who knows when the fog will return."

Angela shrugged. "Ok. Let's do it."

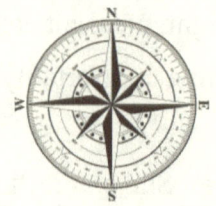

Chapter 19: The Non-Date

"I'm here." Kieran's low voice crackled through her apartment building's ancient intercom system.

"I'll buzz you in." Angela pushed the entry key and quickly threw a few, final things into her beach bag.

She could hear Kieran ascending the stairs to her apartment, his steps echoing off the tall narrow walls that lead to only two front doors: hers and her neighbor's. She always felt secure being able to hear people approaching well before they ever had a chance to knock.

Not that she had anything to worry about. Her apartment was located in the small, safe neighborhood of Encino located on the southern edge of the San Fernando Valley along the Santa Monica Mountains. Ancient oak trees dotted the landscape, which had once been home to citrus orchards and movie studio backlots.

Angela had chosen to live in Encino for the same reasons she had chosen to live in Les Corts in Barcelona: it was safe, well-located, and well-priced.

She opened her door as soon as he knocked. "Hi!" She took one look at his uniform of black t-shirt, black jeans, and black leather jacket, and frowned. "You don't look dressed for the beach at all. Tell me you aren't going to swim in jeans."

He shifted his sunglasses off his face and into his hair where they held back his curls like a makeshift headband. "I've got my trunks on under my jeans, and no, they aren't made out of denim," he said with a playful wink. "And I got us something to snack on," he said, patting his messenger bag. "I picked us up chicken lemongrass *bánh mì*, I hope you like it."

"I love *bánh mì*. Yum!"

"Great, but you'll have to change," he said, giving her a onceover. "You can't ride on my motorcycle like that," he said gesturing to her flip-flops and beach cover-up. He glanced around her apartment. "Hey, nice Peruvian mirror," he said, pointing to the sunburst mirror on her wall. He nodded as he took in more of her décor. "Actually, your whole apartment is really nice. I like your choice in furniture."

"Thanks," she said, momentarily distracted. "What do you mean motorcycle? When you said you were driving, I assumed you meant a car."

He shrugged his shoulders. "I don't have a car."

Angela narrowed her eyes. Ride on a motorcycle with Kieran? He was kind of like her mentor; wouldn't that be awkward? Maybe she should just offer to drive. Then again, she hadn't been on a motorcycle in a long time, and she did love them. Her father had bought her a little 50cc Honda when she was only 11 and she had loved it: the wind in her face, the fun jerking motion as she would shift the little bike into gear. It had always been one of her favorite things to do growing up and she hadn't been on a ride for over ten years. The idea was tempting.

"Come on, it'll be fun. It's a perfect day for a ride through the canyon." He turned his dark brown eyes toward her with just a hint of pleading in them.

She cocked her head. "Are you begging me?"

He nodded. "Yes, I think I am."

He was really being quite adorable, and a ride did sound like fun. "Okay, fine," she relented, but then she turned to him and held up her index finger. "But just this one time. Next time, I'm driving. I'll go change. Have a seat." She pointed to one of the black leather chairs hanging beneath the Peruvian sunburst mirror.

Hopefully he had bought the no-nonsense act because on the inside she was singing.

A motorcycle ride through the canyons on a day like today? What could be better?

She took off her beach cover-up and took a second to think about what she could throw over her one-piece that would be appropriate for a motorcycle ride. She dug around in the back of her closet and pulled out some old, thick black jeans, a long-sleeve cotton shirt, and her well-broken-in, thick, black leather jacket that she hadn't worn in years. It wasn't really her style anymore, but she couldn't bear to part with it…too many memories. She threw her beach towel, hat, and cover-up into a backpack, along with her bottle of water and sketchbook, and walked back to the living room.

"Wow, that was fast," he said appreciatively. "We almost match."

She pursed her lips. "Safety over style, right?"

He nodded. "That's true, let's go. Marilyn's waiting outside."

"Marilyn?"

He smiled gamely. "Yeah, that's the name of my bike."

Angela rolled her eyes as he opened the door for her.

When they got to his bike, he handed her a helmet. "Have you ever ridden before?"

She strapped on the helmet. "Yes, I used to ride a lot when I was young. I had a little 50CC trail bike."

His eyes lit up. "Really? That's great. Then you know all about how to lean into curves, right?"

"Yes. No problem."

He started strapping on his helmet. "Have you ever been a passenger before?"

She pursed her lips as she thought. "Only twice, but they were really short rides."

There was a third ride, but she'd buried that memory so deep, she didn't remember it.

His face got serious. "Okay, well it seems counterintuitive, but it's harder to be a passenger than a rider. In order to ride safely, we need to be in sync, and the best way to ensure that is to ride breastbone to backbone." He pointed to her sternum and then to his spine. "And put your hands here," he said, making a downward chop with the edge of his hands on his hips.

Angela furrowed her brow. She didn't think she'd feel right putting her hands *there*. Suddenly a motorcycle ride with Kieran seemed a whole lot more intimate than she had expected. Her stomach felt queasy in a not unpleasant way.

Traitorous stomach.

He must have sensed her hesitation because he added, "You can also hold onto that metal bar, but I warn you, it's quite an ab workout." He pointed to a curved bar mounted like an upside down "U" to the back of his bike. "Or you can put your arms around my waist. Whatever you prefer."

As he turned back to the motorcycle, she thought she saw him smirking mischievously.

Standing up straighter, she said diplomatically, "I think I'll take my chances with the bar."

"Suit yourself," he said, without a trace of disappointment.

Angela wondered if she'd imagined his smirk.

He continued, "Let me start the bike and then you can get on."

Kieran zippered up his jacket, straddled the vintage motorcycle, and pushed back the kick stand. Grabbing the handlebars purposefully, he put his right foot on the kick start and gave it a graceful downward thrust. The engine roared to life, causing Angela's heart to pound forcefully. She had forgotten how visceral a motorcycle could be, and an exciting tingling sensation swam up her legs and torso in anticipation.

Kieran jerked his thumb backwards and Angela put one arm on Kieran for balance as she threw her leg over the bike. Once settled— her hands firmly gripping the U-bar behind her—she shouted, "I'm ready," over the roar of the motorcycle.

They took off down her tree-lined street and Angela felt her body tingle with the familiar exhilaration of riding a motorcycle. Kieran was right; it was a beautiful day for a ride: the sun was bright, the air was crisp, and the traffic was light.

It was already after 12pm, and Ventura Boulevard was devoid of the commuter traffic that plagued it during rush hour. Within fifteen minutes, they were at Topanga Canyon, the street that would carry them over the hill to the ocean. Kieran wasn't kidding about the ab workout; Angela's stomach muscles were beginning to tire, and the uphill climb was going to be even harder than the flats.

Damn. I'm not sure if I can ride the whole way like this.

As they began to climb through the winding canyon, the uphill incline of the road made it feel as though she was leaning backwards, unsafely; distracting her from enjoying the ride.

When her abs started cramping a few minutes later, she relented, slowly winding her arms around Kieran's waist; not wanting to startle him by the sudden movement. Kieran reached down and patted her arm reassuringly.

Kieran was right; riding sternum to spine was *much* easier. It was surprisingly not awkward hanging onto him this way, their thick leather jackets and jeans a distinct barrier between them.

Maybe I was overthinking it.

She locked her grip tightly around his solid core, responding to his leaning without thought, their bodies in perfect sync.

Now that she wasn't thinking about her posture, Angela was able to fully enjoy the landscape. The scenery of the canyon was beautiful as the open road transitioned from the more common, dry chaparral to a cooler, leafy glen. The temperature dropped noticeably from the mid-70's at her apartment in the Valley into the mid-60's as they climbed through the canyon toward the beach.

They passed through the small town of Topanga with its quaint strip of commerce including a nursery, a few restaurants, a couple of beach-shack-looking stores, and a post office. It reminded her of a highland version of Haleiwa, the famous surf town on the North Shore of Oahu.

As they began to descend toward the beach, the air turned briny; Angela breathed in the fresh sea air. She had made this drive countless times over her life, but experiencing it on a motorcycle felt so different. She felt more connected to the environment around her; it was almost like riding a horse. She had forgotten how much she enjoyed this sensation.

When they turned onto Pacific Coast Highway—PCH to the locals—the view and roar of the ocean were glorious. The water was a deep sapphire-blue twinkling brightly in the winter sun as though its surface was on fire. Seagulls squawked like nagging children overhead, and the crash of the waves on the beach competed with the car traffic for dominance. Angela couldn't stop smiling and the muscles of her cheeks began to burn with overuse.

She couldn't believe what a different experience PCH was by motorcycle than by car. When she drove it in her car, she was just part of the crush of annoying traffic that filled up the road. But on the motorcycle she felt like she was a part of the wind and it was invigorating.

When she saw the sign for Los Leones, she patted Kieran on the shoulder and pointed. He pulled off the highway and wound around to the parking lot. Turning off the motor, he gave Angela his hand to help her off.

Angela took off her helmet and shook out her hair, running her fingers through her long locks. She grabbed her sun hat out of her backpack and pulled it low on her head.

"Like that did you?" Kieran asked with a Yoda-like gleam in his eye.

She cocked her head. "Why do you say that?"

"Because you are smiling like the cat that ate the canary."

She looked down at the ground. "It was pretty amazing. I've never ridden through the canyon or along PCH."

"It was beautiful, wasn't it?" He smiled, his elusive dimples making an appearance.

Angela had noticed that his dimples only showed when he smiled really big. It was kind of an adorable feature actually. She'd never seen dimples as deep as his.

She closed her eyes tightly, pushing the unbidden thought away. She brought her mind back to the motorcycle ride. "It was like I was the wind," she said as she opened her eyes.
"I was one with the wind. It was really cool."

His eyes softened. "I like that. One with the wind. That's a great description."

Angela returned his smile, admiring the liveliness of his eyes. They sparkled with a kind intelligence that was disarming. She was struck with a sense of déjà vu, but she couldn't figure out why. After a pregnant pause, she realized she was staring. He seemed to be looking at her with curious amusement. She cleared her throat. "I can't wait to show you the beach. Follow me."

They walked a few hundred feet to the southernmost beach that made up the long expanse known as Los Leones. Angela showed Kieran the many wonders of the area including its rock outcroppings, broad swathes of sand, and surf-worn nooks. Along the way, she relayed stories of her childhood: the first time she ever had a s'more, learning to jump waves and skip rocks. She pointed out the place she'd learned to boogie board, took him up the rock she'd learned to boulder on, and showed him all the different forms of seaweed whose names she knew by heart: the long strands of giant kelp with their prominent air bladders, the brownish-green feathery boa kelp that looked like a mermaid's long lost wrap; the wide blades of emerald-green wakame looking like soggy lettuce.

Angela did a little sketching of the outcroppings and different types of seaweed. Although she'd sketched this beach countless times before, she always seemed to discover something new. Today she was concentrating on a hardy-looking plant with waxy green leaves that hugged the cliffs like a blanket.

After a couple of hours, Angela pointed to the low cliffs that hugged the north side of the beach. "The tide is too high to walk along the shore to the north beach, but we can go up to the palisades and cross over that way."

After a 15-minute walk, the larger rocks of the north beach began to appear, and a partially submerged sea cave became visible. They continued walking until they came to a sandy beach wide enough to sit on. Kieran grabbed a towel from his bag, spread it out, and placed the food he'd brought on top of it.

He pulled off his shirt. "Man, this sun feels good. Nothing like December in Los Angeles."

Angela sucked in her breath. If Kieran O'Connell was gorgeous with his clothes on, he was positively god-like with them off. She quickly turned her attention back to the absorbing task of unwrapping her half of the Vietnamese sandwich. "Hey, this looks great. The French bread looks legit."

Did I just say legit?

She closed her eyes and took a deep breath, trying to steady her nerves. She wasn't sure why Kieran was so distracting today. Maybe it was because he was half-naked in front of her, or because they weren't working on her manuscript, or *maybe* it had something to do with her argument with Soren a couple of days ago—they still hadn't made up. Her mood darkened immediately.

"This is breathtaking Angela. I can't believe this has been in my backyard all these years and I've never seen it."

Angela opened her eyes and could see in her peripheral vision that Kieran was taking off his boots and jeans. She kept her eyes on the food—not wanting to stare—and tried to keep the conversation going. "Right? That's how I felt the first time I discovered this part of Los Leones. But you should see how huge that cave is during a negative tide, it's like a room it's so large. And when I look out at the sea this direction," she said, pointing to the view directly in front of them, "it feels like I could be in Greece."

"Yeah, I can see that." Kieran sat down across the towel from her and grabbed his half of the sandwich. He kept his gaze on the ocean while he unwrapped it.

With Kieran's attention focused on the view, Angela grabbed another grape from the bag in front of him, using it as cover to study Kieran appreciatively. She never would have guessed how muscular he was under his loose-fitting black on black clothes. His skin was a deeper shade of *café au lait* than her own, with a beautiful coppery tone. His arms and shoulders were muscular but lithe and she had never seen such well-sculpted abs before in her life. *Must be all that motorcycle riding,* she thought, aware that her own abs were going to be hurting tomorrow.

He looked like a Greek statue come to life.

She struggled to return her mind to safer territory what with the buffet of man goods on display before her. It wasn't fair for someone to be this good-looking. It was a safety hazard. Unfortunately, she was pretty sure that this wasn't a complaint that she could file with OSHA.

Suddenly she remembered a topic that would happily distract her.

"Sooo...what made you open Jabberwocky?" she asked innocently as she popped another grape in her mouth.

He turned his gaze from the horizon and gave her a half smile. "Why do you keep asking me that? Don't I look like the children's book type?"

"Not really," she said while chewing. "You look more like the James Dean type."

He raised his eyebrows. "James Dean, huh?"

She nodded her head. "So why children's books?"

The twinkle went out of his eye and turned away from her, looking back out at the ocean. "It's a long story."

A less curious person might have left it at that.

"I've got time," she said, taking a bite of her citrusy-sweet chicken sandwich.

He lifted his hand out of the sand and dusted off his palms. "You definitely need to write your book about this place. The pictures would be stunning. And I love your message of discovering what's around the corner. It's an important lesson, and I like that you are wrapping it in the story of the beach. The idea that important lessons can be learned through observation of the natural world...it's very Emerson: philosophical but approachable."

Emerson? Wow! Angela grew warm at the compliment. It was so nice to know that Kieran really understood and appreciated her. Then she realized what he was doing. "Kieran O'Connell, you are just stroking my ego so you can change the subject."

His face grew dark as he turned away. He was quiet for a few minutes, then he turned back to her and said, "Look, I meant every word of that compliment, but the origins of Jabberwocky…well it's not a story I like to tell." He paused, taking a deep breath. "The bottom line is that while Jabberwocky wasn't my idea, it is my home. I love it, and there's nowhere else I'd rather be."

She could tell from his tone that he wasn't going to say anymore.

Angela was starting to get hot in her jeans and shirt, but she felt surprisingly shy about disrobing in front of Kieran; she wasn't sure if it was his statue-like physique or something else, but when she felt herself beginning to sweat, she took off her jeans, but kept her shirt on.

When she met his eyes, he was looking at her intensely, his eyes smoldering. Her heart sped up.

She usually felt so comfortable around Kieran; she didn't understand why today was any different.

She pulled down her sunhat and turned back to the ocean self-consciously. "Do you want to explore those rocks?" She pointed to a large outcropping, two stories high. "That one over there has a narrow passageway that leads to even more rocks beyond it."

"Sure, let's go." He stood up, dusting the sand off his hands and offered her his hand.

She took it without thinking, a surge pulsing through her arm; she dropped his hand quickly.

He furrowed his brow. "What wrong?"

She shook her head. "Nothing. It was just an awkward angle. I'll get up on my own."

He studied her face intently and then shrugged. "Okay." He turned to face the beach. "I'm just going to go for a quick dip. You want to swim?"

She shook her head. "No way. The water is way too cold for me."

He nodded. "I'll meet you over by the rock."

She watched him jog down to the beach, his back muscles flexing as he pumped his arms. She felt a pang of guilt in her stomach for admiring him.

For all her years of male friendship, Kieran was the first man that had ever aroused such complicated feelings in her: admiration for his business savvy, gratitude for his generous mentorship, curiosity for his mysterious past. Not only that, but he was also funny, insightful, and damn hot. He presented a very compelling package.

But he was not hers to have.

She stood up, brushing the sand off her legs as she walked down to the shoreline. Kieran was just wading out of the water. The sun was low in the horizon, silhouetting him against the blue-black water. His tan muscles were impossible to see from this angle, but she could imagine them as she saw large drops of water falling off him. He ran his hand through his hair, smoothing the black curls against his head.

He was a dripping-wet Adonis.

She shut her eyes tightly and tried to picture Soren's face, but her heart was still heavy with his harsh words.

"Ready to explore?" He flashed her his killer smile, his eyes crinkling up at the corners. Kieran must have read something on her face because his tone became concerned. "Are you okay?"

Angela turned towards the rocks, her sunhat blocking his view of her face. She wiped a stray tear from the corner of her left eye. "Yeah, I'm fine. The sun is just really bright." She hoped her voice wasn't giving her away. "Let me show you the passageway." She walked towards the rock outcropping.

Why do I feel guilty? I'm not doing anything wrong.

She took a deep breath, trying to shake off the dark mood that had come over her.

They spent a couple of hours exploring the outcroppings of the northern beach and skipping stones on the waves. Angela was surprised at how much fun she was having *not* talking about her book with Kieran.

He was no longer just a business contact, he was becoming a friend.

When the sun was low in the sky, Kieran asked, "Are you getting hungry for dinner? There's an amazing restaurant that I found when I was researching which route to take here today."

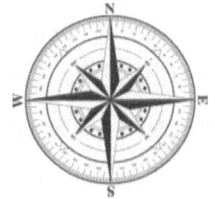

Chapter 20: A Midsummer's Night In Winter

The lights in the trees twinkled magically as they pulled into the parking lot of the restaurant. They walked under a wooden archway hung with gold letters that spelled *Inn of the Seventh Ray*.

A young man with short red hair and a pointy goatee approached them. "Do you have a reservation?"

Kieran nodded. "O'Connell."

A light of recognition sparked in the waiter's eye. "Ah yes, right this way."

Angela was so distracted by the beauty of the location that she didn't think to ask Kieran about the reservation.

"Oh my gosh it's so beautiful," Angela exclaimed taking in the canopy of leafy Sycamore trees that substituted for a roof in this largely open-air restaurant. She walked along the stone pathway, looking around in amazement, surprised that she'd never heard of this place.

A gazebo with a small table stood in one corner, elevated like a place of honor, while along the far edge of the seating area, a dry riverbed—filled with an artful assortment of boulders and fallen leaves—provided a view worthy of a painting. It looked like something right out of *A Midsummer's Night Dream.*

Clearly cupid was screwing with her.

"Here you are," the waiter said, bringing them to a table right along the riverbed. He handed them their menus, took their drink orders, and left.

"How did you find this place?" Angela said, as she studied the delicious dishes described on the menu. Her stomach growled loudly.

Kieran cleared his throat. "Well, there aren't that many restaurants in Topanga, and people raved about the setting and the food. It sounded like someplace you might like."

She smiled at his thoughtfulness. "If the food is half as good as the setting, it's going to be amazing."

The waiter came to take their order and as he left, Kieran turned to Angela with a serious look. "So tell me about your boyfriend."

Angela sucked in her breath, her face flushing quickly. She had never spoken of Soren to Kieran, and for some reason, she didn't want to. She looked down and smoothed out the imaginary wrinkles in the tablecloth. "Kieran, I don't want to seem rude, but I don't see how my personal life is any of your business."

Kieran's eyes widened. He cleared his throat. "You're right; it's none of my business. I'm sorry; I was just trying to make friendly conversation."

Now Angela felt bad. Kieran looked stricken, as though she had verbally slapped him across the face. Maybe she was being too sensitive. If Kieran were a woman—or Marco—she would have answered the question without hesitation.

That realization bothered her.

She sighed. "I'm sorry, that was rude."

"No really, it's fine, you don't have to—"

"No *really*, I was being silly. It's kind of you to ask." *Talking about Soren will help make the boundaries clearer, right?* "My boyfriend," she started, surprised at how strange the word felt. Since she and Soren weren't in the same city, they'd never had to introduce each other before. She continued, "He's in Spain."

Kieran raised his eyebrows and took a sip of water. "Ah, a long-distance thing."

"Yes, he's in MBA school in Barcelona. That's where we met. I was an exchange student there a year ago."

His eyes seemed to dim. "So you've been dating for a year?"

She shook her head. "No, we haven't been dating for a year. We just started dating in July, when I was in London for vacation to visit..um...to visit some friends from school."

No reason to bring up Thomas and that whole debacle.

Kieran seemed to perk up. "Oh, so you've only been dating a short time."

She hesitated before saying, "It's complicated." She shrugged weakly, not sure what she meant by that.

Their history was complicated? Their relationship was complicated? Their feelings were complicated?

If she was being perfectly honest, right now it seemed like all of the above.

He chuckled lightly. "I think what you mean is that you hooked up on your travels. It was a vacation fling, and now you are trying to figure out where to go from there."

Angela's eyes grew wide, stunned by his words.

She angrily wiped her mouth with her napkin. "What? No, it's not a fling, it's just complicated, that's all. He's coming to Los Angeles for Christmas, and we are much more than a *fling*." She said the word "fling" harshly, as though it stung.

Kieran raised his eyebrows, holding his palms up in surrender. "I'm sorry. I was just being light. I didn't mean to hurt your feelings. I'm sure he's a great guy. Why don't you bring him by Jabberwocky when he's in town? I'd love to meet him."

Yeah right. There is no chance in hell I'm bringing Soren to Jabberwocky, she thought as she said, "Maybe."

"Maybe?" His eyes widened. "Why wouldn't you bring him by? I'm sure he's curious about me."

It was Angela's turn to be surprised. "Why would you think that?"

Kieran rolled his eyes. "Because if the woman I was dating was spending a lot of time with another man, I'd want to meet this other man."

She remembered the conversation with Marco from over the summer. He had said something very similar to Angela about their lunch dates and how it would be normal for Soren to be jealous of the time they spent together. She scowled inwardly at the memory.

"Really? Well, that's interesting, but Soren has complete faith in me. If I bring him by Jabberwocky it will be because that's what I want to do, and not because he's checking-up on me," she said theatrically, not completely convinced of the statement herself.

Kieran smirked as he raised his beer to his lips. He took a swig and then said, "Well, good for you. You found yourself the one man on the planet who feels that way."

Although his tone was light, she could feel the sarcasm of the comment. Angela scowled. Why was Kieran baiting her?

Fortunately, just then, their appetizers arrived shifting their attention to the delicious food in front of them. Angela felt grateful for the distraction.

Angela dug in to her soft-shell crab appetizer with gusto. It was dressed with a citrus-flavored aioli that added a wonderful touch of acidic creaminess to the crispy crustacean. "Wow. This is really good. How's yours?"

He chewed his mouthful and swallowed. "Amazing, would you like to try?"

Angela eyed his burrata and fava bean toast. It looked very tempting.

"Here, take a bite. It's delicious." He held his fork up to her mouth; she hesitated and he said, "Go on, I know you want to try it. I can see it in your eyes."

She narrowed said eyes at him, glancing at his fork, and then quickly snapping up the morsel from it. She closed her eyes and inhaled deeply, allowing the flavors to spread across her palate as she enjoyed the watery creaminess of the cheese juxtaposed with the nutty smoothness of the fava beans.

He chuckled, cutting himself another bite of his toast.

Angela opened her eyes. "What?"

Kieran smirked at her. "It's fun watching you eat. You looked like you just had an orgasm over that bite."

Angela inhaled quickly. Kieran seemed to be constantly skating the line of appropriateness today; in fact, this whole day had been firmly in the gray area. Not that she wasn't partially responsible as well.

Then again, it wasn't as though Kieran and she worked in an office or anything. They were both entrepreneurs, and the rules of their working relationship were not clearly defined.

But there was something on the edge of her consciousness that was tugging on her conscience.

You are on a date.

The sudden realization was like ice water in her veins. She knew that while she didn't think of this as a date, Soren would. From the motorcycle ride to the beach exploration to the dinner at this incredibly romantic restaurant.

Oh shit, I'm on a date!

She needed to nip this in the bud and fast.

Putting her fork down, she asked, "Kieran, can we be frank with each other?"

"Of course."

"I think we need to establish some ground rules."

He cocked his head. "Ground rules?"

"Yes, ground rules. If we are going to continue to work together, I think we need some parameters." She paused, waiting for a response.

He put down his fork and turned his attention to her fully. "I'm listening…"

She hesitated briefly and then began with a strong, clear voice. "Look, I think you are a great guy, and I really want to work with you on this project. Your advice and input has not just been gracious, it's been brilliant. My manuscript is a million times better than it was when you first read it and I am incredibly grateful for that.

"And I realize that we are in a creative business, not a corporate office environment, but we need to establish some boundaries. So for the future, let's just say that feeding me and then telling me I had an orgasm is outside of those boundaries, okay? I know it wasn't your intention, but it makes me uncomfortable."

Kieran looked stunned. He gazed down at his lap for a moment, and then looked her in the eyes. "I'm sorry. You're right. That was crossing a line. I guess I just feel unusually comfortable with you." He shook his head, clearly apologetic. "I didn't mean to offend you. I have nothing but the highest regard for you and I really want our partnership to work out. Am I forgiven?"

She exhaled, not realizing she had been holding her breath. "Yes of course. I want this to work out as well. You're forgiven."

Her heart felt lighter. She was glad she'd told Kieran about Soren, and grateful for his heartfelt apology.

"Great. Let's start over. All business, okay?" he asked, a sincere twinkle, replacing the usual mischievous one, in his eye. He held out his hand to her.

She smiled as she shook his hand. "Okay."

"Okay. By the way, I love your idea for a book about Los Leones even more now. I think you should get to work on it right away." He picked up his fork and took a big bite, finishing off his appetizer.

As Angela listened to Kieran jabber on about ideas for her next book, she couldn't help feeling disappointed that he could so easily turn from charming to professional. While she appreciated that he had listened to her she couldn't deny that there was a part of her that enjoyed his flirtation.

What's wrong with you? You just asked him to tone it down.

It was confusing how she could feel so much love and desire for Soren, and yet still be flattered by Kieran's attention.

She looked at the mysterious bookstore owner with the face of a movie star, as she took another bite of her food—feeling too distracted to taste it.

They finished their meal in a subdued manner, the joyful magic that infused much of the day, lost. They talked only about her books and the book business in general, and when the check came, Kieran insisted on paying for dinner, saying it was a tax write-off.

When they pulled up at her apartment building, Angela could tell that she was going to pay for this motorcycle ride tomorrow. Her abs were already starting to feel tight from the ride back since she refused to hold on to Kieran except when it was absolutely necessary.

The moment he stopped the motorcycle, she jumped off, ripping off her helmet quickly. "Thanks for the ride."

"My plea—I mean—you're welcome," he said, as though he thought better of what he was going to say.

She looked away, his dark gaze unsettling. "So I'll see you in a couple days. You mentioned some cover art options would be ready this week."

Kieran didn't respond. He seemed to be staring at her lips. Finally, his eyes flicked up to hers. "Yes, right. A couple of days. I'll call you to confirm."

"Great. Drive safely," she said as she awkwardly stuck out her right hand.

He chuckled lightly as he shook her hand. "Thanks for sharing Los Leones with me. I'll wait until you get through the security doors," he said as he pointed to the front of her apartment building.

Angela turned and pulled open the glass door of her building. As soon as it shut behind her, she turned around to wave.

As she walked to her apartment, she couldn't shake the feeling that she had done something wrong. A guilty feeling churned in the pit of her stomach.

Kieran watched from the curb as Angela vanished deeper into the apartment building. He sighed heavily. He couldn't believe how much effort it took for him not to kiss her as they said their goodbyes. The perfect shape of her cupid's bow lips seemed to beckon to him like a siren.

He sighed, putting his helmet back on, and turning down her street. He replayed the beautiful day, one of the best he'd ever had.

He had initially been disappointed when she refused to hold onto him during their motorcycle ride, but then reality had forced her to do just that and he'd never felt anything as wonderful as Angela's arms wrapped around him. The way their bodies moved together on the curves of Topanga Canyon had been poetic. And Los Leones did not disappoint. The beach was as beautiful as she had described, and spending the afternoon skipping rocks and sitting on the sand had felt almost child-like in its innocent pleasure.

If it had been a date, he would have given it a 10.

He grimaced. It had been a mistake choosing one of L.A.'s most romantic restaurants for their dinner. He had justified the choice because the restaurant had good food—and he knew what a food lover Angela was—but when she was sitting across from him with her sun-kissed skin and her salt spray, mermaid hair in the warm glow of the candles and twinkling, fairy lights, he knew he'd miscalculated. She was ravishing…but she was also taken. Not to mention the fact that she was a business associate.

Damn it, what's wrong with you?

He had always been able to maintain a deep divide between work and pleasure, but he seemed to have no willpower around Angela.

And it wasn't just her perfect lips, her hypnotic eyes, or her enticing body that he was attracted to; it was the whole package. He loved her strong personality, her sharp mind, and her independent spirit.

But he'd overstepped tonight—it seemed to be a reoccurring issue—and it was obvious that if he did it again, she might decide to end their partnership. That much was clear.

And that *couldn't* happen.

He hadn't enjoyed another person's company this much in over five years and he didn't want to lose that. He *couldn't* lose that.

Who knew if he'd ever feel this way again?

Chapter 21: Reinforcements

"Hullo darling." Soren oozed sensual desire over the phone.

His deep voice, and the promise of the pleasure that it would bring, was enough to make Angela's insides churn pleasantly. She could feel her nipples hardening as she answered, "Hello back at you. I've missed you so much."

All was right between them once again. The other night, when she returned from Los Leones, she dreamed of Soren. In her dreams, they made love, and she had woken up feeling happier and lighter than she had since her trip to Barcelona, almost eight weeks ago. She immediately called him, telling him how much she missed and loved him, and they made up quickly. That was a few days ago.

She sighed. This long distance thing was a real mind fuck.

"How much do you miss me?" he asked quietly.

She stood up from her computer—where she was busy transcribing some medical dictation—and walked to the couch, sitting down. She blushed as she said quietly, "So much that I touched myself in the shower this morning thinking about you."

Soren drew in his breath quickly. "Angela!"

She giggled at his tone. "Did I offend you?"

"Offend me? No. Make me one giant, throbbing erection instantaneously? Yes."

She laughed loudly, surprised at how much more comfortable she was talking about sex now that Soren had helped her overcome her reservations about it. "Serves you right. You've absolutely wrecked me with all of this amazing phone sex. I can't wait to see you again and do some of the things we've been talking about."

One particular episode, where she had told him about how she wanted to perform an erotic dance for him, came to mind. It would be a first for both of them. She had bought some gorgeous, black lingerie just for the occasion.

"Enough of this! I can't take anymore. I feel like a bloody teenager with how preoccupied I've become with sex. I can't wait to see you next week," he said in a low voice, full of longing. "I just wanted to call and confirm everything. You have all my flight info, right?"

"Yes, I'll be picking you up at the airport and yes, I can't wait to see you and hold you in my arms."

"I'm so glad you don't have a roommate," he growled.

"Me too."

"What did you get up to the last week? Anything interesting?" he asked offhand.

She knew that what he really should have said was, "What did I miss during the week we weren't speaking", but neither of them wanted to remember the ugly words that had been said during their fight.

A pang of guilt resonated in her chest as her mind flitted to Los Leones. She knew she needed to tell Soren about it, but how to proceed?

"Well, I went on a reconnaissance mission for a new book idea." She hoped her tone was neutral.

There was a short pause before Soren asked, "Really? Where did you go?"

"To a beach that I grew up going to; it's the focus of the whole story."

"Did you go alone?" His voice was even.

She hesitated. "No, I went with the bookstore owner who's been helping me with *The Festival*."

"Oh? What's this store owner's name?"

"Kieran," she winced as she said the name, knowing Soren's jealous tendencies all too well.

"So you and Kieran went to the beach, and then what?" he asked quickly, his tone alarmed.

She hesitated, unsure how much detail to give. She decided vague was best. "And then to a restaurant. It was dinner time when we finished at the beach, and I was hungry."

He was relentless. "Where did you go?"

She stood up and started pacing around her coffee table. "Someplace I've never been before."

"Should we go there when I'm in L.A.? What's it called? I'll look it up online." He said each sentence rapid fire, like an interrogator interviewing a suspect.

Alarm bells went off in her head. He wanted to look it up on the internet? It was so super romantic, he'd certainly freak out.

She ran her hand through her hair. "Why?" She winced as soon as she said the word, realizing her mistake. Her every answer seemed to be fueling his suspicion; amplifying it. She sighed. "I don't remember the name, but I'll ask Kieran. I think you would like it."

"Why do you think I'd like it?" His tone suspicious.

Angela's heart was starting to pound. Maybe the truth was her best option. Just play it off as if it was no big deal. "It was very *hygge*. There were lots of candles, and it was next to a dry creek with lots of lights in the trees," she said with as little enthusiasm as possible.

There was a long pause as she waited for Soren to say something. Finally, he said coldly, "It sounds very romantic."

Her heart felt like it dropped to her stomach. She didn't want to lie, so she said, "It was *hygge*." She knew she was failing at her attempts to sound blasé. If anything, Soren was probably *more* curious about the restaurant now than he was before.

This was not going well.

After a long pause, Soren said in a strained voice, "Angela. I'd like to meet this Kieran fellow while I'm out there. Maybe we can all go out to eat sometime."

Her heart palpitated loudly in her ears. This could not get any worse. Soren meet Kieran? How could any man meet Kieran and not go insane with jealously. He was sex on a stick.

She was screwed…and not in a good way. But what could she do? Soren had her up against a wall…and not in a good way either! She had no choice but to let them meet.

She smiled, hoping that it would lighten her tone. "Great, yes, let's do that. I'd love for you two to meet. He mentioned wanting to meet you too."

"He did?" His voice was icy-cold fury.

Angela's face was hot, her heart was beating as fast as a hummingbird. She needed to get off the phone before she made this any worse. "Yes. It'll be great. I can show you the bookstore he owns. Hey, I have to get back to work. I love you."

"Goodbye Angela."

The phone went dead.

Angela collapsed onto her sofa, resting her forehead in her hand.

Fuck!

Soren hung up without saying "I love you." She knew that meant he was very angry with her.

This was worse than she thought. She needed help, she couldn't do this alone. She needed reinforcements.

Angela picked up the phone and dialed her friend Dalia.

Dalia picked up on the second ring. "Hey honey, how are you?"

Angela sighed heavily. "Not good. I just stuck my foot in my mouth big time."

"What happened?"

"Long story short, Soren wants to meet Kieran when he's here next week."

Dalia clucked her tongue. "Well you aren't surprised, are you?" Her tone officious.

Angela narrowed her eyes. "What do you mean not surprised? Of course I'm surprised."

Dalia sighed. "You're only surprised because you didn't want it to happen. The fact is, it was inevitable. You spend so much time with Kieran, of course Soren is going to want to size-him-up and sniff his butt and stuff."

Angela laughed. "Sniff his butt?"

"Yeah…you know, like the way dogs do when they meet each other. He's also going to want to pee on you." Dalia's tone was matter-of-fact.

"Pee on me?"

Dalia sighed. "Yes…to mark his territory."

"What's with the dog metaphors?"

"We are talking about men here. Dog metaphors are totally appropriate," Dalia said with her usual dry sense of humor.

Angela laughed. "Okay, so I was being naïve to have not expected this."

"I don't think you were being naïve. I think you were *hoping* this wouldn't happen."

Angela sighed. "I hope you know I'm rolling my eyes at you."

Dalia laughed. "Yes, I can tell."

"Okay, well now it's happening. So how can we mitigate the damage? I was thinking I would take Soren to the bookstore and they could meet there."

"Perfect, public is good. Preferably during the day," Dalia added. "And for God's sake, keep it short. Have plans that you have to run to, or make sure Kieran has plans or something. You don't want them talking too much."

Angela nodded. "Okay. Will you come with me? I need you there for moral support, plus, having a stranger there means they'll be on their best behavior. I was going to invite Therese too, but she's out of town for the holidays."

"Of course I'll be there. I should meet Soren anyway, right? I mean, if you are in love with this guy, I should meet him." After a moment, Dalia added, "Why don't you invite RJ? We can go out to eat after Kieran and Soren meet."

Angela's phone rang and she smiled when she recognized the number.

"*Ciao* Marco, *cómo estás*? Merry Christmas!" Angela said, as she broke out in a wide grin, happy to hear from her Roman friend. Although some people might have found it sufficient to refer to Marco as Italian, the truth was he was Roman through and through. He was a chaotic, anarchistic, passionate Roman.

She remembered one time—when they were driving in Barcelona—that described him perfectly.

Marco was on his cell phone, which was pinned to his right shoulder by his jaw. A cigarette was in his left hand and he was holding an espresso in his right, as he shifted the manual car, all while straddling two lanes. He said that lanes were just suggestions, not rules.

"You need to stop doing at least two activities so we don't die," *she said as she grabbed the phone and espresso from him.*

She shook her head at the memory.

"*Ciao guapa*, Merry Christmas. I'm good, how are you?" Marco asked in his musical, Italian-accented voice.

She smiled. "Great now that I'm hearing your voice. To what do I owe the pleasure?"

Angela was straightening up her apartment in preparation of Soren's arrival in a couple of days.

It was Christmas Eve. Later today she'd be headed over to her parents for dinner, tomorrow would be a huge, Christmas open house at one of her aunt's houses—a family tradition—and then on the 26th Soren would arrive. She couldn't think of a better Christmas present.

Marco answered. "Truthfully I don't have a lot of time, my family is all gathered here at my mother's house, but there's something I wanted you to know that I found out a couple of days ago."

Angela tensed. "Is everything all right?"

"Yes, yes, everything is fine. I'm not even sure I should be telling you this since it feels a little bit like gossiping to do so, but I thought you would want to know, since you accused me of keeping important information from you before."

Angela stopped folding her laundry and sat on her bed, one leg tucked under her. "Go on."

"You know the Spanish woman that Thomas was dating?"

Angela rolled her eyes recalling the crazy night in Thomas' apartment when she learned that she had inadvertently been playing the part of "the other woman." She exhaled heavily. "Of course, how could I forget?"

Marco sighed. "Yes well, they are engaged. She's now living in Barcelona."

"What? Engaged?" Angela was surprised by the news, but relieved to find that she didn't care either way. It had nothing to do with her. "Wow, that's an interesting twist."

"No wait, there's more," he said dramatically. After a brief pause he said, "She's pregnant."

Angela sucked in her breath loudly. "What?"

"Yes, she's pregnant and that's why they are getting married. And from what I understand, it wasn't planned."

Angela leaned forward and put her hand to her mouth. "Whoa. How's Thomas taking it?"

Angela could imagine Marco shrugging his shoulders as he said, "I don't know, we aren't that close. He seems like his usual self. Maybe a bit quieter, more serious. It was Enzo who told me."

Angela tsked. Enzo had the discretion of a Las Vegas marquee. "I'm glad he's doing the right thing by her," she paused, adding as an afterthought, "Finally."

Marco grunted his agreement. "Yes. Well I must go, miss you lots. Are you coming to Barcelona anytime soon?"

Angela switched gears quickly. "I don't know yet. Soren is coming here in a couple of days."

"Oh good. And have you been making progress with your business?"

She smiled and nodded. "Yes, very good progress. Writing a book takes a long time unfortunately, but I'm just telling myself that progress is success and plugging away at it."

"Good, good. Well I hope to see you soon. *Ciao, ciao.*"

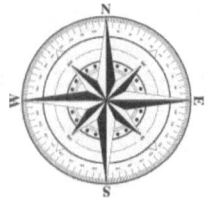

Chapter 22: They Meet

The dark night sky was a dramatic backdrop for the many bright store and restaurant signs on Melrose Avenue beckoning customers to enter.

It was Thursday night and the street was starting to fill up with people going out after work. Soren commented that he had never seen so many tattoos or piercings in his entire life as they drove down the street.

Soren had already made a couple of unflattering comments about L.A. on their drive from the Valley to Melrose—from the "unnatural" landscape, to the crush of cars and people, to the bland architecture. It irked Angela to hear him disparage her hometown. However, the rest of their thirty hours together had been wonderful; so she ignored his comments.

When he arrived yesterday afternoon, it was as if no time had passed. They wasted no time getting back to her apartment and straight into bed. She smiled, remembering how they skipped dinner and barely slept through the night. Her black lingerie was a big hit, and she found a new way to enjoy dancing by performing an erotic dance for Soren.

Angela hoped her downstairs neighbor hadn't heard anything.

After eating a huge breakfast this morning—French toast and Greek omelets—they went straight back to bed. However, when Angela proposed canceling the trip to Jabberwocky in order to stay between the sheets, Soren didn't take the bait.

"You said you wanted me to know about your life in L.A. and meet your friends," he countered, using her own words against her.

Angela pulled her aging Volvo into Jabberwocky's parking lot, expecting to see Dalia's car, but it wasn't there. Her heart sped up. She wasn't prepared to walk into the lion's den without backup. Just then, her phone rang. It was Dalia.

"Hey, you almost here?" Angela asked, smiling at Soren calmly. She hoped the panic she felt was not evident in her voice.

Dalia sighed. "Sorry, running late. What's the plan again?"

Angela rolled her eyes at her perennially late friend, reminding Dalia that they were only spending fifteen minutes at Jabberwocky because they had reservations for four—their friend RJ was joining them—at 5pm in Santa Monica, which was a 20-minute drive away. It was a little after 4pm now.

Angela hung up with Dalia as Soren unbuckled his seat belt. "Everything okay?" He rubbed the back of Angela's hand.

She sighed at his sweet caress. Soren seemed to know her body better than she did. "Yes. Dalia is just running late. She has a very fluid relationship with time."

He raised his eyebrows, his eyes full of judgement. Angela knew how much he hated tardiness. His eyes softened as he looked at her. "I'm looking forward to meeting your friends," he said, leaning forward and planting a sweet kiss on her lips. "You were right. It's nice getting to be a part of your life in L.A. It makes me feel closer to you."

Her heart melted at his words. "I'm so happy you're here, and I'm glad we aren't going to Santa Barbara."

"Me too."

Angela turned to open her door, but stopped when Soren put his hand on her arm. "Wait, before we go in, there's something I want to give you."

He was looking at her with those adoring blue eyes that made her melt from the inside out. He looked hesitant, almost shy as his gaze swept from her to a small silver box in his hands, silently urging her to open it.

"Your Christmas present." His voice was almost a whisper.

She picked up the small box, her heart pounding loudly in her ears. It was the size of a ring box. She felt paralyzed.

There's no way it's an engagement ring, she reassured herself.

She exhaled deeply and pulled on the silky, silver bow. The silver wrapping paper was folded in such a way that the package seemed to pop open as the bow released the tension holding the edges in place. She removed the paper to reveal a black box embossed with silver letters that read "GEORG JENSEN."

She inhaled slowly as she lifted the lid off the box, revealing a silver ring that snaked around twice in a never-ending ribbon nestled against a bed of white velvet. The ring was both graceful and modern, and it was simple enough that she could wear it every day. It was perfect.

She sucked in her breath. "Oh Soren, it's stunning!"

He smiled brightly, clearly pleased by her reaction. "Here, allow me." He took the ring and slipped it over her right ring finger. He kissed her knuckle. "You like it?" he asked shyly.

"I love it, it's perfect. It reminds me of that artist, Escher."

"Yes, actually it shares a name with some of his artwork. It's called Möbius. It is only one continuous surface even though it appears to have a top and a bottom," he paused and gazed at her meaningfully.

Angela felt her senses heighten as she leaned in, sensing that he was about to say something important.

He inhaled deeply. "For me, this design symbolizes us, we are two people, but we are always connected. We are one. The Möbius strip also symbolizes infinity. Angela, you have my heart, and you always will. No matter how far apart we are." He picked up speed as he spoke with more urgency, as though the words would evaporate in his throat if he didn't say them quickly enough. "I just want you to know, that no matter what happens, what I've felt for you is true. I love you."

He leaned forward and brushed his lips gently against hers. A pang of desire thrummed throughout her body. She pulled him closer, probing his lips with her tongue. He mirrored her passion, lacing his fingers through her hair. Angela moaned, her nipples tightening as desire lanced through her.

Angela broke their kiss. "I love you too."

Soren smiled at her widely, his eyes crinkling up. "Let's go inside. I want to see this place I've heard so much about." He arched an eyebrow, but his tone was controlled neutrality.

Angela's stomach was in knots given Soren's past reactions to other men. She knew that his calm demeanor wasn't necessarily a good sign. However, he had been nothing but the perfect boyfriend since she picked it up yesterday at the airport. Maybe she was worrying about nothing. Maybe Soren and Kieran would hit it off and everything would be fine. She sighed deeply.

I hope so.

They opened their car doors into the loud Melrose night alive with the hum of cars and people. The air was thick with the acrid scent of car exhaust and incense.

Soren held out his hand for Angela and they walked the short distance to the back door of Jabberwocky. Angela had never been so annoyed at Dalia's lateness before. She couldn't believe she was walking into Jabberwocky without her wingman.

The purple paint and funky, black puffy letters of the store sign looked different at night, more ominous and mysterious. The sign was lit by bright fluorescent floodlights, which threw large, hovering shadows onto the building, giving the entire façade a slightly threatening feeling.

Soren held the heavy wooden door open for Angela and then followed her inside.

They walked down the short hallway to the main space. Hannah, Jabberwocky's main cashier, was standing at her usual spot in the center of the space, behind the half-circle register counter. Mounds of fluffy, white pillow stuffing were piled about like snowdrifts; sparkly paper snowflakes and candy canes completed the ecumenical holiday décor. About a dozen shoppers were scattered throughout the shop. Elvis was crooning a carol over the speaker system. Kieran was nowhere in sight.

Angela approached Hannah. "Hey Hannah. This is my boyfriend Soren."

The word "boyfriend" still felt foreign on her tongue. She had used it for the second time ever an hour earlier when she introduced Soren to one of her neighbors in the parking lot. He gave her a radiant smile when she said it.

"Nice to meet you," Soren said, offering his hand.

Hannah gave Soren a bored look. "Hi." She then added as an afterthought, "Oh yeah, Kieran told me to tell you he had to run a quick errand. He said if you need to leave, not to wait for him."

Angela perked up at this news. The less time Kieran and Soren spent together the better. "Thanks Hannah," she said.

Soren took her hand and pulled her close. "I really like that word 'boyfriend'," Soren whispered quietly, his lips brushing her ear, sending shivers down her spine. She leaned into him, admiring her new ring surreptitiously.

Just then, Angela's phone rang. "It's RJ," she said to Soren as she picked up the phone. "Hello?"

"Hey Ange, I'm so sorry, but I'm running late on this New Year's Eve project. The client told me they want to see a new draft of it tomorrow and the editor and I still have about twelve hours of work left on it. I'll have to pass on dinner tonight. I'm not sure I'll get to meet Soren at all this trip."

Angela was disappointed, but she knew how demanding RJ's work as an advertising executive was. "No problem. I get it. I'll talk to you next week. Bye"

"Everything okay?" Soren asked.

"Yeah. RJ can't come out tonight for dinner. He's behind on a commercial for New Year's Eve."

Soren tsked. "You Americans are always working. It's the holidays." He shook his head disdainfully.

Angela arched an eyebrow. "For my friends in entertainment and advertising, that just means it's holiday specials time."

The bells of Jabberwocky's front door jingled loudly as someone blew through the front door. It was Dalia. Angela looked at her watch. It was 4:20. She narrowed her eyes at Dalia.

Dalia didn't seem to notice the angry look. "Hey Angie," she said to her friend enveloping her in a big hug. She gave Soren a not-so-subtle once-over before leaning in and saying, "Welcome to Los Angeles," and giving him a kiss on each cheek.

Soren gave Dalia a polite nod. "Nice to meet you Dalia, I've heard a lot about you."

"And I about you," Dalia said with an arch look on her face.

Angela swatted her friend's arm in embarrassment. "Behave Dalia."

Soren shook his head and waved his hand casually. "It's fine. I know I'm being evaluated."

Dalia cocked her head. "So what do you think of our fair city?"

"I don't know how fair I'd consider your city, but certainly you have your share of fair people. I don't think I've ever seen so many good-looking people in one place." Soren said factually, making it clear that he didn't consider that good or bad.

Dalia scrunched up her face with disdain. "Oh yeah. It's because of all the actors. Sorry about that. But other than them, what do you think?"

Angela furrowed her brow, uncertain what Dalia's goal was.

Soren looked up, considering his words. "Well, I haven't seen much. So far all I can say is that it's big and there are a lot of people and cars."

Angela felt herself getting defensive and broke in saying, "There are a lot of really nice outdoorsy areas too. You just haven't seen them yet." She turned to Dalia, "I'm taking him for a picnic tomorrow at the lake near my apartment."

Dalia nodded. "It's beautiful there. And you'll experience one of the best things about Los Angeles: you can picnic here even on the 28th of December!"

Soren smiled mildly. "Yes, well I can certainly see the upside of that. Your winter is as warm as Denmark's summer."

The bells of the front door chimed again, and Kieran entered the store. He looked surprised when he saw Angela, and then glanced at his watch. "Oh, you're still here. I thought you might be gone already. Sorry I'm late."

"It's cool. We were waiting for Dalia." For not the first time in their friendship, she wished Dalia had been on time. "Let me introduce you. This is my boyfriend Soren," she said as the men leaned forward and shook hands briefly. "And this is my dear friend Dalia. We went to business school together."

"Ah yes, the tech friend," Kieran said.

"Yes, that's *moi*," Dalia said flirtatiously, with a sparkle in her eyes and a huge smile on her face. She gave Angela a questioning smile as if chastising Angela for not telling her just how hot Kieran was.

As if words could ever truly capture what one experienced being in Kieran's presence. Everyone *knows* that a volcano is hot, but nothing can prepare you for actually standing near one.

Kieran cleared his throat. "So, Soren, let me show you around the bookstore," Kieran said, as he pointed toward the bookshelves.

The two men walked away, a consistent, visible distance between them, like two positive magnets repelling each other. Kieran pulled out a book here and there, and Soren politely leafed through them.

Dalia elbowed Angela. "You did *not* tell me he was this hot." She lifted her chin towards Kieran.

"I'm pretty sure I did." Angela kept her eyes focused on Soren and Kieran, looking for any clues as to how they were getting along. It didn't appear that they were saying much to each other, they looked more like boxers sizing each other up before a punch is thrown.

"No you didn't. You said he was good-looking, you didn't say he was 'get you pregnant with one look from his smoldering eyes' good-looking." Dalia huffed loudly.

Angela rolled her eyes, feeling a little irritated at the big deal Dalia was making. "Okay, well now you've seen for yourself."

Dalia arched an eyebrow. "I wouldn't mind getting me a piece of that."

Angela sighed. "Please don't make my life any more complicated than it already is. If you really like him, fine, date him, but please don't do anything that will make my life awkward, ok?"

"Damn, you're no fun. Hey, is that new?" Dalia asked, picking up Angela's hand and examining her new ring.

Angela smiled. "Yes, isn't it beautiful? Soren just gave it to me."

Dalia nodded as she twisted and turned Angela's hand. She then glanced down at her stylish, over-sized gold watch; she always kept up on the latest fashion trends. "Don't we need to be leaving for our reservation soon?"

"Oh right, thanks for reminding me." Angela walked up to Soren and Kieran, grateful for a reason to cut their interaction short. "Sorry, but we have a reservation in Santa Monica in about twenty minutes. We should get going." She gave her new ring a nervous twist.

Kieran's eyes flicked to the ring and widened noticeably.

Angela stopped fidgeting and put her hands at her sides.

Soren looked at Angela and then at Kieran, who was just a fraction of an inch shorter and more slightly built than Soren. "Maybe Kieran should join us."

Angela inhaled quickly. *What?!* She hoped she had misunderstood Soren. While the meeting of the two men seemed to have gone well enough, she'd rather not tempt fate.

Soren continued, "Your other friend canceled, right? We have a table for four. Maybe Kieran would like to be our fourth." He turned smoothly to face Kieran, his expression a dare.

Kieran narrowed his eyes. "Sure, why not. I could eat." He arched his brow at Soren, while speaking to Angela. "Where should I meet you?"

Angela and Dalia parked their cars in a dimly-lit parking lot, and walked with Soren the two, short blocks to their destination: a popular vegan restaurant located just blocks from the beach named Real Food Daily.

The air was crisp and briny, and the streets were alive with people returning holiday gifts or taking advantage of seasonal sales. They walked past an adventure travel store, a yoga studio, and a funky bookstore filled with Buddhas and crystals before entering through the doors of a modest, glass storefront into a cheerfully-lit restaurant.

"Welcome to Real Food Daily," the lithe hostess with giant hoop earrings said as she led them to a table on the second floor loft where Kieran was already seated.

He stood as they approached, lips smiling, eyes smoldering.

Why does he always have to look so hot? Angela thought angrily as she watched the hostess smile invitingly at him, twirling a piece of her dark, curly hair around her slim fingers.

Angela grabbed the seat diagonal from Kieran, Soren sat next to Angela, and Dalia took the seat next to Kieran. As she sat, Dalia attempted to give Kieran her most provocative smile, but he was already looking at Angela with a boyish grin.

"I beat you here," Kieran said to Angela jokingly.

"It wasn't a race," Angela replied annoyed.

Dalia raised her eyebrow. Angela lifted up her menu to block Dalia's judgmental look.

"What's good here?" asked Soren.

Angela tried to smile, her stomach a confusing stew of emotions. "Everything I've had has been amazing, but I especially love their Reuben sandwich with mashed potatoes and extra gravy."

"Sold," Soren said, snapping his menu closed as he gave Angela a smile.

After they ordered their food, Kieran turned to Soren, his gaze piercing. "So, what do you think of L.A.?" His tone was already full of judgement.

Chills cascaded down Angela's back.

Soren smoothed out his napkin, before leveling a condescending look at Kieran. "Well, the weather is nice enough. I can see why people like that, but truthfully it's a bit loud and ugly for me."

Angela tensed at Soren's description of her hometown. It stung that he was judging her birthplace, the city she adored, so harshly.

"Wow, loud and ugly? Don't hold back man," Kieran joked, sweeping his gaze from Angela to Dalia meaningfully.

Angela gave Kieran a warning look. He didn't appear to notice.

Soren raised his palms defensively. "I don't mean any disrespect of course; it's just not for me."

Soren's words gave Angela a heavy feeling in her heart. She was about to comment when Kieran said, "No disrespect taken man. To each his own." He waved his hand in the hair lightly, in stark contrast to his words, which dripped with condescension.

A slight ringing began in Angela's ears, as an uncomfortable heat crept up her body. She took off her lightweight cashmere wrap and ran her sweaty palms down her dark wash jeans. She felt like she was watching an accident about to happen, and there was no way of stopping it.

"Of course, there is one thing here that I love," Soren said as he put his hand on Angela's back and smiled at her.

The blood rushed to Angela's face.

Soren leaned in and gave her a deep kiss catching her off guard with its intimate nature. She could feel Dalia and Kieran's eyes on her like hot lasers. When Soren's tongue touched her bottom lip, she pulled back suddenly, her face on fire.

Dalia stared meaningfully at Angela, lifting her hand to shield her mouth from the men, she silently mouthed "pee-ing", and arched an eyebrow towards Soren.

Angela scowled at her and kicked Dalia under the table, jerking her head towards Kieran.

"Owww…So…Kieran, what made you open a bookstore," Dalia asked innocently.

Oh shit. She had to ask that question. Angela took a sip of her water, preparing herself for Kieran's ill humor.

"I'd rather not talk about it," he said tersely, raising his water glass to his mouth.

Soren perked up, recognizing Kieran's sore spot. "Come on Kieran, it can't be that bad," he goaded, childishly.

Angela winced.

Dalia stared meaningfully at Angela and mouthed the word "sniff-ing" silently.

Angela kicked her again…harder this time.

"Owww," Dalia said as she bent down and rubbed her shin.

Kieran's brow knit together. He looked at Dalia. "Are you okay?"

"Um, yeah fine. I just bumped my knee into the table." Dalia turned to Soren. "So, do you have any plans for the rest of your time here in L.A.?"

Angela exhaled her relief. She was unusually tongue-tied tonight. She couldn't think of anything to say to diffuse the situation.

Soren tore his eyes away from Kieran to look at Dalia. He smiled politely. "I'm not sure. Angela has made some plans, but I don't really care what we do as long as we are together. I was trying to get her to go away to Santa Barbara for a few days," he said neutrally, but then added, "But she didn't want to."

Angela could just make out the biting edge of his words. She sighed through a forced smile. "Please Soren, let's not talk about that again."

Dalia and Kieran gave each other meaningful looks.

Their food arrived, and they dug into the vegan comfort food that managed to be light and hearty at the same time, but Angela couldn't even taste her meal. She was too anxious about the unfriendly looks volleying between Kieran and Soren. An awkward tension began enveloping the table. Angela wondered how much longer until she could be alone with Soren.

"This is good," Soren said to no one in particular.

"Yes well, it's not like we are some backwater little city," Kieran said, a touch defensively.

Angela wiped a light layer of perspiration that had developed on her brow. She gave Dalia a pleading look.

"So what do you have planned for Soren's visit?" Dalia asked.

Angela smile gratefully at Dalia. "Soren loves the outdoors, so I wanted to show him all of my favorite nature-y things to do. We are going to have a picnic at the lake near my house, go on my favorite hike—"

"Is that the 405 hike we did?" Kieran asked before taking another bite of his cashew and coconut quesadilla.

Angela could feel Soren's eyes on her. She narrowed her eyes at Kieran. "Yes, that hike," she said through clenched teeth.

"That's a good one." Kieran nodded casually, not noticing Angela's look. He took another bite of his food, and then looked up at Angela, his face neutral. "You know where you should take him? That beach we went to, Los Leones. I'm sure you two will find it very romantic."

The color drained from Angela's face. She felt Soren freeze up next to her. She glanced at Dalia who looked like a deer caught in headlights.

No one seemed to be breathing except for Kieran, who continued eating like nothing was wrong.

Angela felt like she was in a car teetering on the edge of a cliff and any sudden motion would cause them all to suddenly plunge into the abyss below.

It was as though two equally important parts of her life were hanging in the balance: her love for Soren and the future of her business. She didn't want either to be jeopardized.

At this point Angela might have chosen the car scenario over the one she was in now.

Soren was the first to move. He slowly backed his chair up from the table, and folded his napkin with neat precision before placing it next to his plate. The few seconds it took to complete those actions felt like forever to Angela.

He stood up as he said, "Let's go Angela." His voice was eerily calm. He pulled out his wallet and threw two hundred-dollar bills on the table, before pulling out Angela's chair and helping her with her jacket. "It was lovely to meet you Dalia," he shook her hand before turning to Kieran. "Kieran," he said with finality, turning and walking away without waiting for a response.

Angela shot Kieran a dirty look. She turned to Dalia and said, "I'll call you tomorrow."

Kieran looked at Angela with a pained expression, which she ignored. She couldn't tell if he knew what kind of trouble he had just gotten her into.

By the time she got to the front door of the restaurant, Soren had already exited and was walking toward the parking lot with long, angry strides.

"Soren, wait," she called as she jogged after him, looping her arm through his.

Soren didn't slow down, nor did he say anything to acknowledge her presence.

Fuck, he's really pissed. Not sure what to say or do, she walked with him in silence.

They walked in the direction of the beach and after a couple of blocks they were among a throng of people.

Soren looked around, confused. "What's this?"

Angela looked up and down the busy retail pedestrian street. "This is Third Street Promenade. It's kind of like L.A.'s version of La Rambla, " she said, referring to the popular shopping, dining, promenading street in Barcelona.

The lights put up for the holiday season twinkled magically in the trees still thick with leaves. The street was full of shoppers and merry-makers, as well as the groups of singers, dancers, and other street performers who would happily entertain you in exchange for a dollar in their overturned hat or open guitar case. Despite the mob of people, the hum of the crowd was relatively low as people were too busy taking in the myriad sights to talk very much.

"It is like La Rambla," he said reverently.

She could feel him relaxing under her fingers. She was glad she had stayed silent.

They walked around and stopped to admire the windows. When they passed a coffee and gelato place, Angela turned to Soren. "Would you like some dessert?"

He exhaled and looked Angela in the eyes for the first time since leaving the restaurant. His gaze softened and his shoulders fell. "Yes I would like that very much," he said, his voice gentle but resigned.

She sighed; relieved he no longer looked angry. Maybe this night wouldn't be a total loss after all.

They ordered their coffee and gelato, and sat down at a cold, metal patio table to people-watch while they ate.

Angela watched Soren carefully, studying his face for clues about what was to come, but his face was surprisingly serene as he kept his eyes focused on the people walking around. She followed his gaze, looking around at the passersby who all looked relatively normal to her. There were people of all ages, all hair colors, tattooed and unmarked, pierced and not-pierced, all shapes and sizes, gay/straight/nonbinary, unconventional and conventional. It was the world she had grown up in and she thought nothing of the rainbow of differences swirling around her.

But Soren could not tear his eyes away from the constant promenade of people.

Although it may have been a typical mix of people for Los Angeles, he had never seen such a diversity of people in one place before in his entire life. He struggled to process all the visual stimuli he was being bombarded with, holding on to the cappuccino and the gelato like anchors to a world he knew and understood. A simpler world where his senses weren't being accosted with new sights, sounds, and flavors around every corner.

But this *was* Angela's world.

It gave him new insight into who she was and what made her *her*. His lips twitched up as he remembered her saying something similar once in London. Now he understood what she meant.

The problem was, he wasn't sure he saw a place for himself in this world.

The only good thing to come from all the visual stimuli was that he couldn't think about what had happened back at the restaurant as long as his senses were taking in so much new information. It was almost a relief to him because he wasn't anxious to discuss Kieran with Angela right now. They had so little time together; he didn't want to ruin it.

Out of the corner of his eye, he saw Angela twist her new silver ring and his heart panged painfully.

He took her hand and squeezed it as his eyes glistened with emotion. The kinetic vibration of the busy promenade fell away, blocked by the emotions welling up in him. His focus narrowed to just her, like they were the only two people in the world.

He caressed the silver ring with his index finger. He meant every word he said when he gave it to her. He didn't know what tomorrow would bring, and he knew there were no guarantees about how their relationship would progress, but he knew that his feelings for her would always hold a special place in his heart. She had awakened a part of him that he didn't know existed, and for that, he would always be grateful.

He met Angela's gaze, sighed, and smiled uncertainly. All that mattered was that she was his.

Angela gave him a questioning look and he smiled broader. She stood and crossed the short distance between them in an instant, lacing her fingers through his hair and pulling his lips towards her. She kissed him passionately, her lips feverish, her tongue demanding, her hands desperate.

He pulled her closer, wanting to lose the physical separation that existed between their bodies. They had been apart for too long. He didn't want to waste a second being separate from her now.

Even on this street, where almost anything goes, their passionate embrace was drawing some knowing stares. When they finally remembered themselves, they looked at each other and raced to her car, returning to her apartment and allowing their bodies to express what their hearts already knew: fire and ice could coexist beautifully.

Dalia pulled into the parking lot where she was meeting Kieran in her vintage pick-up truck with its manual stick shift. The luxury sedan she drove to work was parked in the garage of her Santa Monica townhome. She preferred driving the little truck in her down time. It reminded her of where she came from, and made her work that much harder when she was at the office.

She grabbed the soft lambskin leather jacket that was a rich olive color, and threw it over her shoulders. Tight, black skinny jeans and black canvas wedge heels accentuated her slim height. She knew she looked good. She took one last look in the mirror, smoothed the edge of her lipstick, and sauntered across the parking lot drawing the eyes of every person around her.

When Soren had stormed out of the restaurant, she had said to Kieran, "Man, I could use a shot of tequila." That's how she ended up here at the fun, slightly-campy Mexican restaurant in Venice known as La Cabaña, famous for its margaritas and handmade tortillas. The interior was brightly lit with festive string lights, and she immediately picked out Kieran sitting in a corner booth. When he saw her, he stood up.

Damn he's hot. I am a really good friend. She sighed, forlorn because she already knew this beautiful man would never grace her own 600-thread-count sheets.

He ushered her into the C-shaped booth. There were two blended margaritas with salt rims and two shots of tequila already on the table.

"I see you are already double fisting it. Was dinner really that bad?" she asked teasingly.

From her many conversations with Angela about both Kieran and Soren, she knew that tonight was going to be memorable, but she hadn't counted on just how memorable. She had sensed that Angela was holding something back, and once she saw how Kieran looked at Angela, she knew exactly what it was.

Kieran smiled knowingly. "Well, it *was* that bad, but actually, one of them is for you."

"Thanks. I couldn't resist teasing you." She grabbed the margarita that was hers and took a big gulp. "And you are right, it was that bad," she said tossing back the shot of tequila.

Kieran raised his eyebrow at her as he lifted his own shot glass. "*¡Salud!*"

Dalia clinked his glass and took another big drink before putting her cocktail down loudly. "Kieran, let's just cut to the chase, okay?" She laughed at the confused expression on his face. Was he really that oblivious to what was going on here?

"What do you mean?" he asked, tracing the condensation on the side of his margarita glass.

Dalia rolled her eyes. "Kieran, you have feelings for Angela," she said with a look that dared him to deny it.

Kieran's eyes widened. He dropped his gaze and took a drink from his margarita glass, surprised at how easily Dalia was reading him. Was it that obvious?

"Look Kieran, I know the timing isn't right and maybe you are trying to keep things professional with her, but it's obvious to everyone else that you have feelings for Angela. Of course, it's not obvious to Angela, she's deep in denial, but trust me when I say that it was clear to me and Soren." She took another gulp of her cocktail.

His shoulders slumped. "You're sure about Soren?" It was a rhetorical question. He knew he'd crossed a line at dinner. It was just that when he saw Dalia admiring Angela's new ring at Jabberwocky, he'd felt like his heart had been smashed. It was like Angela was wearing Soren's brand, and it was a physical reminder that she wasn't his. For the rest of the night he saw red whenever he looked at Soren.

"Yes, I'm sure Soren knows. Why do you think he and Angela left in such a hurry? He wanted to get Angela the hell away from you. His only other option was to punch you in the face. Personally, I was impressed by his restraint. I would have punched you in the face." She arched her brow at him.

Kieran thought back to the restaurant and how he goaded Soren on by mentioning his and Angela's hike and trip to the beach. A small bloom of shame spread through his neck and back. "Yeah, I guess I wouldn't have blamed him if he had." He grabbed the margarita glass and finished its contents, wincing at the aftertaste of the sour mix.

Dalia slapped the table loudly. "That's more like it! Now we are getting somewhere." She picked up her glass and polished off her drink. "*Dos más, con Patron, por favor,*" she said pointing at their empty glasses to a passing waiter. "Look, I'm going to be frank with you because the fact is, you and I need each other."

He furrowed his brow at her. "We do?"

"Yes, we do. You see, Soren's life is in Europe. He doesn't seem to like L.A., so if they get serious, then Angela might just move to Europe to be with him, and I don't want that to happen because I'm a selfish bitch like that," she cackled loudly.

Kieran sat up quickly. He hadn't thought about that. He couldn't imagine Angela living anywhere but Los Angeles. The city was a part of her, like it was a part of him. They were so alike in that way. Plus, if she couldn't be his, at least he could be around her as long as she lived in L.A. If she moved, then he wouldn't even have the time they spent together as friends and colleagues. What would he do if that happened? His heart started beating rapidly.

Dalia watched Kieran's face as he considered this information apprehensively. "I see you are starting to put the pieces together," she said taking a big sip from her new margarita. "Oh yeah, that's good." She looked him in the eyes and leaned forward. "So you see, you and I want the same thing. We want Angela to stay in L.A., so we need to help each other."

He narrowed his eyes at her. Dalia was much shrewder than he'd given her credit for. "How can we do that?"

"You need to show her how you feel." She lifted her glass towards him, her face telling him she was stating the obvious.

Kieran shook his head. "I'm not the kind of guy who breaks up relationships." He winced at the memory of the time he kissed Angela and the elaborate lengths he went through to plan the day at Los Leones. Of course, he hadn't known anything about Soren at the time, but now he did know. If he did anything now, he would be among that group of people he hated the most: cheaters. The hair on his neck stood straight up.

Dalia waved her hand in the air dismissively. "Look Kieran, I didn't say it was going to be clean or easy but the reality is: she's in love with Soren. The only thing that will get her to stay in L.A. is if that changes. What's more important to you? Your morals or hanging on to the girl of your dreams."

He shook his head. "They are both important to me. There's got to be a way to do both."

"Okay, let's try and think of it over another round. *Dos más por favor.*"

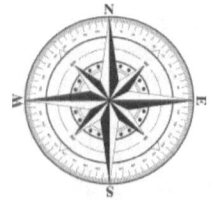

Chapter 23: Mother Knows Best

Kieran walked out of the jewelry boutique on Melrose Avenue with the small fuchsia box burning like a hot coal in his hand. He scowled as he shoved it into his pocket, regret already etched on his tense face.

What the fuck am I thinking?

He ran a hand through his unruly curls and blinked hard, trying to erase her face from his mind; but the more he tried the brighter the image burned. The sun was mocking him too, peeking out at him from between the wintry clouds as if to remind him of her luminousness, as if he could think of anything else.

Ever since the day Angela walked into his bookstore, her face had colored his thoughts. She was the first thing he thought about when he woke up, and the last thing he thought about before going to bed.

Every day he fought to wait as long as he could before calling or emailing her. Fortunately he had a good reason to reach out since they were working on her book together; but a part of him had known that first moment he saw her standing at the cash register, with her mountain of books and that gorgeous hair piled wildly on her head, that there was something about her.

Don't think about it, but it was too late; the image of their kiss was already replaying in his head. It was his own tortuous highlight reel that he experienced over and over and over again. His body reacted to the beckoned memory by flooding him with heat and desire. A familiar dull ache gathered in the pit of the stomach; it had been his constant companion the last couple of months.

"FUCK!!!!" he yelled, momentarily calmed by the physical release that satisfying word always provided with its fricative beginning and its percussive ending. Fortunately, he was on Melrose, where the sight of a man stopped on the sidewalk and cursing the heavens was not likely to provoke much attention.

Why can't I stop thinking about her?

A dull ache thudded in his heart as he recalled his behavior last night at the restaurant. He was usually the picture of cool, but from the moment he met Soren he had wanted to hurt the guy. He was purposefully late to the store, hoping to keep the encounter with his rival short or even miss him altogether. He couldn't deny that he was just curious enough about the other man to want to meet him, but also well aware that he was bound to dislike him if for no other reason than because Angela was his.

But you just couldn't pass up the dinner invitation you stupid ass.

There was nothing wrong with Soren per se, although his dislike of Los Angeles was confounding. He seemed like a nice enough man. He was certainly very attentive to Angela. The real problem was that Soren was what stood between Kieran and the woman of his dreams.

The thought stopped him in his tracks. She really was the woman of his dreams. Up until now, he had been unwilling to admit the degree to which his feelings for her had developed, but as the box in his jacket pocket reminded him, consciously or not, she had worked her way into his heart.

The gift in the box was an apology; an apology for what he had said at dinner the other night…at least that's what he had told himself when he bought it, but deep down he knew it was much more. It was a pledge…a pledge, and a suggestion. It was Dalia's words last night that gave him the idea. "We want Angela to stay in L.A.," she had said.

"Fuck!!!!!"

He pulled out his phone and called the one person who could always make him feel better.

"*Hola cariño. ¿Qué pasa?*" The sweet sound of his mother's voice could always be counted on to calm him.

"*Hola mami,*" he said, reverting to his mother's native Spanish. "Do you have a moment?"

"*Si mi amor,* what's going on?" she asked, her cultured voice always a source of comfort.

"*Mami,* there's no good way to say it, so I'm just going to say it. I think I'm in love."

The sound of his mother sucking in her breath suddenly, made him smile; lightening his mood momentarily. *"¡No me digas!"* She continued the disbelief evident in her voice. "Finally *cariño*! Tell me all about her. When do I get to meet her? You have to bring her for dinner and—"

"*Mami, Mami,* hold on, you are getting ahead of yourself. It's not like that," he interrupted. After a brief pause, and a deep breath, he explained, "She's in love with someone else. I'm the one who is in love with her, and I don't know what to do."

"What? What do you mean she's in love with someone else? I didn't raise a man who would break up a relationship. Kieran Alphonso O'Connell, you know better than that."

He rolled his eyes at his mother breaking out his full name. He could imagine her on the other side of the phone, sitting in her kitchen wearing the stylish pointy flats she favored, the omnipresent, brightly-colored apron that she always wore at home, puffing herself up to her full height of 4-feet 11-inches of righteous indignation. He laughed as he imagined the scene.

Finally, he interrupted her. "*Mami,* it's not like that. I'm not trying to steal her away; I just don't know what to do about my feelings."

"Ah *mi amor*, it's so good to hear that you've met someone you care about. It's been so long since that *puta de madre* Olivia—"

"*Mami* …" he raised his voice in warning not wanting to let his mom get started on his ex-girlfriend.

"I'm sorry my love, it's just that no mother likes to watch her child be hurt." He could hear her collecting herself before she said, "So tell me about this woman."

"*Aye Mami*, she's amazing. So passionate, smart, and beautiful. She writes children's books, that's how we met. I've been working with her on her first book and it's so original and creative. It's set in Spain and it's going to be published in both English and Spanish. I've never seen anything like it."

"Oh, wonderful..." she cooed approvingly.

"I didn't mean to fall in love with her, but we've been spending so much time together that my feelings have kind of run away from me." He ran his hand along the back of his neck as he turned towards Jabberwocky and started walking.

"Does she have feelings for you?"

He raised his brow. "I can't be sure."

"What about her boyfriend?"

"He lives in Europe." Kieran stopped at a light, waiting for it to turn so he could cross the street.

"In Europe? That's crazy. How can you have a relationship with someone living that far away? It's impossible." She huffed.

Kieran sighed. "But she loves him, I can see it."

"Oh my love, I'm sorry that you are in this situation," her voice full of concern. "But you can't do anything except be yourself. You need to let her discover if she has feelings for you. You'll have to be patient. But how could anyone not love my little Pancho," she said, reverting to his Spanish nickname from childhood.

"*Mami*."

She clucked. "Okay, I'm sorry. *Kieran*," she said his Irish name with sarcasm. It had always been a source of contention with her husband that Kieran's first and last names were both Irish. "But I'm serious my love. If you are spending a lot of time together the way you describe, and if her boyfriend is on the other side of the world, it is only a matter of time before she starts to develop feelings for you. I may not know the modern world, but the human heart, it has not changed that much since I was a young woman."

He laughed loudly at his wise firecracker of a mother. She would adore Angela. "Thanks *Mami*, you always know what to say. *Te quiero*."

"*Te quiero más mi amor*."

He hung up the phone, feeling relieved. She was right. If Angela was his heart's desire, he would need to be patient. And he could be.

After five years of feeling nothing, just knowing that Angela existed in the world was enough to make her worth the wait. He also knew his mom was right about Angela and Soren. Kieran couldn't push her. Angela and Soren needed to resolve their relationship on their own.

He needed to make amends for his behavior last night. His apology for Angela was already in motion, but he wanted to make things right with *both* Angela and Soren.

But how?

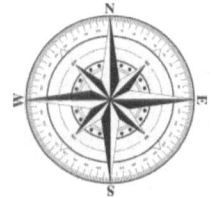

Chapter 24: The First Apology

Angela's phone vibrated, waking her from her half-sleep. She looked at the screen and cursed inwardly, letting it go to voicemail. There was no way she was going to answer Kieran's call with Soren in her bed. Of course, now that she was awake, nature called.

She palmed her phone quietly and got out of bed, shivering as the cold air hit her naked skin. She and Soren fell asleep naked last night, but usually in December, she would be wearing her thin, merino wool pajamas. Of course, with Soren to keep her warm, pajamas were superfluous.

She threw on a silk robe, peed, and headed to the kitchen to check her voicemail. Putting the phone close to her ear she heard Kieran's resonant voice say, *"Please come to Jabberwocky as soon as you can. The graphic artist dropped off the layout early since she's going out of town for the New Year. I thought you might want to show it to Soren."*

Conflicting emotions swirled within Angela. Naturally, she wanted Soren to see her work, but part of her wasn't ready to see Kieran yet. Not after the way he had acted at dinner two nights ago. Then again, she didn't want to lose Kieran either; he was no longer just a business contact, he had also become a friend. She enjoyed spending time with him and felt like he really understood her. But when she thought about how Kieran provoked Soren at the restaurant, the heat rose in her face.

Of course, there was no way of knowing if he'd done it consciously.

Fortunately, the overall evening had turned out well. She twisted the new silver ring on her finger.

The ring was gorgeous and so perfect for her. She especially liked that it was simple enough to wear every day. As much as she loved the emerald necklace Soren gave her over the summer, it was not exactly a daily wear piece. This had more to do with her own low-key style than anything else. There were women who wore giant rocks every day in Los Angeles. Her emerald necklace probably wouldn't even be noticed.

She tiptoed back to the bed and trailed a hand down Soren's naked back and shoulders. This was her favorite part of his body to stare at; it had "man" written all over it. His broad muscles were defined even while he was sleeping. Although usually an early riser, between the time change and their marathon lovemaking sessions, he was sound asleep, his breathing heavy and even.

A delicious tingling began to swirl between her legs, snaking its way up to her lower abdomen where it ached dully. She couldn't get enough of Soren in bed. It was as though the passion he couldn't express verbally saved itself up to be expressed physically, and it was amazing. And for someone who was so reserved in so many ways, Soren was without reserve between the sheets.

She had even learned some new moves from him, she blushed remembering how he grabbed her legs and wrapped them tightly around his waist before putting his long arms over her shoulders and cupping her ass to pull her onto him more deeply. She hadn't even known that move was physically possible. It felt even deeper than when she rode him.

Her breath stuttered as she relived the feeling of him deep inside her.

Then she remembered that he'd be leaving in only twenty-four hours. School would be starting back up for him in only three days and she wasn't even sure when she would see him again.

This might be his only chance to see her book before it was published.

She did some quick mental calculations. It was Saturday; traffic in L.A. would be lighter than usual. She could probably run to Jabberwocky and back before he even woke up. A soft, deep snore seemed to validate her thoughts.

She quietly grabbed some clothes from her closet and left the relative darkness of her bedroom, for the brightness of her living room. It was a little after 9am and the sun was streaming in. She changed quickly, wrote Soren a note, and headed out to her aging Volvo.

Thirty minutes later, she pulled into Jabberwocky's parking lot. The freeways of L.A. were quite magical when there was no traffic. The lights inside were off and the door was still locked. Jabberwocky wouldn't open to the public until 11am today. She knocked loudly on the glass window set in the door.

Kieran walked down the hallway toward her, his typical badass-dressed-in-black self. But he looked different somehow; his usual cocky self-assurance wasn't on display. In fact, if she had to give his expression a name she would say he looked contrite. It wasn't an emotion she had ever seen on him.

He unlocked the door and gave her a weak smile. "Come on in," he said lightly but without his usual jocular energy.

He locked the door behind her and ran his hand through his hair. Fuck he was nervous.

He knew he'd probably played it off enough so that Angela couldn't be certain he'd said those things at the restaurant in order to antagonize Soren, the fact was he knew he'd done it and he felt horrible about it. He couldn't stand the thought of hurting her. He had never felt so desperately bad about anything in his entire life. He needed to apologize and make it right as quickly as possible, which was why he orchestrated this meeting.

He figured that the only way to get Angela to see him while Soren was in town was to lure her with her manuscript. After his talk with Dalia the other night, he called his graphic designer and was able to convince her to work her ass off to complete the layout by this morning. It cost him a pretty penny.

He followed Angela down Jabberwocky's long, dark hallway. She was wearing an oversize chunky black turtleneck, thin wale gray cords and knee high boots with a big heel that made her taller than usual. Her long hair was piled up in a sloppy bun.

God how he wanted to run his hands through her hair.

Even though he was sure she had just thrown on whatever she could grab, she looked positively radiant to him.

She put her bag down on the register counter, turned to him and said tersely, "Where is it? I need to get back."

He started at the sound of her voice. "It's right here." He pointed to the register counter where a thick sheaf of lightly-bound papers sat.

She rushed over and started flipping through the pages. Her face animated as she looked at her story brought to life. A huge smile broke out on her face, causing Kieran's heart to skip a beat.

"Thank you so much Kieran. How did the designer get it done so quickly? I thought it wasn't going to be this far along for another ten days?" she asked as she continued to look at her manuscript.

Kieran looked down at his boots. "I paid extra for her to rush it."

Angela knit her brows together. "Why?"

He shrugged. "It's my way of saying I'm sorry," Kieran said hopefully.

She closed her manuscript and narrowed her eyes. "For what?"

He sighed, shoving his hands in his pockets. "For the other night, at dinner.

She crossed her arms. "Kieran—"

He interrupted her, "Angela, I'm sorry. I regretted the words as soon as they were out of my mouth. I know I crossed the line and I have no explanation for my idiotic behavior. Can you please forgive me?" His heart clenched at the hurt look on her face.

She studied his eyes earnestly. "Why did you say it?"

He ran his hands through his hair in frustration. "I don't know. I saw you wearing that new ring," he said, pointing to her hand. "And I guess I just felt like you might be rushing into things. You are building something great here." He gestured towards her manuscript and sighed. "And you have become important to me. I consider you a dear friend. The words were out of my mouth before I realized it. I'm sorry. It's clear to me that you love Soren and I respect that."

His heart ached painfully as he said the last words, but they were true. As much as he wanted Angela for himself, he knew the only way she would be his completely was if she came to him on her own. Even though every ounce of his being wanted to reach out and kiss her, and even though he suspected that part of her might enjoy it, he knew that action would drive Angela away at this point. So as much as his heart and body wanted him to force the issue, he knew his mother was right: he needed to be patient…very patient.

This wasn't a sprint, it was a marathon.

He watched as her face went from suspicious to uncertain to rueful.

She nodded her head. "I forgive you." She laid a hand on her manuscript and smiled. "This is a very nice apology Kieran. Thank you."

She held out her hand to him and he shook it sincerely, trying to ignore the sensual slither of energy that snaked up his arm.

He cleared his throat. "By the way, I have a little Christmas present for you."

Her face fell and he thought for a second he might have overstepped.

"But I didn't get anything for you," she said, a wisp of guilt floated across her features.

He felt his heart lift, relieved. Shaking his head he said, "Don't even think about it. It's just a little something. I saw it in a window down the street. It had your name written all over it. I thought maybe it would help you write your Los Leones book." He drew the small, pink box out of his leather jacket and placed it in her hands. His heart sped up, anxious for her reaction.

Kieran's eyes were drawn to the movement of Angela's elegant hand undoing the satiny bow. An innocent smile of excitement broke out onto her face. His heart tightened as she smiled at him shyly; completely ignorant of the effect she was having on his cardiovascular system. She opened the box and gasped quietly.

"Oh my gosh Kieran, it's beautiful. I love it," she said as she held up the thin double-strand gold chain that each held a small charm spelling out "Los Angeles" and "California" respectively. "I really love it. It's perfect," she hesitated briefly and then stepped in to give him a quick peck on the cheek.

Kieran sucked in his breath as she leaned forward, willing his body to stay still. Her skin was so soft and she smelled of his favorite flower. The torture was acute.

She put the necklace back in the box and put it in her purse. "And I consider you a dear friend as well."

Kieran smiled, relieved to know she felt *something* for him beyond their business association.

"Thanks so much for this Kieran," she said with her hands on her manuscript now. "It really is a lovely and unexpected present to be able to show the book to Soren before he leaves. I gotta get back to him. Sorry to run out so fast." She gave him a pained expression as she grabbed her stuff. "And thanks for the necklace. I really do love it. I'll give you a call in a couple days once Soren leaves, okay?"

"Okay, talk to you then," he said as he followed her down the hallway to the door. He watched her get into her car and drive away. Relocking the door, he closed his eyes and leaned his head against the glass.

"I am so fucked."

Chapter 25: A Proposal

"Angela it's breathtaking," Soren said in awe.

Angela felt like he could have been talking about himself. He looked like a lion, his blond hair wild and crunchy in that way only salt water can facilitate. He gazed out onto the ocean, his vibrant blue eyes shaded by a pair of silver-rimmed aviator sunglasses with dark black lenses. His white linen shirt hung open to his naval, exposing his golden skin that took sun surprisingly well. He hadn't shaved since arriving five days ago and his scruffy beard only added to his sex appeal.

Angela wanted to jump him right there.

They were sitting on the south beach of Los Leones, the vast Pacific laid out before them with the ribbon-like Pacific Coast Highway stretching to their left and a jagged 30-foot high outcropping of sandstone to their right. It was after 4pm and the sun was heading behind the sandstone, casting a perfect golden light on the almost-deserted beach.

It always amazed Angela that she could be in a city of millions and have a giant swathe of sand like this one almost to herself.

The clean ocean air was electric with negative ions created by the churning surf, and a light breeze blew over the sand causing goose bumps on her arms.

She had to admit that she had been nervous when Soren had asked her to bring him here yesterday. They had been lying in bed, talking about how to spend his last day in L.A.

Her parents had invited them over for lunch again, but they had already spent one afternoon with them. Truthfully, even that one visit was more than Angela was comfortable with. As much as she loved Soren, it was a little weird to have him meet her parents so soon. Her parents had only met three men she dated in her whole life, and no one since Peter Odessa almost five years ago. However, her mother insisted she meet Soren. Lillian was so grateful that Soren called her about the headaches, she practically smothered him with praise.

Once they decided not to see her parents again, he asked her about Los Leones.

"What's so special about the beach you took Kieran to," he asked innocently.

She looked at his face to figure out what his goal was in bringing up the now infamous beach, but his gaze was genuinely curious. She shrugged nonchalantly. "It's a beach I grew up going to as a child. Kieran thinks it should be my next book."

"So when you and Kieran went to see it, you were there for business?" Soren asked uncertainly.

She nodded, pretending as if she hadn't already told him this before. "Yes. When I told him my story concept, he said he wanted to see the location," she said neutrally.

He inhaled deeply. "Is this someplace you would like to show me?" he asked, tenderly.

She looked at him surprised. His tone seemed sincere enough, but she was prepared for the worst. His fits of jealousy had made her gun shy, although she had to admit, he'd handled the night at the restaurant a millions times better than the night with Rolfe.

She looked at him lovingly and took his hand. "Yes, I'd love to take you there. It's a pretty place, and I have very fond childhood memories of it."

He smiled. "Then let's go tomorrow. A trip to the sea sounds like the perfect way to wrap up my trip."

The sound of a barking sea lion broke into her recollection. Sunset was her favorite time of day at the beach; it wasn't too hot and even during high season most people had already headed home. Right now, there were only a few dozen people left on the vast acreage of sand at Los Leones. She stretched out her toes and kicked a bit of sand playfully over Soren's legs.

He raised his eyebrows in amusement as he growled at her and then lowered himself over her, kissing her deeply. She could practically hear him saying the words, "Mine, mine, mine, mine, mine," as he claimed her mouth greedily. She loved losing herself in him. The warmth and weight of his body against hers felt like home.

He rolled off her on to his side and gazed into her eyes. Her face was shaded by a wide, floppy straw hat and her hazel eyes were even brighter with the ocean's reflected sunlight glinting off them. She looked so beautiful with her long, mahogany hair falling in loose waves around her back and her sheer, white beach cover-up did more to enhance than detract from her form, clearly showing her red, string bikini underneath, barely containing her voluptuous body. She looked like a mermaid, washed up on this idyllic beach; a place that she had shared with Kieran already.

He looked back toward the ocean. It was always the same with her. He would always be competing with the other men in her life, but how could he compete when Kieran was here in L.A. and he was in Europe. It didn't matter that they were "just friends" now; Kieran was the one that Angela shared her daily life with. Kieran got to hear about Angela's ideas and see Angela's special beach first.

A melancholy feeling washed over him. He studied the languid curl of the rolling waves.

"Hey, where did you go?" Angela asked, her eyes laced with worry.

He sighed heavily as he ran a hand through his hair. "So this is the place Kieran was talking about. The beach you took him to. This is it."

Even though she said nothing, her concern registered clearly on her face as her eyes and mouth shaped themselves into surprised "O's."

It should have been me, he thought possessively; but then sighed knowing that was impossible, since he was thousands of miles away.

Angela sat up, watching his face as a myriad of emotions cascaded over it: jealousy, anger, resignation. She could feel herself readying her arguments, prepared to defend her working relationship with Kieran, but Soren's attack never came. She was prepared for another of his jealous outbursts, but his silence was unnerving. "What are you thinking?"

Her voice brought him back to reality, and he smiled at her sadly. "I can't fight for you Angela."

His words felt like a slap. "What do you mean?" Her voice cracked.

"Kieran. I can't compete. He's here, I'm there." He motioned out towards the ocean and looked away from her. "It's not that I don't want to fight for you Angela, fight for us, but how am I supposed to do that when I'm not physically here?"

"There's no competition, Kieran is just a colleague." Soren cocked his head at her, making it clear he didn't buy that. "And friend," she added sheepishly.

The impish look on her face disarmed him and Soren shook his head, a sad smile breaking out on his face. "Darling Angela. He's a friend now, but how many more late nights pouring over your manuscript and scouting trips to romantic locations do you think it will take before you develop feelings for him?"

Angela looked at Soren, surprised by his words. He had never spoken to her so calmly about another man and it was…disarming. She was used to his petty jealous fits, feeling justified when she got angry with him in return, but this was something different. She didn't know what to make of it.

She twisted the new ring he had given her nervously, not knowing how to respond to what he was saying. It was like he was looking into her, giving voice to the fears she herself had not been able to admit.

"And I can see that he already has feelings for you love," he said quietly, a look of hollow sadness in his eyes.

She ached for what it must cost him to say these words.

She wrapped her arms around him and held him fiercely to her, feeling his heart thumping rapidly in his chest. She pushed back his shirt to kiss him there, as though she could soothe his heart directly.

"I don't want him, I want you," she urged passionately.

He lifted her chin to look into her eyes. He had told her once that he would always look out for her best interests. As much as it hurt him, he felt like he was doing that now.

"Darling, those words are like gold to me. But how much longer will you feel that way? It's not natural to be away from the one you love. We will be apart so much more than we will be together if we continue this way. How can something as fragile as love be nurtured with so much time and space between us?"

She pulled away from him and studied his eyes. The poetry of his sad words hit her hard. She knew that he was right, and yet she didn't want him to be right. The forlorn tone of his voice only made her want to try harder.

"We can figure this out! We can make it work. Don't give up on us," she pleaded.

He smiled weakly, kissing her on the forehead and pulled her close again. "Always so fiery. That's what I love about your passionate nature. If Kieran and I were in the same city, I would fight for all I was worth. But it's not Kieran I have to beat; it's something much more powerful. It's the insidious but inevitable erosion that distance will have on our feelings for each other. I'm afraid even you, my passionate little fighter, can't win that battle."

Tears pricked up in the corner of Angela's eyes as her heart started beating more rapidly. She couldn't think straight, her emotions were in turmoil. How could Soren say such painful words and follow them up with such physical tenderness? She felt pulled in all directions.

"I don't understand…" She hesitated briefly. "Are you breaking up with me?"

He pulled away to look into her eyes, searching them for something she couldn't name.

"No, but when I look into the future, the view is bleak. How is our position any different from the one you found yourself in with Thomas this summer? You said so yourself that the months apart had left you without feelings for him." He ran his hand through his hair and rubbed the back of his neck.

Her face grew flush at his accusation. "That's not fair! You can't compare how I felt about Thomas with how I feel about you."

"Okay, forget about Thomas. But you can't deny that when you have someone paying as much attention to you as Kieran, for a completely legitimate reason I might add. You can't deny that you won't grow close. I've seen the way he looks at you and the way you act around him. I'm just thinking about where the path we are on is going to lead us, and I'm concerned about what I see as inevitable."

"And you think it's inevitable that Kieran will take your place. Thanks for that vote of confidence," she said sarcastically, angry that he could so easily discount her feelings for him, hurt that it felt like he was pulling away from her, and frustrated by the kernels of truth that she knew his words contained.

Now that Soren was holding up a harsh mirror, she couldn't deny that she and Kieran had grown closer the last two months. While he was nowhere near replacing Soren, his guidance was invaluable, his words of praise like pearls, and the gift of his time precious. Despite her attempts at writing off any attraction she felt for him as simple admiration of his striking good looks, she knew that wasn't completely true.

But none of this changed how she felt about Soren. Her heart ached just knowing they would be apart soon.

She inhaled the ocean air, trying to calm herself. It felt like her heart was splintering into a thousand pieces, and the crashing sound of the waves seemed to echo and amplify her pain.

Tears welled up in her eyes and she looked down to let them fall. She watched as they formed perfect little spheres on the surface of the sand before being absorbed away. She wiped angrily at her face and sat up, hugging her knees to her chest; staring out at the pounding surface of the ocean.

The sun completed its descent and with it, the temperature dropped noticeably. Soren grabbed Angela's wrap from her orange-striped beach bag and placed it around her shoulders, hugging her to his side.

"I don't say these things to hurt you…" he whispered into her ear, holding her tightly.

"I know, but it still hurts," she answered through her tears.

He sighed deeply. "I always told you that I would think about what was best for both of us; that I would protect your happiness as well as my own. That's what I'm trying to do by saying these things. I don't want either of us to get hurt, and I don't want either of us to be put in a compromising situation. I'm already more in love with you than I ever thought possible. Will it be any easier breaking up in six- or twelve-months?"

"But it's like you've already decided that our break up is inevitable. Don't I get a say in this?" she asked quietly, wiping her tears away. She hated being sad, it always felt so weak.

He sighed. "I just don't see any other possible outcome."

She pulled away from him, an angry spark taking hold. "Your logic can be so cold. You're like Mr. Fucking-Spock sometimes." She sniffled loudly, her nose congested from her crying.

"I'm sorry. It's just how I am." He clasped his hands together, sitting up straighter.

The silence stretched between them as they both watched the waves breaking on the beach. Small birds began to gather at the shoreline; running up and down the wet sand, chasing the waterline as it ebbed and flowed. The faintest bit of pink from the lingering sunset tinged the frothy white sea-foam.

Angela felt heavyhearted that this beach, which had always been a place of comfort and solace for her, would forever hold the memory of this heartbreak. Her tears had stopped falling, the angry spark drying her out.

"I'm not ready to give up on us," she whispered through clenched teeth.

Soren put his arm back around her and pulled her tight against his side. He exhaled deeply, relieved and soothed by her words. If there had been any uncertainty in her response, he would have let her go, convinced that it would be better to end it here and now.

"I don't want to lose you now, or ever, but I needed to tell you my concerns." He kissed the top of her head and rubbed her shoulders. Leaning in, he whispered into her ear, "As long as you are certain you want to try, let's fight for us."

She turned to him, eyes searching, and he pulled her to him, kissing her deeply; saying with his actions the emotions he could never describe. How much he needed her. How cold and dark his world felt without her. How lost he felt without his sun to guide him. He laid her gently back on the sand and placed his knee between her legs, resting his weight on her.

Angela moaned at the desperation in his kiss. Soren's outward stoicism hid a physical passion for her that always took her breath away, but tonight there was something else, a ferocity and intensity born out of his fears. She raised her hips to meet his stiffening length. Wrapping her legs around his to pull him closer until there was no space between them, she reached under his shirt and felt his skin shudder at her touch.

He moved his mouth to her neck, pleasuring her favorite area with his tongue and teeth. Swirling, biting, licking, teasing. Her moans grew more feverish beneath him as he bit her hard on her shoulder.

"God that feels good," she groaned breathily.

He ran his hands up her side and glanced around quickly, confirming that they were alone on the beach. He reached into the deep neckline of her diaphanous cover-up and pulled her bikini top to the side. Her nipple puckered instantly at the cold air. He pulled her tight nipple into his mouth and lolled circles around it with his tongue flexed firmly, caressing the fleshy mound of her voluptuous breast as she arched her back, pushing herself towards him.

She pulled him closer to her with her legs, moaning her frustration. His erection pressed against her aching clit, asking for an entrance she was only too happy to grant. "Please Soren, be inside me," she said, aching to close the emotional distance between them with their physical union.

They were still better at expressing their feelings physically rather than verbally.

She fumbled as she searched for the condom in her beach bag. When she found it, she squeezed the condom to the side with her fingers and then ripped the packet open with her teeth.

Soren grabbed the rolled edge and deftly released his hard cock from his surf shorts with a quick flick of his finger against the Velcro closure. He slid the condom on, held himself at his base as he nudged her bikini bottom aside with the tip of his penis.

She gasped as she felt him at her entrance, lifting her hips with urgency.

"Please…" she begged through hooded eyes.

He could never resist her when she gave him that look. He hesitated for a brief second and then plunged deep within her in one swift stroke. God she felt so good. He interlaced their hands and laid their arms out over their heads in the cold, grainy sand. Using their arms as leverage, he rocked his hips from side to side with long, slow thrusts. They stared into each other's eyes, stifled groans escaping the back of their throats.

Despite the deserted nature of the beach, they were aware that it was still possible for someone to walk up on them, and they strained to keep themselves quiet. Fortunately, the sounds of the surf helped to camouflage the muted panting and moaning that they couldn't completely silence.

She clenched her inner walls around his cock, pulling him deeper into her and milking him hard.

"Oh God, Angela…" he moaned, his excitement climbing quickly with the combination of her tightening and the enhanced passion of making up. He unlaced one hand from hers and glided it down her body, finding her clit with his thumb. He rubbed it tightly using her silky wetness to glide over her smoothly and quickly.

Her breath began to hitch as he could feel her body constricting, getting closer to her own release.

"Fuck, yes, that's it…" she gasped.

He sped up the rhythm of his thrusts and his thumb, urging them both closer and closer, higher and higher, on and on until words were meaningless, and white lights flashed across his tightly-shut eyes as they shuddered together, convulsing in their shared climax.

A string of unintelligible words left Soren's mouth, rushing out quickly; words thick with longing and lust and love and hope.

Heaving like one they collapsed spent, intertwined, union.

They laid together—him inside her—as they listened to the roar of the waves.

Angela opened her eyes to a cloudless sky as gentle tears spilled.

"Shhh, shhh." Soren soothed her as he rolled off her and smoothly palmed the spent condom into the plastic bag of picnic trash. He gently covered her breast and then swiftly closed his fly. "Shhhh, I love you. Why are you crying?"

She laughed lightly. "I'm just overwhelmed," she blubbered as she waved her hand. "I just feel so much when we make love. It's as if my body can't contain the emotions so the excess comes out as tears. It's not bad."

She had never before experienced the crying that their lovemaking beckoned forth. Her feelings and passion for Soren consumed and overwhelmed her, taking her breath away.

He wrapped her up in his arms. "I love you too. Now that we've decided to fight for us, I guess there's only one thing for us to do," he said as he kissed her forehead, his voice light.

Angela's heart leapt at his words. "What's that?" she said her voice full of hope.

He stroked her arm. "We need to live in the same city."

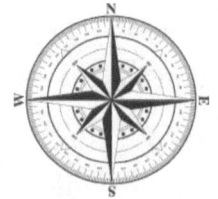

Chapter 26: It's Complicated

"Oh Soren," Angela exclaimed, hugging him tightly. She peppered his face with kisses. "Yes, yes, let's live in the same city. But where should we go?" Her mind raced with all of the possibilities. The world was their oyster, and she couldn't wait to live in the same city with Soren as a couple. But which city would it be: Los Angeles, New York, Barcelona?

"I'm glad you're so excited, but actually there's only one choice because I have really good news," he said, mysteriously.

"Only one choice?" Angela asked confused.

"Yes, Filcher Toffert, the bank I worked for over the summer, has made me an offer and I accepted. I'll start June 1st in the London office." He smiled broadly at her.

"What?" Her voice cracked. "When did you get the offer?"

He moved a lock of her hair behind her ear. "A couple of days before Christmas."

Angela felt stricken, her earlier excitement draining away. "And you accepted it without talking to me?"

"Darling, you've always known I was going to London."

"I knew that was the plan *before* we got together, but I thought that perhaps your plans might have changed now that I was in the picture."

She pulled her wrap around her tighter, suddenly feeling cold.

"What do you mean?"

She sputtered, "I thought maybe you'd consider moving to the States…"

"To California?" The shock in his voice was obvious.

She started. "No, well yes. I mean, maybe. I don't know, I hadn't thought where exactly, but I didn't think London would be our *only* option…after all, New York is a huge financial center too."

He shook his head seriously. "I'm sorry darling, I've already accepted. It's a great opportunity with one of the biggest banks in the world. I've been working toward this goal for the last four years, I can't turn it down." His voice was resigned, and slightly condescending to her ears.

"You can't turn it down or you won't turn it down?" Angela was becoming flush with anger.

She couldn't believe Soren had made a decision this big about *their* future without consulting her. And now he was asking her to give up her city, her state, and her country to move to a city that she didn't even want to live in.

"It's the same thing." His voice was firm.

She inhaled sharply at his response and sat up. "It is not the same thing Soren. You have options, we all have options. But the choice you made has just become a choice for both of us. How could you accept the job offer without even asking me?" Her voice was heavy with anger and frustration.

Soren sighed heavily, the hair on his neck standing up. Was she really accusing him of making a bad decision? Did she really expect him to give up a job at FT to do something as radical as move to Los Angeles? If so, she didn't know him at all.

"Angela, I don't know where this is coming from, but it's been decided. I'm moving to London after graduation in May," he said with finality.

Angela said nothing as she pulled her legs to her, wrapping her arms tightly around them. Soren tentatively put a hand on her arm, but she shrugged it away. "Don't."

"I'm sorry darling, I didn't make this decision to hurt you, but I really had no other choice," he plead.

"There are always other choices," she countered bitterly.

Her pettiness was making him angry. "Angela, the path that I'm on stretches back years before I met you. My path has always been law and then banking. When the offer from FT came, I was beyond elated. There was only one answer I could give. Please try to understand."

She hugged herself tighter, exhaling quietly. His words took the heat away from her anger, like a firm breath blowing the steam off a boiling pot. What he said made sense. How could she expect him to throw away years of work for their nascent relationship? Of course he had to take the job. She could see that.

But something was nagging at her.

"But what about my dreams and my goals? My life is here."

Soren cleared his throat. "Well, I thought that since you are an entrepreneur, perhaps you have more flexibility than I do and maybe...well...I thought you could bring your book business to London."

Her anger quickly flared up again, causing a dull ringing in her ears. "So it's okay for me to give up everything I've worked toward, but not for you?" she yelled, her voice raspy.

Tears of anger, hurt, and frustration began to flood her eyes. She started shivering violently, but it wasn't from the cold.

The sky was now completely dark, twilight having made way for night. The ocean competed with their voices for dominance as it roared more loudly with the rising of an almost full moon.

Angela wiped angrily at her tears. "We should go."

She stood up and grabbed at things randomly: beach bag, towel, hat. Soren stood up as well, picking up their picnic items, and gently putting his hand at the base of her back as they began walking toward the parking lot.

"Don't," she said again angrily, turning her body away to break contact with his hand.

Thoughts and emotions were bouncing around in her like a mosh pit of unruly teenagers. Just as she would grab on to one thought or feeling, another would come by to slam that one out of the way. She didn't know if she wanted to cry or to curse, to sob or to scream, to wilt or to wail, but what she did know was that angry felt strong, sad felt weak.

Truthfully though, she felt too tired to even make a decision as simple as that; instead she chose to embrace the exhaustion that was overcoming her.

"Just don't," she said again, but with a tired acceptance bordering on apathy.

Soren pulled his hand back. He studied her bent form: head cast down, shoulders slumped as vines of despair wound their way around his heart, choking the warmth out of him. He wanted nothing more than to reach out, grab Angela, and hold her tight. He wanted to say words of assurance, certainty, and love; but he couldn't. He knew theirs was not a clear path, it never had been. She had been the dream that he had relinquished long ago. The summer had been a gift so beautiful, he never really believed it was his to accept. Perhaps this is all they were meant to be.

The dreamy bubble of the last five months seemed destined to pop.

They climbed into her green Volvo and turned on the heater. Although the car was old, it still ran like the well-engineered Swedish machine it was and the warmth of the heater felt soothing to them both physically and psychologically. They drove in silence, lost in their thoughts.

As Angela wove the car through the dark, snaking path of Topanga Canyon she allowed herself to be hypnotized by the winding undulations of the road. It was a welcome relief from the cacophonous tumult of thoughts and emotions she had been experiencing. Feeling nothing was better. It hurt less.

She could sense Soren looking at her.

He strained his eyes—trying to read her face as she drove—but the road was too dark. Occasionally a car would pass them, illuminating her momentarily, but her eyes looked empty and glazed over in thought. He didn't want to break into those thoughts.

As the car continued to climb up into the Santa Monica Mountains Angela recalled the last time she had made this journey, less than three weeks ago; the day she had been a passenger on the back of Kieran's motorcycle.

She remembered the freedom of riding on the bike, the wind whipping at her skin. It had been such a light and lovely day, full of fun. Not heavy and hard like today.

Why did everything seem hard with her and Soren? Why were they brought together this summer if they weren't meant to be together? It didn't make any sense.

What Soren was asking her to do, to leave Los Angeles…it was huge. And as much as she loved him, she knew in her heart she wasn't prepared to give up everything—her family, her life, her friends—to move to a city not of her choice.

She approached the turnoff for Inn of the Seventh Ray and an involuntary warmth spread through her as she recalled her meal there. The warmth felt foreign but enticing to her. Her heart was cold with the sadness Soren's decision had created in her, but her body was remembering the joy it had experienced that night and she allowed her thoughts to drift to that memory.

It had been so magical: the lights in the trees, the wonderful food, the aroma of the outdoors mingling with those of their meal. She could feel the features of her face relaxing, her mouth no longer in a tight angry line, the glow returning to her eyes as if they had been relit.

As the car began to coast on its descent into the Valley, she felt a similar lightness within herself.

The lights of the city below twinkled at her, beckoning her to stay. She felt a surge of love for this place—that embraced her as its own—shoot through her heart. Her eyes pricked up with tears again. She didn't know how she was going to choose between the city that had nurtured her, molded her, and accepted her completely, and this beautiful, brooding man beside her. The weight of her decision hung heavy in her stomach like a half-dozen greasy donuts.

When she pulled into her parking space, she turned off the car, and turned on the overhead light. She put a hand on Soren's knee to keep him from moving or speaking.

"I love you, but I am exhausted. I just want to shower by myself and go to bed. I hope you understand."

Soren nodded. A lump developed in his throat at the sadness and exhaustion in her voice. He had never seen Angela like this before. All of her usual fire and passion were gone and it was because of him. He grabbed her hand and kissed her knuckles. "Of course, whatever you need."

They climbed the stairs to her apartment, dropped their stuff in the entryway and separated.

Angela headed to the bathroom where she stripped down and allowed the heat of a pounding shower to relax her. She didn't want to think or feel anymore today. She was empty.

She could feel her troubles being soothed away by the cathartic waters and could almost see them swirling around the drain at her feet. She bid them a silent goodbye and turned off the water.

As she wrapped her fluffy, white terrycloth robe around her, she caught sight of her reflection in the large mirror, peeling silver at the edges where the years of steam had worn away at it.

I'm not going to give Soren an answer until I know.

This conundrum was too much to be reasoned out logically. She bid her brain to do the work and let her know when it was done.

It was a process that she had used many times before, and she trusted it implicitly. Allow her subconscious to process all the logic, facts, and emotions into a single moment of inspiration that it would deliver to her gift-wrapped with a bow. It was the process that had taken her to Barcelona for school, and to London to see Thomas, and now it would be the process that would help her decide between her home and Soren. Because she knew it was a decision that she couldn't make rationally.

She finished toweling off her hair and allowed herself one more glance in the mirror. She felt so disconnected, as if she was all head and no body. She nodded her head to make sure that the body she was looking at was actually hers. The head in the mirror bounced back reassuringly. She inhaled and exhaled deeply willing her mind and body to become one again.

When she exited the bathroom, she saw Soren reading on her couch. She gave a silent prayer of thanks for his thoughtfulness and entered her bedroom alone. She changed quickly into her favorite whisper-thin merino pajamas. They were smooth and light and felt like a second skin hugging her tightly. It was comforting.

She got under the covers of her bed, turned off the light, and fell quickly and silently asleep.

Her subconscious went to work.

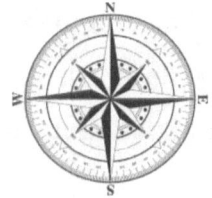

Chapter 27: Bonding Part II

"MMMMmmmm," she groaned as she stretched catlike in her bed. Her eyes fluttered away the sleep as she felt the weight of Soren's arm pinning her down across her waist.

It was so nice to have him close.

She inhaled deeply his familiar cool, woodsy scent. Her back was warm with his reflected heat. She lifted the blankets away from her chest to allow some of the warmth to escape.

He was still sound asleep.

I wonder when he came to bed last night.

She remembered falling asleep quickly, a combination of emotional, physical, and mental exhaustion taking their toll. Her heart ached with the knowledge that he'd be leaving today.

They never seemed to have enough time.

She lifted up his arm slowly, allowing her some wiggle room to turn over so she could face him. Everything seemed so simple right now, in the fresh newness of the morning, his eyes closed, his soft breathing on the pillow. Right now, she knew that she loved him with all her heart. She didn't know if it would be enough, but she knew that she wanted to try.

She ran her finger over his smooth, broad forehead, down his cheek, and along his stubbly, square jaw. A sweet ache shot through her chest as she studied his face. Today she didn't need to know all the answers. They could take it one day at a time.

She leaned forward and pressed her lips gently against his. They were so warm and soft. He moaned invitingly and she kissed him again, snaking her tongue into his mouth, a pleasant sense of déjà vu reminding her of their first night together; it seemed like a million years ago. She smiled as she ran her finger over his eyebrow and nose, finally causing sounds of wakefulness to emerge from his throat.

"Mmmm, goooood morning," he said groggily as he pulled her to him. He couldn't believe how deeply he slept here; the combination of being on vacation, sleeping next to Angela, and a 9-hour time change had created a sweet lethargy in his body that was not unpleasant. It felt so good to have Angela next to him. He wished he could wake up with her every day.

With that thought the events of the night before flooded back, snapping him fully into the present. He blinked his eyes rapidly.

The sun had been up for hours and was attempting to force its way into the bedroom through the crevices of the vertical blinds.

"Good morning sunshine," Angela said in a silky-smooth voice. She smiled brightly at him as he finally managed to open his eyes.

He basked in the familiar warmth that her gaze elicited from his body. Last night—when she shut herself off from him—his body and heart had been cold in comparison. He smiled back at her.

"Hullo my darling. I see the tables have been turned on me here in Los Angeles. Here it is you who are the early riser." He hugged her close and inhaled the familiar rose scent that always lingered on her body.

She gave him an ironic look. "Early? I don't think anyone would call 9am early. But it has been nice to wake up before you. I love listening to you talking in your sleep."

"I talk in my sleep?" he asked, his eyes wide.

"Yes, you do." She managed a straight face.

He narrowed his eyes. "Really, what do I say?"

"You say things like 'Oh Angela, you're the only one for me. I'll do anything for you'," she said with a mischievous grin.

"Well, the sentiments are true even if the method of delivery isn't," he said as he pulled her to him and kissed her passionately, overjoyed to put last night's conversation behind them. "Angela darling, I'm so sorry. I don't know what I was thinking—"

She interrupted him, "I know you would never do anything to intentionally hurt me. Let's not talk about that now. I love you, you love me, that's all that matters. We can figure everything else out. Okay?"

He answered by lowering himself down to her and brushing her lips with his gently. She gasped and the sound sent a thrill down his spine. He leaned down and gently kissed her forehead, her left cheek, her right cheek, her nose, her chin, honoring all the parts of her, searing the memory of each of them into his brain so he could recall them individually when he was in Barcelona again. He pressed his lips chastely against hers and then trailed a sweet chain of kisses down the right side of her face toward her neck. He stopped just before he reached her neck and hovered a hair's breadth above her skin.

She gasped at the sensation of his lips lingering just above her neck. She could feel the electricity vibrating in the space between them. Pushing her neck outward she closed the gap, inhaling sharply when his lips made contact, the soft fleshiness of his mouth contrasting with the slightly-painful burn of his stubble combining into a pleasurable sensation that seemed to pry her open from the inside out.

He opened his mouth widely, clamped down on her sweet spot— that place halfway between her neck and shoulder—and bit her with achingly-sweet pressure.

"Yes," she said with a gravelly vocalization that sent an erotic lance of desire down his abdomen and made his erection pulse. He kneaded this erogenous zone with alternatingly soft and hard bites, licks, and nips causing her to writhe beneath him sensually.

Every undulation of her body sent flames of longing through him, sparking him with every unintended touch to thigh, shin, and forearm. His body was like a tuning fork and she was the hammer causing resonant vibrations to course through him with every tap. He was quickly losing the ability to think, allowing himself to become an instrument of pure emotion and sensation.

"More," he said semi-consciously, pulling at her clothes, wanting nothing to come between them. Her hands labored clumsily alongside his own.

Clothes floated to the ground like falling leaves, followed by pillows, blankets, and sheets.

He knelt over her and took in the view of her naked form; raking her body with his eyes; trailing flames in their wake. "You're so beautiful Angela. I love everything about your body." He dragged his hands over her as he spoke, "From your gorgeous breasts," he ran his hands around her voluptuousness, swirling the skin around her nipples until they puckered tightly. He drove his pelvis forward involuntarily as his erection reacted to her arousal. "To your incredibly soft and wondrous skin." He trailed his fingers gently down the center of her abdomen, circling under her rib cage and then back up along her sides, his hands making mirroring movements across her stomach.

Angela gasped. Soren's gentle, deliberate ministrations on her body were driving her into a frenzy of want. She inhaled, trying to steady herself, but her hips wanted to buck, wanted to feel him claim her fully, wanted to grind herself into him into physical oneness. Her hands splayed to the sheets and clung to the fabric like an anchor.

She arched her back and released a long moan. "Soren, you are driving me crazy."

He smiled smugly, as he answered through half-closed eyes glazed over with desire, "You drive me crazy all day long."

He lowered his face toward her stomach and licked her belly button sending waves of pleasurable pain through her stomach, pinging forcefully off her clit, and releasing her wetness.

"Fuck Soren," she said desperately, the sounds of her want fueling his own.

He kneaded her hip bone with his thumb as he danced his tongue over her abdomen, causing her to roll from side to side as she gasped with deep laughter at the erotic tickling sensation.

He buried his head in her mound, inhaling deeply the subtle muskiness of her sex.

"Oh God," she moaned, her head lolling back, overwhelmed by the pleasure shooting through her body.

He pressed his nose and mouth deeper into her vulva, pushing downward through the triangle until his lips found what they wanted, her bare lips. God how he loved the feeling of his mouth against her smooth, swollen sex. He stopped himself and took a few breaths, willing himself to calm down. Licking her turned him on to an extraordinary degree, if he wasn't careful he could easily orgasm as he pleasured her.

He lapped softly at her outer lips, hot and plump with her desire for him. Angela slapped the sheets violently, moaning with abandon.

"Soren, you fucking tease," she said with laughter in her voice. She groaned as he skimmed her swollen outer lips, sending shudders vibrating through her pelvis and thighs.

"Hhhhmmm, I could do this all day long," he said, smacking his lips.

He darted his tongue beneath her folds and tapped her clit gently. She gasped in response.

Tap, gasp, tap, gasp, tap, gasp. Swirl, tap, suck, lick.

"Soren pleaaaaase."

The sound of her begging made his cock throb compulsively. He wanted to lose himself in her, have her undulate around him, but not yet.

He lightly slid the pad of his thumb up and down the length of her outer labia, rubbing her slickness against her soft skin with a teasing touch; slowly decreasing the pressure until he was just barely touching her; until there was just the slightest whisper of skin against skin.

Angela squirmed with the sweet torment, struggling to push herself against his hand and increase the pressure against her sex. As his touch lightened, the torment increased in direct proportion until she was as tightly wound as a torsion bundle awaiting release.

She pulsed her inner walls in frustration, which sent chills down her back, bringing her just to the edge of her orgasm...that sensational fall that she was seeking.

Finally Soren removed his finger altogether and hovered barely an inch above her skin. He watched her eyes, closed with intensity, her pelvis bucking, searching for his hand. His erection was painfully hard.

Watching her in the midst of her pleasure was the most beautiful image in the world. He wanted to sear this memory of her into his brain to call up at his leisure in the many months they would be apart.

"Fuck Soren, please. I want you inside me," she gasped through gritted teeth.

He took his hands and dragged them down the front of her body from her neck, over her breasts and stomach, down her thighs.

Angela sucked in her breath quickly at the surprise attack; her body undulating in the wake of his touch, like the ground rolling under the pressure of a tremor.

Swiftly he took his middle finger and plunged it inside of her, causing her to inhale loudly. His cock jumped in response. He twirled his finger clockwise, stimulating every surface of her inner walls and then flicked his wrist at the end of each turn.

Plunge, twirl, flick, plunge twirl, flick, plunge, twirl flick.

Angela's breath got deeper and faster, matching the rhythm of his finger. Each plunge was met with an inhale, each twirl with a buck of her hips; each flick was met with an exhale. Soren was in total control of her body; her breath followed his movements exactly.

Soren sped up his finger and listened to her breath match its rhythm as she climbed higher and higher. She stretched and flexed her legs, holding on to the sheets to still her body and allow her concentration to focus just on Soren's hand and her impending orgasm. Her entire world existed only there at this very moment.

With his free hand, he reached up and caressed the outside of her breast, skimming her powdery-soft skin and then pinching and twisting her nipple firmly.

She clenched her vagina around his fingers in response as she exclaimed, "Fuck yes."

He skimmed and twisted repeatedly, increasing the rhythm of his fingers until he could tell by Angela's incoherent stream of breathy babble that her orgasm was close.

He grabbed her hips and rolled her over, lifting her up onto her knees. Pinching her nipple hard, he slid a second finger into her and began to pound into Angela from behind.

Angela threw her head back as she ground against his hand; her long hair midnight against her honeyed skin.

The feeling of Soren's fingers fucking her was divine, but the real mind-blowing pleasure was coming from the hilt of his fingers, where his knuckles kept beating against her entrance, the dull throb of pressure resonating through her entire sex, sending forth deep vibrations that seemed to liquefy her from the inside out.

"Harder, fuck me harder," Angela pleaded.

Soren complied. Angela was so wet and open, his fingers slid in and out of her easily, the tender folds of skin pulling him in and releasing him as if they had a mind of their own. The view of her face and body was incredibly erotic from this angle.

One side of her face was pressed down into her bed, the visible cheek pink with sexual exertion. Her palms were splayed out on either side of her face. Her knees tucked under her and her back slanted upward like an isosceles triangle; ass and hips thrust into the air to meet his hand.

What. A. View.

He removed his hand from her nipple and encircled his penis with it; tightening his fingers around the base to temporarily slow his own excitement as he continued to fuck her with his hand.

"I want you now," she said with languid need.

"I want you to come," he said forcefully.

At his words, she moved one hand to her clit. She could barely concentrate on the little bundle of nerves, so engrossed was she in the powerful pounding at her door.

Fuck that feels good.

She sped up her finger to match the rhythm of his merciless thrusts until finally she flexed her back upwards, like a cat stretching, and came with a loud shuddering groan. She moved her hand to the bed to support herself as the waves of orgasm rippled through her, extended by Soren's continued fingering which he had slowed down to match the waves of her orgasm.

She laid flat on the bed, craving the fullness of his cock inside her. "Condom, now."

He chuckled inwardly. Who knew safe sex could sound so enticing?

Soren quickly sheathed himself, lifted her ass up gently, and thrust himself into her completely.

They groaned deeply in unison.

"Fuck me hard," she groaned loudly.

He thrust into her with long, hard strokes, each one eliciting a deep, gravelly groan.

Angela was surfing the low tide of her orgasm now, the ripples continuing with Soren's thrusts, wave after wave continuing to crash over her as he thrust into her again and again, stretching her fully.

She braced herself against him as he sped up, his own release approaching, as he thrust once, twice, thrice…pushing into her fully, her cheek sliding forward on the bed as he groaned throatily.

He collapsed over her, his slick abdomen dampening her back. She reached her hand around and caressed his thigh.

Together they fell over onto their sides, still connected. He pulled her back close to him and hugged her tightly.

"You're incredible," he whispered into her ear. "That was amazing."

She mewled softly at his words and snuggled her back into his chest, pricks of joyful tears in the corners of her eyes.

Her heart clenched.

Right now, this was all she needed.

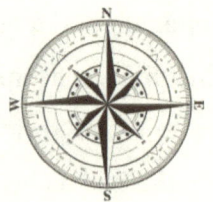

<u>Chapter 28: Goodbye Again</u>

The freeways were clear and the sun was shining its bright, but cool, wintry light.

Angela pulled her car into one of the cavernous, concrete parking lots and found a spot tucked in a dark corner, cars surrounding them on all sides for privacy.

Soren's flight departed in four hours.

Air travel had changed so much in the three months since September 11th. The long lines at security made travel something to be tolerated and no longer enjoyed; and there was certainly no way for her to accompany him to the departure gate. They would have to say goodbye here, in the solemn, stone confines of the parking structure. It seemed slightly better than the bright, institutional sterility inside the terminal. At least it was cool enough that she could leave her windows up, keeping the gas fumes at bay.

She cut the engine, turned her head to him and said with a mischievously-arched brow, "Backseat?"

Soren smiled broadly at her and nodded his head.

They opened their doors and jumped into the backseat, immediately embracing fiercely, clinging desperately to each other.

"I'll miss you so much," Angela said.

"I'll miss you more," Soren said with a deep, gravelly voice full of emotion, knowing it was true. He squeezed her tighter, not wanting this moment to end. "Angela, I don't want to pressure you. You need to make the decision that is right for you, but I don't want to lose this opportunity to tell you how much you mean to me."

Angela pulled back to look Soren in the face.

He reached for her hand and held it gently in his palm. He looked into her eyes and said, "Angela, I've never felt this way before, and there were certain things that I didn't get to say at the beach last night." He gave her a shy smile remembering the fight they had before continuing, "I don't want you to move to London just because it will be convenient for me. I want you to move to London because I miss you desperately when we are apart." He struggled to find the words to describe the depth of his loneliness.

"I never feel as alive as I do when I'm with you. Everything feels more significant with you around. I'm happier, more driven, more satisfied. I don't want to imagine life without you. I don't want to go back to my cold, disciplined life. You are like my own personal sun. I never want to be without your warmth, I love you Angela, and I wish we could be together always," he said tenderly.

Angela sighed, her feelings in turmoil. Her heart ached painfully and she couldn't decide if it was breaking with sadness at his departure or if it was exploding with joy at his ardent words. She could feel the tears pricking in her eyes, her nerves overwhelmed with emotion. She had never received a declaration of love as clear as the one that Soren had just said to her. He was putting all his cards on the table, and his courage and honesty astounded her.

Soren was the most thoughtful and honest man she had ever met, and she loved that about him. There were no games, no hidden agendas. She always knew where she stood. But there was one thing that still wasn't clear to her.

"Soren, even if I were to say 'yes' today to moving to London, I don't see how it would be financially feasible. I can't afford to move to London, rent a flat there, and start my business all at the same time. Here I have everything dialed in. I have my part-time work that lets me write. My apartment is affordable." As the words came out of her mouth, she realized just how true they were. Even if she was prepared to give up her family, her hometown, and her friends, how was she supposed to just pick up and move to one of the most expensive cities in the world? Now that she was thinking about the issue rationally, she saw the impossibility of it all.

She shook her head. "There's just no way I can make it work anytime soon. I'd need to do a lot of research, try and get a job in place before I leave..." She trailed off as her mind began to spin with everything she'd have to figure out if she wanted to move to London or anywhere else for that matter.

Soren spoke quietly with longing in his eyes and a shy smile dancing upon his lips. "No Angela, darling, you don't understand. I'm not asking you to move to London. I'm asking you to *move in with me* in London." He paused to let the words sink in fully.

Angela gasped, finally understanding what it was that Soren was asking. Her mind went blank with shock. Move in together? Her and Soren? In London? She didn't even know where to start in considering his offer. They had only been dating for a handful of months, and the number of days they had been in the same city together as a couple was less than three weeks. Granted, they had known each other before that, but still. She didn't take the idea of moving in with a man lightly. She had never lived with a boyfriend before. Of course, moving in with him would make things easier financially. At least she wouldn't have to find an apartment and the rent would be shared.

Soren studied Angela considering his offer. Her face was nakedly making a list of pros and cons; running an MBA-worthy cost/benefit analysis of his offer.

But Soren wanted to make something else clear.

"Angela," he said softly, breaking into her thoughts.

"Yes?"

"I just want to be clear what I'm offering you so that you have all the information you need to make a decision. If you decide to come to London, I will pay for everything: your flights, shipping whatever you need, the apartment, everyday expenses. You will be completely free to work on your books. You won't have to get another job to support yourself. I love you. I want you with me. I want you to be happy. I love your spirit and your books. I know how important your business is to you. I want you to succeed in all areas of your life. I know I'm asking you a huge thing to move to London, so I want to make it as easy for you as I possibly can." He sighed and gave her a look that seemed to plumb his very depths. "I just want us to have a real chance, and I believe we need to be in the same city for that to happen. I know it's soon, but I don't want to lose you. So while it's not ideal I'm willing to try if you are."

Angela gasped at his offer, and her brain went blank, overwhelmed by this new information.

"Darling, you don't have to answer me now. I just wanted to say these things to you in person." He leaned forward and caressed her jawline with his finger.

He knew that their relationship was young for such an offer. Of course, if they had been a normal couple they would live in their own apartments while they allowed their relationship to develop, but that was not a luxury they had. He sensed they were at a delicate phase, and he feared what would happen with so many miles between them—and a rival as worthy as Kieran close to home. He had never lived with a woman before, but he also knew that he had never felt about another woman the way he felt about Angela. Soren was willing to take things to the next level—albeit prematurely—in order not to lose her. It was a risk worth taking.

He caressed the back of her hand. "We have five months before I'll be in London, so we can figure this out leisurely. He kissed her sweetly on the nose. "And don't forget, there is lots of good Chinese food there," he said with a wry smile and a twinkle in his eye, hoping to bring some levity to the moment.

She laughed briefly. "Okay, I'll think about it," she said breathlessly, struggling to process all of this new information.

Financially it made her decision easier, but in other ways, it made it harder.

She had never lived with a man before, and while the idea was exciting it was also nerve-wracking. She had lived alone for the last three years and she cherished her freedom both physical and financial. Her parents had raised her to take care of herself, and the idea of Soren paying for everything made her uneasy.

In fact, she couldn't decide if the main feeling she was having was one of excitement or one of fear at his generous offer.

I don't need to decide now. Just think about it.

Suddenly she remembered something. She grabbed her purse and pulled out a small, flat box about the size of her palm wrapped in metallic blue paper.

"Your Christmas present," she said sheepishly. "It only arrived the other day."

He gave her a big, puppy dog smile and took the box into his hands.

Angela had never given him a gift before. His heart sped up with excitement. He unwrapped the present and picked up the dainty silver object within. He held it up in the air and smiled with delight.

It was a silver snowflake ornament, and its fanciful filigree design sparkled brightly. On one side was a picture of the two of them, from her trip to Barcelona two months ago. In the picture, Angela was kissing Soren on the cheek and the look on his face was one of perfect contentment. He had never seen himself look so happy. Beneath the picture, the words "First Christmas" were engraved. The words made his heart skip with happiness, because implied within them were the notion of a second Christmas and a third Christmas.

"It's beautiful darling. I know exactly where I'll put it. I'll hang it off the lamp on my nightstand, so it's the last thing I see when I go to sleep and the first thing when I wake up." He gave her a light kiss on the lips.

"Read the other side," she said uncertainly.

He turned it over and saw an engraving in delicate cursive script. It read, "If I know what love is, it's because of you. Yours, -Angela".

He gasped at the beauty of the words. "What a lovely sentiment. I love it. I'll treasure it always."

Soren looked at his watch. "I have to go soon," he said his voice thick with regret. He reached forward and pulled Angela to him again, wanting to memorize the feeling of her body against his.

The way her voluptuous breasts felt pressed against his chest, the smooth caress of her hand snaking through his hair, the feeling of her strong legs, wrapped around his own, pulling him closer still.

It was as though they were magnets and every surface of their bodies wanted to be connected.

Their attraction was undeniable. They allowed their bodies to say the goodbye in a way that couldn't be said with words. Quietly and desperately kissing and searching.

"One more time, please." Angela's voice was thick with need.

He nodded his head in agreement.

She reached into her bag and pulled out a condom. She held the wrapper in her mouth and undid his belt and pants quickly. She pulled out the condom and pinched its tip lightly with one hand as she wrapped her firm grip around the base of his erection with her other. She unrolled the condom swiftly down his length.

Soren gasped. He never realized how erotic putting on a condom could be, but the certainty with which she handled him made his penis throb with desire. He grabbed her hips and pulled her over him. She lifted her dress and pushed her flesh-colored thong to the side, bracing herself on the back of the seats as he slowly lowered her down onto him.

"Fuck," the word escaped Angela's mouth as she reveled in how full she felt.

In this position, she could clamp down fully on him with her internal muscles and the sensation was delicious. Slowly she raised herself up and lowered herself down, trying to keep the car from rocking and giving away what was happening inside. Grateful that the limo tint on her windows, and the packed parking stalls, gave them a measure of discretion. Slowly she worked her way up and down his shaft, as he attacked her neck with his mouth with pleasurable abandon. Angela could feel herself climbing quickly, the stimulation of his happy trail against her clit bringing her quickly to her edge.

Soren grabbed her ass and pulled her closer. Pulling down the front of her dress, he released a nipple from its cup and slipped it in his mouth. He alternated between swirling teasing and all out desperate sucking as his own need built within him.

Angela picked up the pace, finding the rhythm that would keep the car from bouncing, stabilizing herself against the upholstered ceiling of the car allowing her to push down more fully on Soren.

"God I love watching you ride me," he said, as he watched her face, eyes half-closed, mouth open, desire plainly-written on her features as a delicate sweat broke out on her forehead.

She grabbed one of his hands and pressed it against her mouth to stifle the moans that she could no longer hold back. She bit down on the heel of his palm, lost in her experience. The painful sensation immediately turned into a jolt of pleasure, causing Soren to groan deeply.

Her speed became desperate as she got closer and closer, twisting and rocking, her clit explosive with built-up tension begging for relief.

"Yeeeeees," he said with throaty yearning.

She registered his words unconsciously and thrust down once…twice…three times…moaning hard as she toppled over the crest of her orgasm into release, sweet release, as wave after wave rocked through her body sending pleasurable ripples of tingling energy through her from her sex up through her shoulders and scalp. She collapsed onto him with a strangled moan and he hugged her tightly as his own climax rocked thorough him and he bucked slightly finally letting out a low groan.

They clung to each other, intertwined, until their breath returned to normal.

Angela felt warm, slow tears streaming down her face. What was it about Soren that making love with him always made her cry? She lifted herself off him, grabbing a handful of paper napkins from her glove box, dabbing at her tears with one as she handed the others to Soren.

He removed the used condom, straightened his clothes, and pulled her to him, desperate to soothe her tears, which always caused a deep ache of protectiveness in him. "It always makes me sad when you cry."

She shook her head. "Don't feel sad. These aren't tears of sadness. It feels amazing actually. Every time it happens I feel like I love you a little bit more," she said shyly, as the lasso that attached itself in Barcelona tightened around her heart one more time, binding her to him.

He held her tightly. "Well if that's the case, cry all you want," he said as he caressed her cheek with a slight smile on his face. "I'm going to miss you so much. My roommates are going to hate me when I get back. They say I'm a grumpy arse after I've seen you. And I know I'm going to be even worse after this amazing trip." He paused a moment, and then said impulsively, "Promise me you'll come to Barcelona in the spring, and don't let money be an issue. It would be my joy for you to be there. I'll pay for the ticket. I'll pay for any ticket that brings you to me."

She kissed him deeply, communicating her "yes" physically as she smiled at him sweetly, happy to accept *this* generous offer. "Of course I'll come to Barcelona, just tell me when."

Her answer was met with a smile unlike any other she had seen from Soren, he looked incandescently happy. She really did make him happy. She could see it on his face, and the knowledge melted her heart. But there was something else there too…what was it? Finally, she named the emotion she saw: relief. He was relieved that she had said yes.

God she loved this man.

He brushed her cheek with the back of his hand. "Great then, it's a plan. I'll send you the dates for Spring Break." He glanced at his watch. "I could stay in this backseat with you forever, but I should go. Who knows how long it will take me to get through security."

They straightened their clothes and got out of the backseat, avoiding eye contact with a family with three young children who stared at them curiously as they passed by.

Angela couldn't help but giggle as she walked around to her trunk to open it for Soren.

He took out his bag, closed the trunk, and grabbed her with his free arms into a final kiss. "Woman, what you do to me," he growled seductively.

She fluttered her eyelashes at him and said quietly, "I feel ravaged and I love it."

He shook his head. "March can't come soon enough."

After a final hug, they separated. The cool air of the parking lot quickly extinguished the feverish warmth where their bodies had been touching.

"I love you," he said as he turned to walk toward the terminal.

"I love you too," she said giving him a small wave.

She watched as he crossed the street to the entryway. He turned one last time and blew her a kiss, before she lost sight of him in the crush of airport traffic.

Continue Angela and Soren's journey by purchasing
BECKONED, Part 4: From Barcelona with Love
AVAILABLE NOW! SmartURL.it/BeckonedBarcelona

A Special Request: Please Review

Thanks for reading. If you enjoyed this book, it would mean the world to me if you would rate OR review it at Goodreads and Amazon. Indie authors like me **need** your positive words to keep writing. It encourages other people to buy our books (cha ching) and keeps us motivated. Thanks! Aviva

<u>Keep reading for a sneak preview from</u>

<u>BECKONED, Part 4: From Barcelona with Love</u>

It was never going to be easy...

Fire and ice have nothing on Angela Holguín and Soren Lund who first met as MBA students in exciting Barcelona. But their timing was off, until Destiny put them back in the same city: London; and their passion ignited.

Now Distance has come between them with Soren in Barcelona and Angela in Los Angeles. And now that Angela has a handsome new business partner, the stakes are even higher. Things come to a head when Angela and her partner travel to Barcelona for business and it is there where she will have to decide between the opposing forces that beckon. Will Soren's offer of life in London pull her to Europe, or will her business–and the siren song of the sea–keep her rooted to Los Angeles?

SNEAK PREVIEW
"BECKONED, Part 4: From Barcelona With Love"

"I'm not sure yet…When do they want to know by?...Okay, I'll get back to you by the end of the week." Soren hung up the phone and scowled mildly, just as he did most things: mildly.

Anyone who knew him would say he was as steady as they came. Of course, Angela brought out another side of him that no one would ever guess at. She was like a flame to his wick. He even surprised himself with the level of passion he felt for her.

However, that passion seemed to come at a price: uncertainty. At first he had thought the uncertainty was just the by-product of a new relationship and the long distance between them; but a new thought was beginning to percolate up from the depths of his subconscious: the realization that the uncertainty might just be a by-product of him and Angela.

However, it wasn't a fully formed thought yet; it was still just an annoying itch that he couldn't scratch.

He dialed her number.

"Hello there darling, how have you been?" She cooed into the phone.

As always the sound of her honeyed voice was enough to placate the raw edges of his nerves. He exhaled deeply. "So much better now that I hear your voice."

She giggled that adorable laugh that ignited the desire in him to take care of her. "You're so sweet. I miss you and can't wait to see you."

"And me you. Only a week until I can hold you in my arms." His body tingled as he thought about their bodies pressed together.

Angela would be coming to Barcelona to spend his spring break with him and it couldn't come soon enough. They had been apart for over two months and he ached to see her.

"And the timing couldn't be more perfect. I finished the manuscript and got it off to the editor," she said, her excitement evident in her voice.

"You did? Why darling that's wonderful. How exciting for you." Soren felt a tiny ache in his heart that he couldn't be there to celebrate with her. "I wish I could have been there for that."

"It's okay, we'll celebrate when I'm in Barcelona. You can take me to that great restaurant in the Barri Gottic; the one with the secret underground room."

"Yes, whatever you want, but I still wish I could have been there in person." Part of him wanted to ask if she and Kieran had celebrated already, but he realized that no good could come of that question, so he let it pass with a sigh. "There's something else though."

"What?"

He hesitated and then said, "Darling, I know I said there was no rush, but I just got off the phone with my real estate agent in London and she has found a wonderful 3-bedroom apartment for us. It's in an old building that I know you will love and the location is fantastic. The thing is, I only want to commit to it if you want me to." Even as the words came out he knew that he was pushing. It felt so innocent to ask her if she had decided wrapped up in the convenient excuse of the apartment, but he also knew this could go either way for him.

"Why do you need me to help you decide?"

Soren shifted awkwardly. "Because if you aren't coming to London I was going to get a 2-bedroom flat, but if you will be joining me I wanted to get a 3-bedroom so that you could have an office."

On the other end of the line, Angela sucked in her breath and felt a pain in the pit of her stomach. She recognized this feeling. She remembered it from her days with Peter. Soren's words were manipulation gift-wrapped in the gloss of generosity.

She felt herself grow cold. She didn't know what to say. She hadn't expected this from Soren. He had always been the man who looked out for her needs as much as his.

"Angela?" he asked, his voice heavy with uncertainty. "Are you there?"

Her mouth felt dry. She didn't know what to say.

He sighed. "Angela darling, never mind. I'll make the decision on my own. I'm sorry to have asked. Please don't give it another thought."

"Okay. I need to go," she said dully.

"Okay. I love you. Congratulations on your book," he answered.

"Thanks. I love you too," she said mechanically.

Soren slammed his hand down on his desk.

What did I do?

He laid his head back against his desk chair and sighed. He knew he was making mistakes, he could feel it. He had always believed that no good could come out of rushing something, and yet here he was, breaking his own rule.

But what else could he do? He could feel the competition with Kieran like it was an actual physical object. It reminded him of his time in Barcelona with Angela, when they were students, and he let her slip through his fingers. He couldn't make that *same* mistake again.

Of course, perhaps now he was making a different mistake.

He needed more information.

He flipped to the number he needed and dialed. The man on the other end picked up immediately.

"Yes Mr. Lund," the voice answered in his typically clipped— but polite—tone.

"Jameson. I need something."

"Go ahead," Jameson said with his military precision.

Soren sighed, debating if this was a good idea.

"Mr. Lund?" Jameson asked into the silence.

Soren smiled. It amused him when Jameson called him "Mr. Lund." They'd known each other so long now, that he'd always felt like he was more like a friend. After all, Jameson was his father's security guard, not his.

"Yes, sorry Jameson. I need something for myself. It's personal." He leaned back in his desk chair. His Barcelona apartment was quiet, his flat mates all out for the night.

"Yes sir, what do you require?" Jameson's icy calm was almost soothing.

Soren squinted his eyes hard and rubbed his temples with his thumb and index finger. "Do you know anyone in Los Angeles who can do some light surveillance?"

"Of course sir, I have a few excellent contacts down there. Who's the target?"

"Ms. Holguín," Soren said evenly.

"Angela?" Jameson asked, the professional tone softening slightly.

Soren knew that Angela and Jameson had become friendly over the summer. "Yes Jameson, Angela. Is that going to be a problem?"

"No sir, not at all." His icy calm back in place.

Soren sighed. "Jameson, I need someone like you. Someone who can read people. I don't just want to know what she's doing. I want to know *how* she's doing. I want to know…" Soren trailed off, unsure of exactly what information he was looking for.

"Sir?"

"I guess I want to know if she's happy in L.A. Maybe I should say *happier* in LA. I need to know if she's happier in L.A. than she was in London. Does that make sense?"

Jameson cleared his throat. "Sir, may I ask a question?"

Soren sighed. Was he that aloof that Jameson—a man he looked up to—felt he needed to ask permission to ask a question? In a softer tone he answered, "Of course Jameson. You never need to ask."

"Sir, it would make this easier if I knew what you were looking for *exactly*."

Soren balled his hand into a fist and placed it on his knee. He inhaled deeply. "Jameson, Angela has a business partner that she spends a lot of time with. A bloke named Kieran O'Connell. I need to know if he's more than a friend."

"Soren…"

Jameson only used Soren's first name when he was going to give him a compliment or advice. Soren sensed some advice was coming.

"Soren, I don't think Angela is the type of woman you need to have followed—"

"Jameson, I know where you are going with this. Look, I don't think Angela is being unfaithful to me, but I do think that Mr. O'Connell has feelings for her, and I want to know if there is any possibility that she might reciprocate these feelings…in the future. That's why I'm saying I need someone like you. I need someone who can read Angela. And I need it done this week."

"Understood sir. I'll get right on it."

BUY IT NOW!

SmartURL.it/BeckonedBarcelona

OTHER TITLES FROM AVIVA VAUGHN
Novels

BECKONED join the conversation at
Facebook.com/groups/AvivaVaughnBookClub
-Part 1: From London with Love AVAILABLE NOW
-Part 2: From Bath with Love AVAILABLE NOW
-Part 3: From Los Angeles with Love AVAILABLE NOW
-Part 4: From Barcelona with Love AVAILABLE NOW
-Part 5: Adrift in Costa Rica AVAILABLE NOW
-Part 6: Adrift In New Zealand AVAILABLE NOW

Short Stories

-PRESSURE (available now and included in Beckoned, Part 4)
-Knotty Naughty Bits Volume 1: a collection of tangled
romantic shorts PREORDER NOW SmartURL.it/KNB1

Links

Subscribe to Aviva's list to be notified of new releases and special
offers—and get her favorite **FOOD | BOOK | TRAVEL tips** by
clicking SmartURL.it/BECKONEDfan

Website: AvivaVaughn.com/
Facebook Group "Book Club" (where I do lots of "behind the
scenes stuff") and share early material for feedback:
Facebook.com/groups/AvivaVaughnBookClub
Reader Survey: Like to give feedback? Want to help me decide
what to write next? Fill out this survey
SmartURL.it/ReaderSurvey

Corrections

For the grammar-philes, **please send any corrections to**
Corrections@AvivaVaughn.com. To see if the correction you
found has already been caught, **visit**
AvivaVaughn.com/corrections . Thanks for your eagle eyes!

Other Links

If you suffer from headaches from sexual activity, please consult with a physician. Nothing written in this work of fiction should be construed as medical advice.

Love my writing?
Consider becoming a patron at

Patreon.com/AvivaVaughn

Hi Reader!

It means so much to me that you are here! It means that you love BECKONED and appreciate how unique it is.

If you want more "behind-the-scenes", VIP access, then consider becoming a "patron" and help me bring more of my creative imaginings to life! There's even an opportunity to name a character in my book. To find out more, click **Patreon.com/AvivaVaughn**

XOXO,

Thank you to my "Superfan" level patrons

1. Christiana Garcia
2. Anonymous
3. J. Merriweather
4. YOUR NAME HERE
5. –
6. –
7. –
8. –
9. –
10. –
11. –
12. –
13. –
14. –
15. –
16. –
17. –
18. –
19.
20. –
21. –
22. –
23. –
24. –
25. –
26. –
27. –
28. –
29. –
30. –
31. –
32. –
33. –
34. –
35. –
36. –

Soundtrack

Playlist available on YouTube at **SmartURL.it/Beckoned3Music**

Scene	Song
Chapter 9	*I Love L.A.* by Randy Newman
Chapter 12	*Crash* by Dave Matthews Band
Chapter 16: Bar scene	*California Gurls* by Katy Perry
Chapter 19: The motorcycle ride	*Under The Bridge* by Red Hot Chili Peppers
Chapter 20	*Noche No Te Vayas* by Trío Ellas
Chapter 28	*Come Away with Me* by Norah Jones

Book Club Questions

Hey book-clubbers! Aviva here.
I'm a book-clubber myself, and I love it when books include built-in questions.
Here are some questions from me to you! Have fun.

1) Is a "romance" still a "romance" if the ending isn't "happily ever after"?
2) Would you leave your country for love no matter where you were asked to go?
3) What's your favorite thing about Soren?
4) Have you ever had phone sex?
5) Are you more comfortable talking about sex than having it? Discuss.
6) Are Angela and Soren long-term material? Discuss.
7) What's your favorite thing about Kieran?
8) What makes a good sex scene?
9) Have you ever felt like someone tried to "buy" you?
10) Team Soren or Team Kieran?
11) What was your favorite scene from *BECKONED*, and why?

If you'd like me to SKYPE, FACETIME, ZOOM, GOOGLE HANGOUT, or whatever else there is, into your book club. Please send a request to BookClubRequest@AvivaVaughn.com with the time, time zone, date, city, and expected number of people. Thanks!

<u>Thanks, Gracias, Dojeh, Merci, Toda, Gratzie, Shukraan</u>

My sincerest thanks and gratitude to anyone reading this sentence now. I hope BECKONED will live on in you in some way.

If you enjoyed this book, it would mean the word to me if you would rate and/or review it on Goodreads, Bookbub, or wherever you purchased it. Thank you in advance!

Thanks to the universe for unlimited creative expression.

To my family: I can see the light at the end of the table. Thanks for helping to make BECKONED possible.

To my friends, colleagues and mentors in the indie publishing world: I'm eternally grateful to be a member of your tribe. It is your shoulders I stand on. I promise to pay it forward to the next generation.

To my dear, dear friends and first-draft readers: I ADORE you. Thanks MM for all of the encouragement.

To my professional beta reader and hand holder Melissa Natzke. You continue to help me improve BECKONED. Thank you.

Wishing you love and romance,

www.ingramcontent.com/pod-product-compliance
Lightning Source LLC
Chambersburg PA
CBHW051952240626
47153CB00005B/1726